J.F. Hurst

John's Gospel: Apologetical Lectures

SALZWASSER
VERLAG

J.F. Hurst

John's Gospel: Apologetical Lectures

1st Edition | ISBN: 978-3-75250-121-6

Place of Publication: Frankfurt am Main, Germany

Year of Publication: 2020

Salzwasser Verlag GmbH, Germany.

Reprint of the original, first published in 1869.

JOHN'S GOSPEL:

APOLOGETICAL LECTURES.

BY

J. J. VAN OOSTERZEE, D. D.,

PROFESSOR OF THEOLOGY IN THE UNIVERSITY OF UTRECHT.

TRANSLATED, WITH ADDITIONS,

BY

J. F. HURST, D. D.

EDINBURGH:

T. AND T. CLARK, 38, GEORGE STREET.

LONDON: HAMILTON, ADAMS, & CO. DUBLIN: J. ROBERTSON & CO.

———

MDCCCLXIX.

THE TRANSLATOR'S PREFACE.

THE following work is a translation, from the authorized German edition, of four Apologetical Lectures on John's Gospel, delivered to a large audience in the Odeon at Amsterdam, Holland, at the close of the year 1866, by Dr. J. J. Van Oosterzee, Professor of Theology in the University of Utrecht. They were designed chiefly, though not exclusively, as a reply to the Lectures on the Biblical Account of the Life of Jesus, especially on the Gospel of John, which had been delivered at the same place by professors and preachers of the so-called Modern Tendency. The author, with due regard to the requirements of a popular audience, avoided all abstruse and technical treatment of his subject, preferring to give the *results* rather than the *method* of his learned investigations.

**

There are few theologians more capable, by acquirements, native talents, and piety, for defending Christian truth than Dr. Van Oosterzee. In the present work he furnishes a new proof, that, while he refuses to renounce any cardinal point of evangelical theology, and gives abundant grounds therefor, he is ready to make any concessions that candor requires. It may not be out of place here to give a brief account of his life, theological position and literary labors, by a personal friend of his, the Rev. Dr. P. Schaff, of New York, who says:

"Dr. John James van Oosterzee was born at Rotterdam, Holland, in 1817, and brought up in the faith of the Reformed Church. He studied at the University of Utrecht, and commenced his theological career in 1840 with an able Latin dissertation, *De Jesu e virgine Maria nato*, in defence of the gospel history against the mytho-poetical hypothesis of Strauss. He labored as pastor first at Eemnes, and at Alkmaar, and since 1844 in the principal church of Rotterdam, where he continued eighteen years. In 1862 he was called to his alma mater, as Professor of Theology. He opened his lectures in Utrecht with an apologetic oration, *De scepticismo hodiernis theologis caute vitando*, 1863. He is generally considered as the ablest pulpit orator and divine of the evangelical school in Holland now living. He combines genius, learning, piety. He is orthodox and conservative, yet liberal and progressive. He seems to be as fully at home in the

modern theology of Germany as in that of his native country. To his attainments in scientific theology he adds a general literary culture and fine
poetical taste.

"It is as a pulpit orator that he first acquired a
brilliant and solid fame. He has been compared to
Adolph Monod, in his more calm and matured days,
when he stood at the head of the Evangelical Protestant pulpit of Paris and of France. His sermons
on Moses, on the Seven Churches of the Apocalypse,
and on other portions of Scripture, passed through
several editions, and some of them have been translated into the German language. He was selected
as the orator of the festival of the Independence of
the Netherlands, where he delivered in the Willems
Park at the Hague, in the presence of the whole
court, an eloquent and stirring discourse under the
title *De eerste Steen* (The First Stone).

"In the midst of his labors as preacher and pastor,
he prepared a number of learned works, which gave
him an equal prominence among his countrymen as
a divine. His principal contributions to theological
science are a *Life of Jesus* (3 vols. 1846 — 1851;
2nd Ed., 1863 — 1865), which is mainly historical
and apologetic; a *Christology*, or *Manual for Christians who desire to know in whom they believe*, which
is exegetical and doctrinal, the first part of which
discusses the Christology of the Old Testament; the
second, that of the New; the third part states the
results, and forms a complete work in itself, de-

scribing the Son of God before His incarnation, the Son of God in the flesh, and the Son of God in glory (The third part has been translated into the German by F. Meyering under the title: *Das Bild Christi nach der Schrift.* Hamburg, 1864. It is well worthy of an English translation.); and *Commentaries* on several books of the New Testament, of which we shall speak presently. These and other works involved him in controversies with Dr. Opzoomer and Professor Scholten of Leyden, which bear a part in the conflict now going on between Supernaturalism and Rationalism. He has already contributed several parts to Dr. Lange's Bible-Work, which are undoubtedly among the very best, viz., *Commentaries on the Gospel of Luke*, the *Pastoral Epistles*, the *Epistle to Philemon*, and the Doctrinal and Homiletical Sections to the *Commentary on the Epistle of James*. He also wrote a reply to Renan's *Vie de Jésus*, under the title: *History or Romance?* It was translated from the Dutch into the German, and published at Hamburg, 1864, and republished by the American Tract Society, New York, 1865. He also founded and edited, in connection with Professor Doedes, the Dutch Annals of Scientific Theology from 1843—1856. His essays on Schiller and Goethe, and similar subjects, prove his varied culture and deep interest in the progress of general literature and art. His merits as an author have secured him a place in several literary societies, and also the decoration of the order of the Dutch Lion, and the Swedish order of the Pole-star.

"Dr. Van Oosterzee may be called the Lange of Holland. He is almost as genial, fresh, and suggestive as his German friend, in hearty sympathy with his christologico-theological standpoint, and philosophico-poetic tastes, and equally prepared by previous studies for the task of a commentator. If he is less original, profound, fertile in ideas, he compensates for it by a greater degree of sobriety, which will make him all the more acceptable to the practical, common-sense of the Anglo-American mind. His style is clear and natural, and makes the translation an easy and agreeable task, compared with the translation of Lange's poetic flights and transcendent speculations. The Dutch mind stands midway between the German and Anglo-Saxon."

If Holland and Germany were the only countries in which evangelical truth is contested, the present translation would not have been necessary. But in Great Britain and America many of the sceptical arguments so warmly advanced on the Continent have their champions, and special pains are made to give them both a hearing and footing among those who are not confined to theological circles, and particularly among the moderately educated and the young. Of late, this is particularly true of John's Gospel, though it must be confessed that, in the present, as well as in other instances, those who combat it in those countries are too often the servile imitators of sympathizers on the Continent, marching in their rear, and being content to carry on their part of the conflict by using weapons already wrested from their friends in the van. "The authors of the *Essays and Reviews*," says Hengstenberg, "have been trained in a German school. It is only the echo of German infidelity which we hear from the midst of the English church. They appear to us as parrots, with only this distinction, common among parrots, that they imitate more or less perfectly. The treatise of Temple is, in its scientific value, about equal to an essay written by the pupils of the middle classes of our colleges . . . . . . The essay of Goodwin on the Mosaic cosmogony displays the naïve assurance of one who receives the modern critical science from the second or tenth hand." [1] The equally glaring instances of this servility, which we utterly repudiate as a trait of the Anglo-Saxon mind, is furnished by an article in the *Westminster Review*, (April, 1865) on St. John's Gospel, in which the writer attempts to extinguish John's whole claim to credibility and authenticity, and even confesses that he uses only the arguments of the Tübingen School.

Dr. Van Oosterzee, in the Preface to the Dutch edition of this work, says: "Even the best apologists for Christianity cannot, of themselves, convert

---

[1] *Evangelische Kirchenzeitung, Vorwort*, 1862.

the enemies of the truth into friends, yet we achieve
great success if we succeed in dissipating the mist
which conceals it from many who are striving for
it, and if we can strengthen the conviction of hesi-
tating minds, that, though great floods have poured
over the country, not a foot of land has been carried off by them. The purpose of these Lectures
will have been accomplished, and I shall be de-
votedly thankful, if they should contribute even
slightly to the attainment of this great result.
Apart from all the fruit which they may bear in
other minds, I can say with confidence that these
feeble utterances of my own conviction have proved
a great blessing to myself. I am more hopeful
than ever of Lücke's prophecy: 'As long as the
Church possesses a living theology, every doubt on
John's Gospel will be solved and every question
will be answered.'"

I sincerely trust that the Apologetical Lectures
on John's Gospel may not only not have finished
their good work of "dissipating the mist" that ob-
scures the truth, but that, so timely in their appearance on the Continent, they may be found equally
so, and be blest with a bountiful harvest, in the
new field on which they enter.

It would have been impossible to complete
the translation by the present time if I had not
had the services of Mr. John P. Jackson, of New
York, but temporarily residing in Germany, who,
both in stenography and correcting the proofs, has

rendered me valuable assistance. To make the
volume more useful to the English reader, I have
added Notes whenever advisable, a Table of Apologetical Literature on John's Gospel, and an Index.

FRANKFORT-ON-THE-MAIN, GERMANY.

December the 1st, 1868.

PREFATORY LETTER OF THE AUTHOR TO THE TRANSLATOR.

MY DEAR SIR:—

I have learned with much pleasure that my Apologetical Lectures on the priceless Gospel of John have been thought worthy of the honour of an English translation, and I shall be thankful to God, from the bottom of my heart, if He will grant that this testimony to the truth, though a very weak one, may prove a blessing to those who speak that language. The conflict concerning the verity of the Gospel and the credibility of the Gospel History, and particularly of the Johannean Christ, is constantly waged with more energy on the Continent, as well as across the English Channel and beyond the Atlantic Ocean; and hence it is very proper that all of the adherents to, and advocates of the truth in other lands should unite more closely to

defend the good cause of revelation, as far as they
can, against the fanaticism of negation, which, like
every other fanaticism, has its stalwart foes as well
as its deluded champions.

You have already observed that my Lectures
were not delivered to a learned, though an educated
audience, and comprise the results of scientific
study, but yet not the researches themselves. It
seemed most appropriate that the public to whom
they were addressed should be directed to the *internal evidences;* and while I could not dwell at
length on the external evidences, this deficiency in
my work has been recently supplied from another
quarter in a way which deserves our thanks and
hearty appreciation. I may call attention to two
friends of the Gospel of St. John who have defended it, in a very superior manner, both patris-
tically and critically. I refer to *Die Zeugnisse für
das Evangelium Johannis, neu untersucht,* by Prof.
C. J. Riggenbach, D. D., of Basle University, published in Basle, 1866; and to the small but highly
interesting work of my friend in Groningen University, Prof. Hofstede de Groot, D. D., on *Basilides
als Zeuge für das vierte Evangelium,* translated into
German, accompanied with a letter to the celebrated
Dr. C. Tischendorf, and published at Leipzig in
1867. Both these works prove that the hostility
to the authenticity of John, though it is now carried
on even as far as to remote Iceland, is nevertheless designed to be a defence of modern natu-

ralism, which assails this rock of the Church with truly titanic fury, and has taken as its motto:

"Superos si flectere nequeam, Acheronte morebo."

You inquire of me as to the results which I judge followed these Lectures. I am sorry to say, my dear sir, that I cannot decide on this point very positively. My opponents have replied to me with dignified silence, and have regarded my work as *non avenu*. But as for many who have grown weak in faith and have stumbled, I have learned, with great gratitude, that their faith has become strengthened; while I have heard of but one slander, which soon met with its merited punishment. On every side I see that the study of John's Gospel is now conducted with increased zeal and love. It may interest you to hear that this little book has been translated also into the French by Prof. Sardinoux of the Theological Seminary at Montauban, France. You are already acquainted with the German translation.

It will be a source of great joy to me if stronger and more eloquent voices than mine shall be heard in this and other lands in defence of John, whose cause is hotly contested but by no means lost. I am firmly convinced that this cause is identical with that of Apologetical Christianity, and, in a good sense, of modern Supernaturalism. For the present, I have nothing further to say than simply, through you, to communicate my salutations of fraternal love and fellowship in the Lord to all my English and American friends, whose acquaintance I have had the good fortune to make by my participation in Lange's Commentary on the Bible, which, as I hear from yourself and others, has found an entrance into very wide circles among your fellow - countrymen; ὡς ἀγνοούμενοι, καὶ ἐπιγινωσκόμενοι (2 Corinthians vi. 9).

Let us extend to each other the hand at the foot of His cross who comes to us amid all the violent storms of our age, and will live and reign for ever. I can only express the earnest hope that your translation may be followed by the good fruit which you have aimed at in undertaking it.

Very Fraternally Yours,

J. J. VAN OOSTERZEE.

UNIVERSITY OF UTRECHT, HOLLAND.

July the 6th, 1868.

TABLE OF CONTENTS.

I.

THE AUTHENTICITY OF JOHN'S GOSPEL.

"The unique sublimity of the Fourth Gospel was regarded by the early writers, with some few exceptions, as a special seal of its Apostolical character. It is remarkable that it is this same circumstance which has made this Gospel an object of special suspicion on the part of Rationalistic criticism; or, we should rather say, that this criticism has itself produced these suspicions."

J. P. Lange.

In announcing a course of Apologetic Lectures, I do not fear the objection that I have undertaken an entirely superfluous task. You are all aware to what a height the controversy on religion and Christianity has risen in our day, and you may well wonder that in our country the attempt has scarcely been commenced which has been made elsewhere, especially in Germany and Switzerland, and has for some years been followed with happy results. Yet, the people of the Lord are feeling, to an increased degree, the necessity of being directed in such a way "that they may know the certainty of those things wherein they have been instructed." They are constantly confronted by the same questions, which very properly excite their interest, yet cannot be treated at sufficient length from the pulpit. What wonder if the platform has risen into a power side by side with the pulpit, which, — I do not say it without shame and a sense of my own neglect, — down to the present time has been used perhaps more in opposing than in defending the good cause. Truly, he who has anything to advise in defence and support of his holy faith may well make use of this means. This has been my conviction, at least, for some time, and your presence on this occasion proves that it may also have been yours. In fact, though slight and unprofitable questions have often been discussed here, yet enough has happened within the last few months to make us turn from them with a feeling of indifference and even repugnance, in order to investigate a totally different department. What is even the fiercest battle in the social and political world compared with the conflict concerning the most important questions of life; what is the most dangerous sickness compared with the torture of infidelity, which takes from the sick man his only trust in life and death?

The more convulsions and transitions we pass through or expect in the change of things about us, the more we feel compelled to inquire after the firm ground of those things which we have heretofore believed and hoped could not be changed. The more dark and threatening have been the times in our century, the less able are we to do without a solution to the enigma, a light in the darkness. And this light and key can only be found, as I am deeply convinced, in the Word of Truth. Whoever, therefore, tears to pieces this Word, leaf for leaf, before my eyes, takes away from me the very thing which I can least do without in troublous times. And he who restores to me even a single fragment of this precious treasure has secured to me a spiritual capital, the value of which never declines even in the most critical times, but is always sure, and advancing in value.

In announcing Apologetic Lectures on the Life of Jesus, I believe there is little necessity for either an elaborate or personal explanation. Every one knows that just this is the central point around which the battle in our day is being fought out, with as yet indecisive results. Even the new romance which Renan has served up for us as history, and which he has entitled The Apostles, cannot alter our conviction on this point. It is certain, that though the history of the Apostolic Age is important, it will never set so many tongues and pens to work as the history of Christ himself, or as even the Johannean question alone. Of course, if the Gospel History stands firm, we have a standing-place where the words, deeds, and experiences of the Apostles can be explained and portrayed. But if, on the contrary, Christ is nothing more than modern naturalism represents him to be, we may be quite unconcerned as to whether the Gospel owed its first triumph over the Jewish and Gentile world to fanaticism, or to deception, or to a conjunction of favourable circumstances, or to a combination of all these. Though these two questions are intimately connected, they are far from having equal importance. The greatest of the Apostles is, in reality, nothing less than the arm by which the sword of the Spirit was wielded; but Christ is the living Head of the Church. Take from me the Acts of the Apostles, and my picture of the origin of the Church may be clouded, but there yet remain the Apostolic Epistles. These give a general outline of this same picture, which is confirmed and illuminated in all its minuteness by the Acts of the Apostles. But, on the other hand, if you take from me the four Gospels, or even that of John alone, my whole confession of Christ will suffer from a defect whose disastrous consequences for the doctrines of faith and morals can scarcely be calculated. In fact, the Christian theologian, especially the author of a Life of Jesus, who passes over everything which has recently been urged against the Christ of the Apostles, incurs the danger of making a very unfavourable impression in consequence of his timid or apparently helpless conduct. And yet there would be no less cause of complaint on his account than on account of the holy cause which he defends.

I confess that I have long been indulging the thought of delivering such Apologetic Lectures on the Life of Jesus before a cultivated, though perhaps not strictly learned, audience. Need I fear being misunderstood if I say that I do not take in hand this voluntary task without some degree of hesitation. Let me add, at the same time, that it is by no means a doubt of the merits of the cause which I defend that produces in me a certain degree of hesitation, but solely the fear that my manner of defending it will be so inferior to the importance which it merits. It is, perhaps, less difficult to speak to learned people on a scientific question in an appropriate manner than to convey the results of learned research in a popular form in such a way as to avoid both the danger of obscurity and superficiality. I am afraid that the Babel-like confusion of tongues prevalent in our times has arisen, to a great extent, from discussing before a mixed audience controverted points, which had needed more mature consideration in the council of the learned; and I might almost affirm, that though ignorance in our day slays its thousands, it is half-knowledge which slays its tens and twenties of thousands. Yet the question has been presented before the judicial seat of the Church, and what Bacon has said of philosophy may apply with equal force to theology, — that "a little taste may lead away from God (as He has revealed himself in Christ), but that a deeper draught leads back to Him."

In examining the sources for a Life of Christ,

there is one side of the question which can be
brought only partially and with difficulty within the
range of every man's vision; but there is another
side of the same question which the simple man
can discern just as well, and perhaps even better,
than the learned; for the sharpness of the learned
man's eye is not always equal to the extent of his
studies.

The external evidences for the authenticity of
one or more of the Gospels, — which priceless
treasure they possess, — are, and must ever remain,
such as it is difficult to pass a fair and independent
opinion upon as long as we have no knowledge of
the history of the second and third centuries; and,
if you will allow the expression, this cannot generally be expected of a layman. The internal proofs,
on the contrary, are not borrowed from old and
unknown writers, but from the contents of the Gospels
themselves, and are so numerous, and at the same
time so convincing, that they can be examined and
proved, in many cases, by every unlearned yet
unprejudiced person just as easily as one can distinguish cold and warm, bitter and sweet. To
portray the full value of all the Biblical accounts
concerning the life of our Lord is a task whose
satisfactory discharge, — at least within the limited
space of a few hours, — exceeds my power. But
to examine closely at least some sources, — especially those which are on the one hand valued most
highly, and, on the other, most violently opposed,
— is an undertaking which perhaps does not lie

beyond my power, and certainly not beyond your interest. It is both an unfruitful and unrefreshing task to contend against those who argue from totally opposite views and principles, too many of which are furnished by the history of the last few years. But where the negative school ring out their notes with increasing clearness, you cannot name a nobler task for the Christian chime of our day than to produce a clear and candid testimony of what we have felt in ourselves to be the Truth and the Life, and to aid in defending anew our well-grounded faith against manifold contradictions.

I have now reached the point where I can declare my design, how I believe that I must accomplish my task, and what I desire of my hearers. It is my plan, in this and the following Lectures, to direct your attention to the Gospel of John, with the fixed purpose of learning where and how far it is entitled to our confidence and esteem, as a historical source of the Life of our Lord. I wish to lead you as little as possible into a department where you can see with your own eyes only with difficulty, but to point you to the Gospel itself as the best advocate for the Gospel. I do not design to pronounce a criticism on, or still less attempt a direct refutation of, what I believe has been untruly and unworthily said concerning the fourth Gospel in recent years, as well in Holland as in other countries. If I can only succeed in shedding a clear light, the darkness will disappear of itself. I will go to work positively rather than polemically; sincerity, and not animosity, shall be my watchword. The question with which we have to deal is not the seeking of one's own honor, but the authoritative exercise of the honor of the Holy Scriptures; not in tearing down, but in building up, — in establishing a proof of the strong foundation on which faith in the Apostolic Christ is grounded. You cannot desire that I should remain immovably cold in discussing a question which is vital in the fullest sense of the word. Yet, in conducting the defence, I wish to preserve all that composure which the consciousness of a good cause can afford, and least of all to forget the Apostolic sentiment: "I speak as to wise men; judge ye what I say." In making up your judgment, do not be arbitrary but candid; withhold your final decision until the end is reached, and you shall have weighed everything honestly; and in the full consciousness of the narrowness and defectiveness of all human knowledge, let your heart unite with mine in uttering a response to the silent prayer: "Sanctify them through thy truth; thy word is truth."

As we now pass on to speak of the authenticity of John's Gospel, nobody will deny, in view of what has been said, that we enter a department of very exciting questions; neither can it be denied that the credibility of the fourth Gospel deserves to be regarded as a subject of the highest importance. Of course, the importance of this, as well as of every other question, can be exaggerated; the loss of a single Scriptural book is by no means the downfall of Christianity. We readily grant, to a certain degree, that we should not be deprived of Christ even if we had not John's Gospel; the Christian Church existed at least half a century, though under totally different circumstances, without this Gospel having lived and flourished.[1] I am, indeed, of the firm opinion that the first three Gospels prove sufficiently that Christ is infinitely more than the theology of the present day would make of him, so long as we are permitted to receive their accounts without mutilation, and without being met at each of their expressions that has a superhuman character by the dogmatic utterance: "As for me, I do not believe that Jesus spoke these words." Further, if there be left in our hands only the four Pauline Epistles, whose authenticity even the Tübingen School could not deny, — I mean those to the Romans, Corinthians, and Galatians, — I can justify my faith in the supernatural origin of Christianity and in the superhuman character of its Founder with them alone. It is simply not true that the so-called "modern tendency" will have triumphed in case John's Gospel shall be proved to be unauthentic; even then there would still remain facts and questions which no impartial inquirer can examine without at once becoming convinced of the untenableness of this tendency.

[1] According to Tholuck, *Glaubwürdigkeit der evang. Gesch.*, p. 323, the present Greek Church derives its notion of Christ almost exclusively from the first three Gospels, without having, by this means alone, ceased to exist. Whether it flourishes in the absence of the Johannean element, is quite a different question.

But can we stand indifferently at a distance from the fourth Gospel if we inquire into the history of Him whom we confess to be our Lord and Saviour? We live in a time when the love of many has waxed cold, and when much that was once dear to them has lost its former value in their estimation. Yet the mind of the Church can hardly be so deeply sunken, so cold, and so puffed up, — if you will allow the expression, — that the loss of a Gospel of which the celebrated Herder, the apostle of humanity, once said, "an angel has written it," would not deeply affect their hearts. If we would not be led astray by high-sounding terms, we cannot conceal from ourselves the fact that we should certainly have lost this Gospel, lost it forever from our faith and life, if it had turned out to be no more than a theological romance, or the historically coloured drama which some men now-a-days declare it to be. There is much said about what a "conscientious man, who has the mournful privilege of thinking,"[1] can or cannot do in our times. But I ask, How long will such a conscientious man regard it worth his trouble to call Christ "The Bread of Life," "The Light of the World," "The Good Shepherd," and "The Life," if it is true that these and other terms mean nothing more than the private opinions of an obscure writer of romances, who lived in the latter half of the second century, and who led the Church and the world astray by his pious deception? It seems to me that

---

[1] Pierson.

a conscientious man will by no means commit such dishonourable quibbles when sitting in the instructor's chair of truth, supposing such a thing possible, for a really conscientious man would catch him in the very act of his Jesuitical mental reservation, and would despise the impostor.   •

If we need any further proof of the importance of our subject, it would be the ardour with which this Gospel has been opposed during the last three years, and which Renan has now carried to the furthest extent. So much learning and acuteness would not be applied to prove the possibility of the unauthentic character of the fourth Gospel if such men were not of the opinion that it is utterly impossible to secure a complete triumph to their so-called modern view as long as this Gospel remains firm in its place. What the resurrection of Christ is in the historical sphere the authenticity of John's Gospel has now become in the critical department, — it is the all-pervading shibboleth; and we can hardly deny the remark of Strauss, that we must first be clear on John and his relation to the synoptic Evangelists before we can say a word concerning the history of our Lord. He, indeed, is foolish who can make himself easily contented while things are in such a state. If any one who is on the point of taking away our most precious jewels, tells us that their loss would not amount to much after all, and even that we owe him hearty thanks for relieving us of a coloured glass-bead, he can nevertheless hardly expect that we should unhesitatingly take this assurance of love without some inquiry into the matter.

One more remark before proceeding to our immediate subject. The opposition to John's Gospel, — for we still adhere to this term in our preliminary remarks, — is by no means new, and yet it is not so old that it has a long history behind it. It began in England in 1792, by a certain Evanson; and Bretschneider, an author not unknown in our own country, continued it in 1820, though he had been in a slight degree preceded by certain other German writers. The invaded territory, however, was so zealously defended on different sides that the last-named opponent publicly withdrew his objections, and declared that his purpose of becoming more strongly convinced himself was now fully gained. There now came on a period of peace to the fourth Gospel, which lasted fifteen years; but it was disturbed in 1835 by Strauss, in the First Edition of his Life of Jesus. Yet so strong is the power of truth itself upon its most obstinate opponents, that Strauss felt himself compelled by the strong refutation he met with, to declare, in his Third Edition (1838), that he was no longer of the opinion that this Gospel was unauthentic, and that he now doubted the correctness of his own previous doubts concerning it. But in the Fourth Edition, on the contrary (that of 1840), he withdrew this confession, yet not, as it seems, because of new arguments, but owing to the influence of painful experiences in his personal life. And in his popular treatment of the same work (1864),

nearly twenty five years later, he unhesitatingly extended a friendly hand to the criticisms of the Tübingen School, which had arisen in the meantime,
and had hoped to dissect the Gospel of John into
an "artistic composition." It was especially this
school, which, being supported from several quarters,
made such a spirited attack on the authenticity of
John's Gospel that there was some ground for
speaking of a "modern revolt" against the Johannean
Christ. But here again it became apparent how
fire, while it burns up the straw, only gives a more
splendid polish to the gold. To say nothing of the
defence of the Gospel in other lands, it was attempted in our own country, especially by two Leyden Professors, Niermeyer·and Scholten, and followed
by good results. Strong views were heard from
Professors in Utrecht and Groningen; and in Amsterdam this Gospel found in Da Costa a warm defender. Ten years ago, and even later, all the prominent theologians in this country harmonized on
the great fact of its authenticity and value. Even
between the different schools and tendencies there
prevailed unanimity in this respect, while in Germany, theologians of the first rank, such as Lücke,
Ebrard, Ewald, Bleek, Hase, and many others, regarded it both a pleasure and an honour to conduct
the defence of John.

You may ask, then, whence does it come that
the storm has arisen anew within the last few years
and months? Has there been a sudden discovery
of difficulties in this Gospel which nobody had antic-

ipated before, and which are not reconcilable with its Apostolic origin? Or, have new witnesses from antiquity been suddenly heard against it? And, if all this has not occurred, have the earlier witnesses for it become antiquated, refuted, and brought to silence?

Neither the one nor the other has taken place. The subject itself, with its pros and cons, stands pretty much as it did before; it is only the eye by which it is observed that has become gradually changed, or, rather, there are eyes which now see through a certain kind of spectacles that render it impossible to regard this Gospel as anything else than an unhistorical, and therefore unauthentic, writing. You have no doubt sometimes heard in by-gone years of "orthodox-phobia;" but, indeed, the "miracle-phobia" of later date is scarcely a less prevalent and obstinate evil. Sceptical criticism is controlled by philosophical attacks and views which assume at the outset that this or that should, and could, by no means have happened. In regard to every work of so high antiquity as this Gospel, questions and phenomena very easily arise, which, as soon as one once begins to doubt, awaken only mistrust, and perhaps justify it to a certain degree. Perfectly new weapons against the fourth Gospel have not, so far as we know, been devised in the most recent time; but we must say, for the honour of those who are engaged in the attack, that the old ones, which have been many times wrested from the hand by our predecessors, have been sharpened anew, and are wielded with so much skill against certain points. that the latter may seem really to be threatened. In the critical method there is an art which can hardly be better described than by the expression of "the art of grouping figures," which we must be careful to distinguish from "the art of verifying dates." But there is not any special dexterity in so presenting the proofs for a good cause in the shade, and the grounds against it so in the light, that the well-meaning, but not properly instructed, observer derives an unfavourable and perhaps deeply painful impression. It is not so difficult to describe what is clear in an obscure way, the simple in an intricate style, and that which is universally recognized as having but little foundation in such a light that the uninitiated man scarcely knows how the matter stands. And certainly the acuteness of the critically analytical mind has never greater ⁀hope of victory than when it enters into the service of systematic scepticism, under the influence of fashion and the spirit of the age.

You will be able to decide hereafter how far these general remarks apply to this subject. It is very certain that such a materialistic age as ours can exhibit little sympathy for such a spiritual Gospel as that of John. Modern naturalism knows perfectly well that it may as well make its will if this Apostle has really spoken the truth. And it is quite natural that naturalism would sooner pronounce sentence of death on the Christ which John describes than subscribe to its own death-warrant. It is urged, that we must impartially inquire as to whether the grounds for the authenticity of the fourth Gospel are satisfactory; but the people who do this quite involuntarily increase the number of the conditions on which this authenticity is to be determined; and, indeed, they find it necessary to increase these conditions, because the recognition of authenticity would necessarily lead to the renunciation of the modern idea of God and the general view connected with it, — a result which is very naturally avoided by these men.

Is it our opinion that the method adopted in opposing the fourth Gospel in our day deserves the name of "partizanship?" We must confess, that, at least now and then, we cannot banish this word from our lips without an effort, when we perceive how easily sometimes the most cogent reasons in favour of this object of accusation are pushed aside, or declared to be devoid of the slightest force. It seems at least undeniable, that the perception of the necessary failure of Renan's well-known romance, — because he firmly adheres to John, — has increased the opposition of his sympathizers to this Gospel to a degree not known before. It was an opposition which was prepared with care, announced with boldness, and begun, continued, and maintained with skill and talent, but at the same time has been popularized with so much adroitness, and made use of by minds of such small dimensions, that we are involuntarily reminded of the well-known expression of the poet: "Though kings build, hod-carriers have to do the work." Will not John, who has fallen so low with some, again rise in value, since it is plain that Renan, in his Apostles, adheres incorrigibly to the authenticity of John's Gospel, — thus proving that even the most audacious revolutionist may show himself conservative on this important point? Such a thing is not impossible. Many learned men of the present day have accustomed us to a change of face with every new edition of their works; and who knows what we may experience within a few months to come? We will quietly await the future; meanwhile, let us take John's Gospel itself into our hands, and ask the author the same question which he reports the Jews to have asked his contemporary of the same name: "What sayest thou of thyself?"

"What sayest thou of thyself?" — John has as little to say of himself, as the author of his Gospel, as Matthew, Mark and Luke · have had to say on their authorship. Even the usual title, "The Gospel according (κατὰ) to John," which may be attributed to later origin, and variously construed, does not here warrant any absolute certainty. We must therefore set out upon a voyage of discovery, in order to trace out previously the still anonymous author, — a task all the more difficult, but at the same time the more fascinating, because he purposely keeps more in the background, instead of coming to the light. In the last chapter, which we have good grounds for believing was written by the same hand which had written the twenty preceding

2

ones, the author characterizes himself (chapter XXI.
20—24) as "the disciple whom Jesus loved, who
testifieth of these things, and wrote these things." [1]
But it is very probable that he only reveals the
secret of his name in this way for the very reason
that it was not unknown to his first hearers. Even
this silence leads us to suppose that the author must
not have been an obscure person, but one who was
pretty well known; and it therefore decidedly indicates the Apostolic origin of the Gospel. Or, why
should Falsarius, who would make the impression
that he was no less than the Apostle John himself,
not have been ready to ornament his writing with
this highly revered name; as, for example, the writer
of the Second Epistle of Peter, — granted, for the
sake of argument, though we do not accept it, that
this Epistle is not authentic, — immediately begins
by designating himself as "Simon Peter, a servant
and apostle of Jesus Christ." It seems to me, that
if, in this latter case, the mention of the Apostle's
name gives us ground for supposing the Epistle to
be authentic, then the absence of the name in this
Gospel justifies us in assuming its authenticity. Yet,
we only say this in passing. We desire perfect
certainty far more than bare possibility; and we
shall not find it difficult to perceive this certainty
as soon as we look at the great unnamed one, who
here stands before us, plainly in the face.

[1] Compare, on the authenticity of the 21st chapter of
John, J. J. van Oosterzee, *Life of Jesus*, last (Dutch) Edition (1865), Part III; also the literature given in the same place.

It certainly stands upon the very face of the Gospel that its writer must have been a Jew, — a Jew living in Palestine at the time of our Lord. Although he nowhere indicates his purpose to write for Jews, he, not less than Matthew, continually cites the Old Testament, and shows unmistakably that he was not merely intimately acquainted with the Alexandrine translation but also with the original Hebrew text. On the smallest points he shows an extensive acquaintance with Jewish manners and customs. Writing after the destruction of Jerusalem, he paints the Holy City, with its inhabitants and localities, in such living colours thait tappears to us sometimes as if the city and temple stood before us. One of the most prominent Oriental scholars of Germany, Henry Ewald, says: "We discover throughout, in the author, a man who possessed an accurate knowledge of the state of Galilee and Judea at the time of our Lord, — a man who possessed such knowledge as could only be found in an eye-witness of that time." [1]

It has been unjustly maintained that he speaks of the Jews in a spirit of animosity. We grant that we do not find that warm sympathy for Israel which Paul exhibits; but it is owing to the influence of totally different experiences and circumstances of

[1] Likewise Weizsäcker, *Ueber die Evangelische Geschichte*, 1864, p. 263: "We find ourselves so completely transported to the Jewish circle of ideas and to Jewish life, that, in this respect, we must recognize not only the design of portraying these matters thoroughly, but also the peculiar memory which furnishes the material for such portrayal."

life that the feeling of nationality is more outspoken
in Paul than in John. At the time of Paul, Jerusalem was still standing; but when John wrote, —
we are here dealing with him in particular, — the
city, the temple, and the visible partition-wall
between the Jews and Gentiles, had fallen; the
chosen people were no more God's people, but were
suffering the penalty of their rejection of the Messiah;
and so completely did a glowing love for Christ
pervade the writer that it outweighed his feeling
of nationality. Moreover, it is well known that,
where the Jews are spoken of in the fourth Gospel,
we must have in mind chiefly the Jews of hostile
feeling, the party of the Sanhedrists (for example,
chapter v. 15, 16, 18), who are also described in
the other Gospels in a very unfavourable light; and
what bosom-friend of Jesus could represent this
party mildly and forbearingly? Yet sorrow, mingled
with the deepest indignation, is perceptible enough
in the lamentation: "He came unto his own, and
his own received him not" (chapter i. 11). No
wonder, since he shows plainly that the old Israel-
itish expectation of the Messiah is also perfectly
his own. Even his incarnate Logos is the same
Christ of whom Moses and the Prophets bare witness;
who says of himself, "salvation is of the Jews;" and
who places himself in the same line with the people
of Israel when he makes use of the profound expression, "we know what we worship." So with our
writer himself; his whole language proves him to
be a son of Abraham, but an Israelite who has

found his Messiah, and in him the Light and Life
of the world. The fundamental Jewish type of his
individuality, which is controlled by a new, Christian,
and philosophical element, nowhere disappears, but
ever and anon presents itself anew to the attentive
eye in a surprising manner.

It is just as plain that this Israelite must have
belonged to the most intimate circle of the friends
and contemporaries of our Lord. The reflection of
the Light of the world strikes upon us as from the
very face of the man who exclaims in holy ecstacy,
"And we beheld his glory" (chapter I. 14). It is,
in fact, perfectly gratuitous to associate this declaration with a merely intellectual intuition, that has
as good as nothing to do with sensuous contemplation. It rather sounds like a note of the permanent remembrance of personal, living experience,
— as a voice from the heart of the Apostolic circle.
He who utters it speaks at the same time in the
name of others with whom he felt himself to be
one, yet not by virtue of the gift of intuition, but
because he was in possession of a matchless privilege. Yet he subsequently looks away from them;
he appears before us standing alone, and says:
"And he that saw it bare record, and his record is
true: and he knoweth that he saith true" (chapter
XIX. 35). He thus speaks as an eye-witness of
such a material fact as the piercing of our Lord's
side, with its well-known consequences. We continually recognize him as such because of his use
of the present tense, in which he generally records

his accounts, but still more in the manner in which
he invariably transports us to the scene of the
circumstances themselves. What can be more visible
than his description, in the seventh chapter, of the
state and struggle of parties in Jerusalem; what
more plastic, fresh, and outspoken than his account
in the ninth chapter of the man who was born blind,
of his parents, of his conduct before the Sanhedrim,
and of his meeting with our Lord? In fact, such
accounts may be compared' to a freshly-plucked
cluster of grapes, on which the morning dew still
glistens; and I deeply pity him who, on carefully
reading them, does not receive the slightest degree
of this impression, but can think only of the artistic
creation of an anonymous compositor, who, — oh,
unheard of connection, — combines such incomparable talents with such unskillful simplicity.

It is undeniable that our author moves as a familiar acquaintance among the friends of our Lord,
and in every case appears to know something more
than his predecessors relate. With the exception of
Peter, these chief characters are described only in
general outline by the other Evangelists; but here
they appear before us animated and active. We
here become acquainted with Bartholomew, not mentioned by him elsewhere, by his precise name of
Nathanael; Thomas, elsewhere mentioned only by
name, here appears before us three times, twice incidentally, and once as a principal character when
the risen Christ makes his appearance. [1]   At each

---

[1] John XI. 16; XIV. 5; XX. 24—29.

of these times, however, he is presented so strikingly
and naturally in the same character that the writer,
like a skillful artist, paints for us a likeness in
but three strokes of his brush that is distinctly different from all the other portraits of him, and can
only be explained on the ground of its having been
the fruit of personal recollection. There is here
presented to us a treasury of details which may be
apparently of but little consequence, but they are
explicable only on the ground that they arise from
the natural necessity of the witness to write down,
even to the smallest particulars, those recollections
which were so invaluable to his own heart.

Notice the number and size of the stone water-
pots of Cana, whose contents were changed into
wine; the value of the pounds of myrrh and aloes
which Nicodemus used at the burial; and the correct number of the fish caught in the Lake of Ti-
berias. In fact, if we would not incur the folly of
an allegorical interpretation of John's mention of
numbers, — which, strangely enough, is favoured
by our modern Rationalists, — we must recognize
the truth of this conclusion: just because there seems
to be no reasonable ground for presenting such apparently small details, they must have had their
natural ground in the personal interest of the author.
In addition to this, comes the fact that he knew
very well not only what, and how, but also when
the events transpired. His Gospel deals in such
chronological indications as have an importance
more from a psychological than from a historical

point of view. They furnish proof of his unmistakable effort, when writing, to place again before the eye the facts themselves as exactly as possible, in their natural relation, and to enable his readers to live in the midst of them as if they had been themselves eye-witnesses with him. Even in the first chapter our attention is directed to the regular succession of days, and even to the tenth hour; then (chapter IV. 6) to the sixth hour, when our Lord sat at the well; and then to the seventh hour (verse 52), when the fever left the nobleman's son. All these dates appear to be without any conceivable purpose, — but for this very reason they possess great importance, for they involuntarily remind us of an eye-witness.

And it is remarkable that we meet with these chronological intimations chiefly at the beginning and the end of the history. Are we not also accustomed, when we call to mind our early experiences, to notice with pleasure the individual parts at the beginning and end, while those of the intermediate time become proportionately indistinct, even in the best memory?

I believe we can scarcely err when we seek this Apostle in the Apostolical circle. The most of the Apostles are distinctly mentioned in this Gospel. Thaddeus is mentioned once; Philip twice; Andrew four times; Thomas five times; the betrayer eight times; and Peter thirty-three times. We have not the slightest ground for regarding one of these as

the eye-witness who here furnishes the account.[1]
We only miss two principal names: James, the son
of Zebedee, — who had been earlier beheaded by
Herod (Acts xii. 2), and who therefore cannot at
all come into consideration as the author of this
last Gospel; — and John, who, with Peter and
James, was the most intimate disciple of Jesus and
one of the so-called "pillar-Apostles."[2] That his
name is totally ignored in the fourth Gospel is
utterly inexplicable unless he wrote it himself. From
all that has been said, it can scarcely admit of a
doubt that he, and no one else, was the "other
disciple," whom we find so frequently mentioned
with Peter; who stood by the cross with the women;
and first believed at the empty sepulchre in the resurrection of the Master. This follows indirectly,
but yet without a doubt, from the mention of the
memorable *tenth* hour (chapter i. 40), in which the
friend of Andrew and Peter was brought for the
first time to Jesus, — a statement which is either
totally without occasion or purpose, or it is the
writer's ineffaceable recollection of the happiest hour
of his life.

But John's authorship of the fourth Gospel appears, above all, from one feature, which is so perfectly artless that the perception of it almost compels us to say of our author: "His language betrays
him." And what is this? While the other Evan-

1 Lützelberger's notion that it was Andrew, has been
refuted by Bleek.
2 Galatians II. 9.

gelists speak of the precursor as John the Baptist, — and very naturally so, in order to distinguish him from his companion of the same name in the circle of Apostles, — this writer nowhere regards it necessary to add this surname to the forerunner of our Lord. In all other cases he is exact and complete enough in giving names. He speaks of Thomas, "called Didymus," of Judas "not Iscariot," and of Peter as "Simon Peter;" and why does he never speak of John the Baptist as *John the Baptist,* who was universally known and honoured by this name? There is only one conceivable reason: *Because he himself was John,* and was known as such to his hearers, he did not regard the distinction as at all necessary; indeed, it may never have occurred to him to draw the distinction, because, unlike the remaining Evangelists, he did not know two Johns, apart from himself, of whom it was necessary to speak to his readers.

Now tell me, can you suppose that an impostor who appeared under the name of John, and mentioned the precursor of Jesus about twenty times, should ever have thought to himself: "I will take care always to speak of the Baptist without this surname, since I can take cognizance of only one John, as I myself have undertaken to play the part of the other?" In this case, we should indeed have to do with . one of the most cunning deceivers, who would be less in place before the judicial bench of criticism than before the police-court. Even our most hot-headed opponents must confess that the writer

of the fourth Gospel *wished* to be regarded as no
one else than John; yet, if "the style is *still* the
man," it is incumbent upon us of the present day to
explain psychologically how he could have so imitated this one without himself having *been,* and *lived*
the original, and how so much subtleness of character could be united with so much frankness of expression. You may rest assured, that, if the negative
critics did not possess their special reasons why a
certain somebody could never have written this
Gospel, the most critical acuteness could scarcely
find an end to the multitude of internal reasons
which prove that the author could have been none
other than the son of Zebedee. The question is still
propounded: "Why, then, did he not mention his
own name?" The answer is easy. Why should
the Apostle have done what was not customary in
his day, and what was utterly superfluous for readers who were acquainted with him? He certainly
never reckoned on severe critics without special gifts
for their occupation, and still less on readers who
only recently knew which one of the Apostles was
the disciple "whom Jesus loved." This honourable
epithet was infinitely dearer to his heart than any
other; he therefore made use of it with special
pleasure when it was necessary to speak of himself;
and that man cannot be a very acute psychologist
if he regards as immodest boasting the choice of a
term that expresses the deepest sense of gratitude
for the highest manifestation of favour.

When we look at these features it is simply

impossible to be mistaken about the person. We may therefore confidently group in this first conclusion the result thus far gained: The light which the Gospel itself sheds upon its author warrants us in adopting no other opinion than that it was written by John, the son of Zebedee. [1]

"But," it may be said, "You can possibly be deceived. Perhaps, what we learn elsewhere concerning John is of such a character that we must come to the conclusion that it was not possible for such a person as this one to have written this Gospel." Let us see.

We become acquainted with the Apostle John more or less from the first three Gospels, from the Epistles of Paul, from his own Epistles, and especially from the first one; at least, until within a few years ago, no prominent theologian had ever doubted that this first Epistle was written by the same person who wrote the Gospel. We become acquainted with him from the Book of Revelation, whose authenticity is acknowledged by almost every opponent of the fourth Gospel; we know him, finally, from the accounts of the Church Fathers, who tell us concerning this Apostle such things as cannot be doubted. From a combination of all these scattered colours there stands before our eyes a perfectly clear life-

---

[1] Compare K. L. Weitzel, *Das Selbstzeugniss des vierten Evangelisten über seine Person*, in the *Stud. u. Krit.*, 1849, III. p. 578 ff. — An example of how even very freethinking critics have perceived the unmistakably Johannean character of the fourth Gospel, may be found in Credner, *Einl. N. T.*, 1836, I. Sec. 93, p. 208.

picture. Quite apart, therefore, from the fourth
Gospel, there appears before us the person of John.
Well, let us ask, whether we find John in the fourth
Gospel exactly as he is known to us from the other
sources mentioned? Our answer is, judging from so
many varied characteristics, if we only knew that
this John had simply written a Gospel, we should
be driven to the conclusion that it is a Gospel which
possesses just the character that we meet with in
the fourth.

Now for the proof. It may be said, "The author
of this Gospel could only have been a friend of
Jesus." But it is exactly as such a friend that we
become acquainted with John through the synoptic
Evangelists.

"The writer manifests a culture and intellectual
development quite above the other Evangelists."
But, according to the synoptic Evangelists, the
son of Zebedee belonged to the moderately opulent
class of fishermen. [1] His mother was none other
than the judicious and vivacious Salome; and he
tarried for years in the cultivated city of Ephesus,
where he must necessarily have come in contact
with the philosophical tendency of his times. Therefore, it could not have been difficult for him to rise
to more than an ordinary degree of culture.

Again, "The author exhibits in almost every line
a spirit and holy zeal for the Lord's cause, united
with a glow of the most intense love for the person

1 Mark I. 20; Luke V. 10; Mat. XX. 20; Mark XVI. 1.

of the Master." But just this is the energetic
Boanerges-character as represented by the synoptic
Evangelists, according to whom John also wished
that fire from heaven should descend upon the in-
hospitable village of the Samaritans, and who would
not tarry under the same roof with that arch-heretic,
Cerinthus; but he is also the patriarch who grouped
his last will and testament in the commandment
of love.

Still more. "In the first three Gospels, the Acts
of the Apostles, and the Epistles of Paul, John is
everywhere the man who says much less than the
impetuous Peter; he repeatedly appears with Peter,
but always allows the latter to conduct the conversation; [1] he is the witness whose receptivity
surpasses the spontaneousness of his mind; he is
the quiet observer, — I was almost going to say,
the silent man." But this is exactly such a person
as our writer proves and declares himself to be.
Call to mind the silent John at the Last Supper of
our Lord, in contrast with the inquisitive Peter,
Thomas, and Judas (not Iscariot); and think of the
many remarks introduced in relating facts connected
with himself, which are sometimes enlarged by the
self-confession of earlier error or defective perception. [2]
We might mention, in this connection, the strange
confession of Falsarius, who hoped to awaken unlimited confidence in his account by writing in the
person of the most distinguished Apostle.

1 Acts III. and IV.; Galatians II.
2 John II. 21, 22; XII. 16.

If the First Epistle of John, not to mention the
Second and Third, was really written by this
Apostle, (and this has been acknowledged by everybody, with the exception of the latest advocates of
a single school), then the beginning, key-note, spirit,
and whole tendency of the Epistle presents such
surpassing elements of harmony with the fourth
Gospel that the identity of authorship is clearly
perceptible on every page. So mcuh is this the fact
that we can hardly silence the question, whether
one of these writings did not serve as an accom-
paniment to the other?

And now what idea must we form of John according to the Apocalypse, a writing whose Johannean origin has been left untouched by even
the negative criticism of our times? Certainly, that
he is a man who confesses with loud voice the divine nature and majesty of Jesus, — for which
reason the writer received at an early period the
name of "The Theologian;" — who finds specifically
in the work of redemption and reconciliation the
very center of the whole of Christ's labors; and by
whom the love for Christ and the desire for his
Second Coming are spoken louder than by any other
voice. Observe, that the same fundamental features
appear here as on almost every page of this Gospel,
notwithstanding the infinite diversity that must
necessarily arise from a difference between history
and prophecy. No one of impartial judgment denies
that the divine nature and dignity of the Messiah
can scarcely be declared more clearly than is done

in the Apocalypse. Then, we find here the same
key-note which echoes more majestically than anywhere else, except from the prologue to the fourth
Gospel; and most assuredly no one can call it
accidental that the only place in the New Testament,
with the exception of this prologue, where the name
of Logos is attributed to Christ, is in the Book of
Revelation (chapter xix. 13).

Still more. From tradition we become acquainted
with John as the most long-lived of the Apostles,
who evidently, therefore, — if we believe in the
continuous guidance of the first witnesses of our Lord
by the Spirit of truth, — must have stood higher
than all others, have looked deeper than all others,
and have been further removed than all others from
the contracted Jewish views which, in the earlier
period, had undoubtedly been as distinct in him as
in his fellow-apostles. I ask you, does not this
very fourth Gospel make on you the impression
that it was written by a man whose youth was
long behind him, who had seen Jerusalem lying in
ruins below him, and who had almost completely
ascended in the person of Him on whose heart he
once lay, as if to listen to the throbbings of that
heart, and at last to explain, after years of silence,
what he had seen, and heard, and lost in his in-
describably blissful contemplation of the One so un-
speakably beloved.

But I desist. Such harmonies, only a few of
which I here touch upon, can be seen in abundance by any one who takes pleasure in the study

of them. I think they prove so much, — according
to some, so little, — that inward harmony is perfectly demonstrable if we inquire after truth and
life. You will hardly be able to deny that, in this
case, the harmony is as unintentional as it is incontrovertible. We, at least, maintain that one of the
most excellent theologians of our day does not say
too much when he writes thus: "There has never
been between a book and a writer a harmony more
striking than between the fourth Gospel and the
person of John, such as the history of the first century has made him known to us."[1] And holding
myself fully responsible to answer any denial that
may here arise, I may add, on the ground of what
has been said, this second formal conclusion: What
the Gospel itself gives us ground for deciding upon
its author, is established in a multiform and surprising manner by what we learn elsewhere of John;
and the one proof, therefore, naturally and necessarily supports the other.

Here, however, the opponent of the authenticity
of this Gospel finds it impossible to look on in
silence. Thus he exclaims to us: "What is the use
of all these and other grounds; what is the use of
the witnesses of an author with reference to his
own work, if this work shows that the author is
constantly in antagonism with the work itself? And
just see how this Gospel bears upon its very face
the most direct proofs that it could not have been

---

[1] Edm. de Pressensé, *Jesus Christ*, etc. Paris, 1866. p. 223.

3

written by John." This is the exclamation of a continually increasing number of voices at our left; and
yet at the right we hear constantly repeated, in all
manner of forms, the sentiment of Ebrard: "There
is no book in all pagan and Christian antiquity
which can produce more positive and numerous proofs
for its authenticity than just this fourth Gospel."
The controversy here gives promise of great ardor,
but, on this account, it is all the more interesting.
Let us try to arrive at certainty on this point, and then
we shall see on which side lie the truth and the right.

We at once hear from the camp of our opponents the cry: "This Gospel is unauthentic, for it
contains a number of historical, geographical, and
statistical mistakes which it is impossible to expect
from a contemporary of our Lord, and least of all
from John." Granting that this is so, then we ask
every impartial man this question: Must not the
mistakes be very gross, and the errors quite distinct,
in order to be able to outweigh the proofs which we
have already presented, and which pronounce more
distinctly for the authenticity of the Gospel the longer we reflect upon them? Let me concede your
point for a moment, just for the sake of an example. A very aged inhabitant of our metropolis, who
passed through the scenes connected with the independence of the Netherlands, in the year 1813,
subsequently went either east or west, and there
published a book descriptive of the events of his
youth, on the occasion of the fiftieth anniversary, in
1863. In numerous instances he proves plainly that

he was an eye - witness, but he once makes a mistake by mentioning the Nobleman's Canal, for example, where he should have said the Emperor's Canal; or, in giving an historical account of an event, he places it on the 15th of November, while others show that it occurred on the 16th. Now I ask, would not this aged man have good ground for complaining at the criticism which would push aside all his authenticated claims to belief and reliance, because of such a small matter, and say that he could not have lived at all amid the events of the year 1813? Very well; in the most unfavourable case, the matter would stand just so with the fourth Gospel, — yet, even then, it need not give us a single sleepless night.

In the most unfavourable case, I say. Yet do we really find this to be the fact? Of nearly all the doubtful passages an explanation can be given which is at least just as acceptable as that which the negative criticism presents; and in every instance there is only a show of disadvantage to John. Against a hundred internal evidences of authenticity, we can scarcely gather together ten suspicious grounds of the kind mentioned, and one after another of these falls away on coming to the light. It is inferred, for example, from the expression (chapter xi. 49): Caiaphas "being the high-priest that same year," that the author had in mind an annual change of the high-priest's office, — which would be in conflict with history. But what prevents us from maintaining that he here speaks emphatically of "*the*

3*

[remarkable] year," the year of the death of our
Lord? Or, if this be objected to, who can say that
there was not a sort of secret and base exchange-
between Annas and Caiaphas, which, at that time,
might have been tolerably well known, although
not mentioned in history, just as many private machi-
nations in the ecclesiastical and political spheres of
later date have not been chronicled?

One more example. "'John also was baptizing
(chapter III. 23) in Enon, near to Salim;' but there
existed no such city as Enon. Jesus visited Bethesda
(chapter v. 2), but Josephus is silent on this place
of baptism." Very well; uncertainty is no proof of
falsehood, and silence gives us no right for negation. Enon is not once mentioned here as a city;
and if it was so little known that it had to be more
definitely denoted by the addition of the local speci-
fication, "near to Salim," then it should cause us no
wonder that it is not mentioned by any other topog-
rapher. Or, does our knowledge of the Holy Land
present no other chasms besides this; and, among
other places of baptism in Jerusalem, may there not
have been one by the name of Bethesda, though Josephus may have had no occasion to make mention
of it? Must we infer that the "sheep-gate" which
Nehemiah mentions, did not exist (Nehemiah III. 32;
XII. 39), because the Jewish historian is silent concerning it?

A third example. "John, according to most MSS.,
relates, at the beginning of his history of the passion
of Christ, that He went over the brook of The Ce-

·dars (τῶν κέδρων), which, however, did not exist
anywhere in the neighbourhood of Jerusalem, and
which, accordingly, could have been invented by an
ignorant writer, who confounded the well-known and
dark Brook Cedron with an imaginary brook of
·"The Cedars." The reading (chapter XVIII. 1) on which
this objection is made, is not firmly established, but
is probably to be regarded simply as an error of later
·copyists, who did not understand the subject, and
who, being naturally unacquainted, — from the ab-
·sence of their own inspection, — with the Brook
·Cedron in the neighbourhood of the destroyed city
of Jerusalem, regarded that word as the plural (κέ-
·δρων) of the Greek word *cedar*, and easily placed
the article in the plural instead of the singular number. The article in the singular stands, however, in
the celebrated Alexandrine MS.; we find it likewise
in the recently discovered, but invaluable, *Codex Si-
naiticus*. Therefore, having this twofold and extremely important testimony, we have simply to
place the article in the singular instead of the plural, and the whole invented cedar-forest, from which
our opponents discharge their poisoned arrows, suddenly sinks into the dark brook, — The Cedron.

    We take no pleasure in adducing many more
proofs of this kind. Even if the microscope could
discover a single worm-eaten spot in the coronated
pine-apple tree, that queen of fruits would never-
· theless still remain. "One must have the soul of a
registrar," as Tholuck somewhere says, "to suspi-
ciously allow the cloud of witnesses for the truth,

— of whom we have mentioned only a small num-- ber, — to be outweighed by such small matters. We give only a single proof of how doubts of this kind, closely considered, become demonstrations of authenticity and credibility. It excites suspicion that the well-known Samaritan city is called Sychar in the fourth chapter of John, while everywhere else it is called Shechem. "If John were the real writer," we are asked, "should he not have known the true name?" We answer, that in the Talmud this city is called Sychar; and in more than one way, — with an account of which I will not now burden you, — this change of name can be explained. The city bore also two other names; what wonder if our author does not quote the old Hebrew, but a later Hebrew word, by which the city was called either by the inhabitants themselves or by the Jews, — thus proving that John was perfectly at home in his own department?

It is objected that there is a suspicious sound in the words attributed in chapter VII. 52. to the Sanhedrim: "Search and look: for out of Galilee ariseth no prophet," while both Hosea and Nahum were of Galilean origin. But who does not see that the fathers of Israel, in their zeal, forgot history for a moment; and who can help finding in this very circumstance a psychological proof of the truth of the whole question, instead of charging the narrator, on such doubtful ground, with no acquaintance with the sacred history of Israel? If, as negative criti- cism will have it, the author has always so carefully placed his words upon the gold-balance, that, as we have seen, he never calls the precursor John *the Baptist*, but, with acute consideration, simply John, then it is utterly inconceivable that he could have invented an expression of the Sanhedrists in which there is such a gross historical blunder. It is also unreasonable to find fault with him for expressing himself unfavourably on Nazareth (chapter I. 47), though we elsewhere hear of nothing unfavourable of this little city. Certainly, what we read in another passage (Luke IV. 29) concerning the murderous design of the Nazarenes against Jesus, does not speak very favourably for the prevailing spirit of the inhabitants; and even if this were not the case, what becomes of all historical certainty if the smallest specialty becomes an object of suspicion if not testified by more than one witness?

If all the remaining objections of this character were mentioned, be assured they are not more important than the ones we have presented. If you look at the subject in the most unfavourable light, — in which light, however, it does not really stand, — we would have just as much right to conclude from a few such phenomena that this Gospel is unauthentic, as to infer from the supposed obscurity connected with some false or rare coins in a bag full of precious metals, that the whole bag had been sent out of a counterfeiter's workshop.

Yet we must be perfectly candid. There have been still more important objections than these adduced against the authenticity of John. "This Gospel is unauthentic," we hear from an objector, "for its philosophic colour, its historical material, and its doctrinal character are of such a kind that it could not possibly have come from John. How could the fisherman of Bethsaida have written such a philosophical introduction; how could the Apostle of Christ have wrapped himself up in the robe of the Alexandrine philosophy; and how could a Jew of that period have expressed himself in such pure Greek?" As far as this last objection is concerned, we have this to say: Supposing John to have written this Gospel, he certainly did it after spending a number of years in Ephesus, Asia Minor. It was, therefore, not impossible for him to perfect there his knowledge of the Grecian language, the foundation of which he had certainly laid very early in his native country; indeed, the Greek was much more spoken in Jerusalem in the apostolic age than Hebrew, which gradually became the exception instead of the rule (Acts XXII. 2).

As for the author's ideas, profundity of intellect and sentiment are not always the heritage of the higher classes. The history of philosophic thought proves that the sanctuary of theology and theosophy frequently comprises within its walls men of humble origin. We need recall only the names of Spinoza, Jacob Bœhme, and Moses Mendelssohn; and yet we can say, that we have no warrant for calling John a *poor* fisherman. The more fervent was his love of Christ, the more intensely it must have excited him to profound reflection on what had been revealed to him. It is just this love that animates and excites a thirst for knowledge, as it also best enables one to comprehend the endeared subject by the force of sympathy. Augustus Conti, an Italian thinker of our day, has said: "*Che ben ama ben sa,* — *He who loves well knows well.*" A residence of a number of years in Ephesus could certainly have been of great influence on the development of such a receptive and contemplative nature as that of John. He there first came into contact with that false Gnosis which was soon to spread so much devastation; and just there he must have felt himself all the more impelled to oppose this glittering error by presenting the truth in its full splendour, yet in all its depth. Who can blame him for doing this in forms derived from the philosophy of his day, just as Paul in Athens appeals to the sentiment of a heathen poet (Acts XVII. 28)? He would by no means have done this if he had not found in this use of language a trace of higher truth, and regarded this form as by far the best adapted to his first readers. Indeed, we also meet with a doctrine of the Logos in Philo, the Jew, as well as in John, yet, in this case, the harmony is confined almost exclusively to the term. Between the Logos of John and that of Philo there is such a deep abyss, — to prove which would lead us too far from our appropriate theme, — that it is impossible to doubt the independence of the Apostle even when he makes use of this form of expression. Closely regarded, he never once thought it necessary to bor-

row this method of clothing his thoughts from the
Alexandrine philosophy. Even in the Psalms and
Proverbs of the Old Testament he met with the representation of the Word of the Lord as an animated and active being, and of the Wisdom of God,
boldly personified, as sharing in the work of Creation and as an object of God's indescribable good
pleasure. What wonder if John, illuminated by the
Holy Spirit, should use this representation, — which
he had been familiar with from his youth, — where
it seemed especially adapted to his purpose of portraying the glory of Christ conformably to the customary use of language and the necessities of his
times? He has here in mind not a speculative, but
a practical design; he purposes to show that the
person of Christ affords what the philosophy of the
times was still seeking; and he develops no abstract conception of God, but encloses the historical picture of Christ in the philosophical frame of
his age.

But if we lay this form aside for awhile, we
shall find that the import of what John says of the
Logos, both before and after the incarnation, is not
at all different from that presented in the preaching
of Christ by the other Apostles, and especially by
Paul in his Epistles. From this point of view,
scarcely a serious objection can be raised against its
special use in the fourth Gospel; but if objection is
made, we must by no means make concessions on
this point. If it is perfectly safe to suppose, at the
outset, that Jesus was a mere man, and that, accord-

ingly, an Evangelist who was really his apostle
and bosom-friend could not possibly have perceived
and admired in him anything more than a man,
then even John himself could not have believed, as
somebody has expressed it, "that he had sat at the
same table with the world's Architect." But it seems
to us that to this criticism there is just this important objection: It assumes what must first be proved;
namely, that Jesus was not the Son of God, the
Logos, the Architect of the world, and that therefore John could not subsequently have recognized in
him this character, or have described him as possessing it.

Can you call such criticism logical and purely
historical? With all due respect for its acuteness
and learning, I must denominate it extremely partisan and dogmatical. To him who is really impartial, John's profound expression, "The Word was made
flesh," is really nothing less and nothing more than
what Paul says in a more popular manner: "When
the fulness of the time was come, God sent forth
his Son. . . in the likeness of sinful flesh." We believe that no one has yet shown that John could
not, and should not, have said the same thing in
his own way.

Indeed, if we further investigate the historical
matter and doctrinal character of the fourth Gospel
in their minuteness, we shall see anew, by every
comparison, that the Christ of the fourth Gospel is
fundamentally the same as the Christ of Peter, of
Paul, and of all the Apostles. It is true that not

all of them have looked with the same profound gaze upon the glory of His person and the object of His appearance. But no irreconcilable contradiction exists here; and we may confidently ask any one to show that John, in his confession of the supernatural character and majesty of our Lord, stood alone among the Apostles. He who is called "The Word" by John, is called by Paul "The Son," and "The image of the invisible God," and in both cases in the metaphysical sense. And, according to the son of Zebedee, He who "was with God," and "was God," and "dwelt among us," was, according to the son of Jonas, "manifested in these last times for you," — an expression which, taken in connection with every declaration of Peter, refers clearly to the mystery of preëxistence. [1] Is it not remarkable that the same elevated christological representation which we meet with in John is already met with, in substance, not only in the Epistle to the Hebrews and in the Epistles to the Colossians and Philippians, — which were written, without doubt, by Paul long before the fourth Gospel, and even before the writing of the synoptical Gospels, — but also in the Epistles of the same Apostle, whose authenticity nobody doubts? [2] It is clear that Peter, Paul, and John, in their harmonious description of Christ, stand upon the same ladder, but on different rounds; so much

---

[1] 1 Peter I. 20. Compare ver. 11.
[2] See, for example, Romans VIII. 3, 4; IX 5; 1 Corinthians XV. 47; 2 Corinthians VIII. 9; Galatians IV. 4. Compare Philippians II. 5—8; Colossians I. 15—20; II. 9.

is this the case, that the one who stands relatively
lowest sees more in Christ than mere humanity,
while he who proclaims his divine majesty the loud-
est, does not cease to know him as truly man. It
is evident that we can not yet go into particulars;
we hope to do that hereafter, when we shall also
look closely at the real stones of offence, — the miraculous deeds and experiences of our Lord. We
shall be contented if you grant that the objections
which are raised against the miraculous and supernatural contents of this Gospel can be raised in
greater or less measure against the most, if not all,
the books of the New Testament. But if the matter
stands so, then you may decide for yourselves
whether there is any cause for calling to mind the
well-known proverb: "That which proves too much,
proves nothing."

Yet there seems to be one book of the Bible
which is used as a special weapon for opposing the
authenticity of John. And we can all the less leave
it unnoticed, because it is held up in opposition to
his Gospel under the name, and, as it were, by the
hand of John himself. "This Gospel is unauthentic,"
we hear, "for if the Apocalypse is by the Apostle
John, it is then self-evident that the Gospel could
not possibly have come from the same hand. The
Gospel and the Apocalypse! What a contrast! Here
is the most spiritual Gospel, there the most sensuous
expectation; here the Good Shepherd who lays down
his life for his sheep, there the Mighty Ruler who
breaks the nations like a potter's vessel; here, —

yet, where all is contrast, the mention of particulars becomes wearisome and to no purpose." No wonder, indeed, that a few years ago this critical oracle found a re-echo: "No result of science is more certain than that the Gospel and the Apocalypse *could not* have come from the same hand." Is it impossible? We are properly warned from time to time to be a little careful in using this word. Shortly after the above sentiment was heralded, and, naturally enough, had to be subscribed to on penalty of the loss of all scientific reputation, the Hague Society for the Defence of the Christian Religion awarded a prize to the work of an acute scholar who, unfortunately, has already died. The conclusion, in this work, after a thorough investigation of all the particulars, may be compressed in these words: "The differences in the Johannean writings, — the Gospel and the Apocalypse, — are perfectly natural, intelligible, and necessary; but the coincidences, on the other hand, can only be explained by ascribing these writings to the same author." [1] People who are acquainted with this subject know at once that I am speaking of Niermeyer's sterling Prize Essay, which appeared as long ago as 1852, but, in our humble opinion, has become so little antiquated that it still supplies a treasure of serviceable

---

[1] Comp. A. Niermeyer, in the *Verhand. v. h. Haagsch. Gen.* Part XIII. p. 390; and especially J. P. Lange, *Über den unauflöslichen Zusammenhang zwischen der Individualität des Ap. Johannes und der Individualität der Apokalypse. Vermischte Schriften.* Vol. II. p. 173 ff.

weapons for even apologists who do not harmonize with this accomplished scholar on the date of the Apocalypse. We refer all who are interested in the subject to the work itself, in order to pass a judicious opinion on this much-discussed difference.

Let us look back at what has been said on this point very recently. We purposely desire, in the present instance, to make use of no smooth expression when we say that it is simply *not true* that no supernatural character and dignity are ascribed to Christ in the Book of Revelation. The former leader of the Tübingen School, who maintained this, and had to do it in order to sustain his system, here finds himself in an obvious difficulty, and does not know how to get out of it. It is also very clear that twenty places to one prove plainly the contrary. The names here given to Christ, the attributes ascribed to him, the works performed by him, and the honor paid him equally with the Father by all creatures in heaven and on earth, — all this, when looked at in clear light, deserves no other name than that of blasphemy if he of whom the author says it, was, in his opinion, nothing more than an ordinary man. "Whoever will maintain this," we may say with a German theologian, against Strauss, "as a critical opinion, must be either perfectly blinded, or does not wish to see. There is no third condition." [1] He who will look at the matter clearly must perceive that, as far as Christ's nature and

1 Dr. Otto Thenius, *Das Evangelium der Evangelien.* Leipzig, 1865. p. 54.

majesty are concerned, he is set forth in the Apocalypse not a finger's breadth more subordinately than
in the fourth Gospel, while the unmistakable and
grand deviation of the two writings can be explained, to a great extent, by the difference in design,
contents and purpose. May we not add, that Falsarius, who would publish the fourth Gospel under
the name of John, and who was acquainted with
the (undoubtedly authentic) Apocalypse, would have
been very careful to see that an obvious harmony
existed between the two writings? Truly, he who
would oppose the fourth Gospel must get his arms
from some other arsenal than the Apocalypse if he
has any hope of victory.

We believe ourselves now fully justified in drawing our third conclusion: Apart from the miraculous and supernatural contents, as well as from the
difference between John's and the first three Gospels,
the fourth Gospel, considered in and of itself, contains nothing which would have been impossible for
John, — as we become acquainted with him elsewhere, — to write, and which compels us to deny the
authenticity of this writing.

One step more, and our design will be accomplished for the present occasion. As you observe,
we have thus far appealed almost exclusively to the
internal evidences lying within the scope not only
of learned, but also of unlearned men. Yet, it is
especially in this department, as friend and foe remember from experience, that the conflict must be
decided. We frankly avow, that the inward proofs

are so manifold and striking that a doubt on the authenticity of John's Gospel would seem to us almost inconceivable if we did not know that there are other and concealed grounds, apart from those which are usually exposed to the light. Yet we are far from supporting our conviction of the authenticity of John's Gospel exclusively on these internal evidences. We urge, that what has good reasons for being deduced by internal evidences is impressively corroborated by external ones. As we said at the beginning, the value of the external and historical evidence can only be appreciated in its whole scope by him who possesses more than a superficial knowledge of the history and critical aids of the second and third centuries. Yet we would not be altogether silent concerning them, especially in view of the fact, that, since the publication of Tischendorf's work, — which has been more derided than refuted, — the investigation of the subject has directed the eyes of many anew to this field. [1] The contempt with which some opponents of the authenticity of this Gospel mention these witnesses of antiquity, gives us special grounds for supposing that these witnesses must be no small thorn in the side of the negative school. Here, however, — as you will appreciate and readily consent to, — we shall

[1] C. Tischendorf, *Wann wurden unsre Evangelien verfasst?* Compare *Allg. Kirchenzeitung,* 1865. No. 70. [The English translation of this work: *When were our Gospels Written?*, was issued in London (Relig. Tract Society), 1866, and in the United States in 1867. The American Edition, translated by the Rev. W. L. Gage, has reäppeared also in London. — J. F. H.]

not make use of an extended inquiry, but only present you with a brief indication of our view, the defence of which would be very easy if any one should oppose it.

I would ask whoever desires what is almost tangible, to take into account the following facts:

1. It is a fact, that there is connected with the Gospel itself an external witness, whose great value has been many times recognized by the most prominent men. Even if one adhere, with us, to the Johannean origin of the postscript (chapter XXI.), he will hardly be able to overlook the fact that the last two verses have been written, or at least enlarged, by another hand. We have specially in mind here the words in verse 24: "This is the disciple which testifieth of these things, and wrote these things: and we know that his testimony is true." Those who here speak, and 'in this declaration present the completed writing to. its first readers, are, indeed, not mentioned by name; but they would hardly have thus written if they had not known that such an assurance on their side would have been of unquestionable value and importance. This assurance must, therefore, have come from the most intimate circle of the first disciples of John, perhaps from the elders of the Ephesian Church, who pledged themselves (as also the writer himself) anonymously, but yet collectively, for the authenticity of the Gospel as a work of this Apostle, as they possibly gave it into the hands of the Church after his death, and provided it with this seal of its authenticity. The

weight of such an attestation is as clear as noon-
day, and it does not speak much for the imparti-
ality of a certain criticism if, in the examination of
internal evidence, it simply passes over in silence
this first and most ancient one. [1]

2. It is a fact, that the first Epistle ascribed to
John was written by the same hand as the fourth
Gospel. The most remarkable coincidences in contents and form declare the identity of the author. [2]
If, now, the Johannean origin of this Epistle stands
above all reasonable doubt, in consequence of the
testimony of the witnesses of the early Church, —
among whom are Papias and Polycarp, — and has
scarcely been doubted by any one, with the exception of the Tübingen School, then is also the Johannean origin of the fourth Gospel established in the
same way. Both writings stand and fall together,
— that is, they *stand* together.

3. It is a fact, that the authenticity of this Gospel
was neither denied nor doubted by any one in the
second century, except the sect of the Alogi, who
did not do it on historical, but doctrinal, grounds, and
regarded this Gospel as the work of Cerinthus, a

[1] Compare Tholuck, *Glaubwürdigkeit der evangelischen Geschichte*, 1837, p. 293; and also Beyschlag's remark in his
Die Auferstehung Christi, p. 37.
[2] Compare Grimm, *Ueber das Evangelium und den ersten
Brief des Johannes als Werk eines und desselben Verfassers*, in
the *Stud. u. Krit.*, 1847. I. — Düsterdieck, *Die drei Johannes-
briefe*. Göttingen, 1852. I. p. xxxv. ff. — Da Costa, *De
Apost. Joh. en zyne Schr.* Amsterdam, 1854. p. 169 ff. —
Compare also especially Ebrard's article: *Johannes der Apostel*,
in Herzog's *Real-Encyclop.* VI. p. 732 ff.

4*

heretical contemporary of John; hence, they considered it a product of the first century. Although this almost total absence of combating it does not altogether prove its authenticity, the presumption of its unauthentic character is by no means favoured by this phenomenon.

4. It is a fact, that the oldest Gnostics living in the first half of the second century prove that they were acquainted with this Gospel, as they made use of its terminology, quoted it, commented upon it, and made use of it in a way which would be utterly inconceivable if they had not recognized it as a work of the highest value, — that is, as of Apostolic origin. We find traces of this use of it even in the first quarter of the second century by Basilides, the Gnostic, who was in part a contemporary of John, the Apostle who lived longer than the others. Basilides even quotes two passages from John's Gospel.

5. It is a fact, that Ignatius, who wrote at the beginning of the second century, made use of such expressions as prove acquaintance with those words of our Lord which are contained in this Gospel alone; that Justin Martyr, who died A.D. 140, was not only acquainted with the fourth Gospel, together with its doctrine of the Logos, but appealed to the Acta Pilati, whose anonymous author was acquainted with the contents of this Gospel; and that the most distinguished Church Fathers of the second century, — Theophilus, Athenagoras, Apollinaris, Tatian, and others, — made use of this testimony in the most

positive manner. The silence of two of them, Papias and Polycarp, can excite no serious suspicion when we consider that there has come down to us only a fragment of the former writer, and but a single Epistle of the latter; yet both of these writings show familiarity with the First Epistle of John, to whose intimate connection with the fourth Gospel we have already referred.

6. It is a fact, that Irenæus, the Church Father, a disciple of Polycarp, cites this Gospel in the second half of the second century more than sixty times; that the oldest Syriac translation of the New Testament received it during this period without objection, together with the other canonical Gospels; that about the same time the oldest canon of the New Testament, of which a fragment (that of Muratori) has come down to us, mentions the Gospel of Luke as the third, and makes that of John follow as the fourth. Irenæus compares the four Gospels to the four winds and the four cherubim, but this detracts nothing from the value of his testimony. Convinced by historical reasons of the existence of a quatenary number of the Gospels, he indulges in this spirited comparison, but shows, at the same time, that he by no means accepted a quatenary number of the Gospels on a *priori* grounds.

7. It is a fact, that this Gospel was first quoted about the year 180 as the work of the Apostle John, *under his name*, but that for a considerable time previously it had been considered of like character to the first three Gospels, — which would have been

utterly impossible if its Apostolic origin had been
seriously doubted. There were other writings of the
New Testament, — and, among them, those whose
authenticity is far above all doubt, — which, at the
beginning, were but little, or even not at all, quoted
under the name of their authors. For what was almost never contradicted, did not always need to be
expressly mentioned; and as in the beginning the
stream of oral tradition ran still purely and quietly,
the Church was less directed to the written than the
spoken word of the first witnesses of our Lord.

8. It is a fact, on the one hand, that the Pa-
tristic literature of the second century was controlled in such a manner by the idea of the Logos that
everything compels us to suppose a common original fountain of this idea in the doctrine of an Apostle
of our Lord; and, on the other hand, that the appearance in the Apostolic period of so prominent a
fictitious writing as that of the fourth Gospel, without
the name of the author being once mentioned, must
have been a highly improbable, if not inconceivable,
exception. It cannot be denied, that the Johannean
conception of Christ remained tolerably foreign to a
large portion of the Christians of the third century,
but, for this very reason, we can the less imagine
that an anonymous writer of a romance in the middle
of the second century appeared unexpectedly one
beautiful morning from his concealment with such a
writing as this, which was even in advance of a later
period. The Christian Church gradually worked itself
up to the high standpoint of John, and relied upon

it for a succession of centuries, until the year 1792 (as we have already seen), when a sceptical Englishman gave the signal for a controversy, which has recently been transplanted from the theological schools to the bosom of the Church itself.

We might say still more, yet enough has been advanced for our purpose. It does not, indeed, excite our wonder that even a learned opponent of the fourth Gospel can regard its external proofs, considered in themselves, so satisfactory that the least doubt cannot be raised on this score. We do not believe that Lücke has expressed himself too strongly when he called this Gospel a "rock on which the hammer of criticism will sooner be broken to pieces itself than break the rock." And now I can conscientiously place before you this fourth and last conclusion, as the result of my investigation:

That which the Gospel itself leads us to suppose concerning its author; that which is established by what we elsewhere learn concerning John; and that which, on no essential point, contradicts the contents of the Gospel, when we consider it in and of itself, apart from the question of miracles, are established by the testimony of Christian antiquity in such a way as justifies faith in the authenticity of the Gospel to a high degree, and will continue still more to justify it, on further and impartial examination.

Here we remain for the present. But shall we consider the case decided for ever, and the adherents of the opposite view stricken to the ground by one blow? We will willingly leave to others the passion for scientific murder and destruction. We hope to discuss hereafter many difficulties which we have not yet touched. But we can now confidently assert this much: We would heartily congratulate all those who are engaged in the study of the writings of classical antiquity if they always enjoy such strong proofs of the authenticity of its master-productions as, through the wise providence of the God of Truth, prove the authenticity of this much-mistaken Gospel. As a matter of course, if one is disposed to do so, he can always find subterfuges, and start exceptions, and allow the great force of evident probabilities to be overbalanced by merely abstract probabilities. Yet, as far as we are concerned, we doubt whether stronger proofs can be justly demanded in favour of an historical statement (which is to be distinguished from a mathematical one) than those to which we have now called your attention. In our opinion, the good cause of John's Gospel is more threatened by bitter enemies than ever before; yet by no means do we regard its cause as lost. And since we may now see, in advance, on which side will incline the scales of truly impartial judgment, we reverently acknowledge the deeper truth which lies concealed in that false supposition, that "John expected to live until the second coming of our Lord," and we can say with a profound feeling of admiration, love, and gratitude: "This Disciple shall not die." [1]

[1] On the External Evidences, read the valuable treatise of Hofstede de Groot, Professor in Groningen, entitled,

A Witness of the Longest - Lived Apostle as the first Witness of the Antiquity and Authority of the Books of the New Testament, together with other Witnesses thereon before the Year 138, in the Dutch Theological Review, *Waarheid in Liefde*, 1866, p. 449 ff.; also its continuation under the title of *The Antiquity and Authenticity of John's Gospel according to External Witnesses before the Middle of the Second Century,* p. 593 ff., in the same periodical.

The following German literature should also be compared: H. Ewald, *Ueber die neuesten Zweifel an der völligen Aechtheit des Ev. Joh.* in the *Jahrbücher der bibl. Wissenschaft*, 1865, p. 212 ff. As a popular work, we may recommend *Vom Evangelio des Johannes. Eine Rede an die Gemeinde*, by C. A. Hase. Leipzig, 1866.

II.

JOHN AND THE SYNOPTIC GOSPELS.

"THE altogether peculiar majesty and glory of Christ which are portrayed in the Gospel of John were certainly not concealed from the other Disciples; but John alone was capable of reproducing them as a picture. Every man can see the delicate haze of an Alpine mountain glowing in the twilight, but not every man is able to paint it. John had the nature of a living mirror, which did not merely receive the full glory of our Lord, but knew how to reflect it upon others."

A. EBRARD.

"This Disciple shall not die." With these words of faith and hope I recently closed my first Lecture, which was designed to prove the authenticity of the Gospel of John, as far as the limited time would allow.

After further reflection upon the highly important subject which at that time engaged our attention, I do not recall that sentiment. Yet, it does not by any means declare that John should attain to immortality without having to die. On the contrary, as the history of our Lord is one of triumph, so is also the history of his true witnesses the same, though it must be after a conflict which is constantly renewed. It is a victory of rising again from an often-prepared grave. At the beginning of the present century there appeared in Germany a frivolous work under the title of John the Evangelist and his Expositors before the Final Judgment. [1] But if we take the title in a serious sense, and imagine the Apostle as standing with his interpreters before the great judgment-bar, we can well suppose that he would have ample grounds for complaining at not a few among the number. It is certain that but few writings of the New Testament have been regarded and decided upon in such a divergent and often contradictory way as that to which we now direct your attention anew. Call to your remembrance once more the enthusiastic panegyrics which have been pronounced upon the "Spiritual Gospel" all the way from Origen down to Matthias Claudius, and contrast them with the severe charges which have been heaped within the last few years upon the "fourth," — for so this Apostle is frequently called, with unmistakable contempt, — and you can scarcely conceive how so much honor and derision can be applied to one and the same person. We can scarcely suppress this exclamation: Through what un-

---

[1] Vogel, Superintendent in Wunsiedel.

happy change of fate, the eagle, whose bold flight
has been watched by so many millions of eyes with
admiration and interest, seems all at once to have
have been nothing but a raven, which was dressed off
for centuries with feathers not its own, until a sharp
eye at last discovered the deception! Truly, the
Apostle John, in view of his reception within the
last few years, may repeat the sad lamentation
placed in the mouth of faded fame by one of our
tragedians: —

> "How sudden is my fall! How far am I cast
> down!"

If not "down to yesterday," at least down to only
a few years ago, scarcely any one hesitated to
give the crown of honor to the "only tender chief-
Gospel," as Luther called it. And though no prominent theologian has failed to observe the great
diversity between the synoptic accounts and that of
John, yet the value of the latter has always been
recognized; indeed, it has not been unfrequently the
case, that, owing to Schleiermacher's influence, the
preference has been given either consciously or unconsciously to John. But, at present, it seems to
have become settled in some quarters that there has
been a general deception, — that the New Testament really contains a double picture of Christ: the
synoptic on the one hand, and the Johannean on
the other. The diversity between the two, which
has been studiously widened as far as possible, is
held to be a permanent and irreconcilable conflict,
which invariably results in favor of Matthew,

Mark, and Luke. The Gospel of John, on the contrary, when compared with its predecessors, is getting to be thought rather an obscure and mystical writing, having no purely historical, but only a dogmatical and philosophical, character, and presenting to us the conception of Christ as entertained by the anonymous author and kindred spirits rather than a visible picture of Christ in the framework of his age. It follows from this, that, where we have to do with a knowledge of the life of Jesus, the first three Gospels (very naturally, on condition of a necessary critical sifting) must be sought for counsel, while, on the contrary, we can at most conclude from the fourth what Jesus was *thought* to be in the second century, but not at all *who Jesus really was.*

What shall we answer, in reply to these and other assertions, that, by the confident tone in which they are presented in manifold ways, are very well adapted to make some impression on him who hears them for the first time? We might call to mind the fact, that the believing Church of all centuries does not appear to have specially observed this irreconcilable conflict between the synoptic and the Johannean Christ, since it has been built up alternately by reading and reflecting on the words and deeds of the one as well as the other, and has drawn from both together an image of Christ before which it still bows in reverent admiration.

The perception of this fact proves at least that the diversity mentioned above does not endanger the profound sanctity of the Christian consciousness of faith, and it awakens the supposition that the conflict here is more apparent than real. [1] Yet the correctness of this supposition must first become apparent by thorough examination, and you may now imagine what the subject is which we present at this time for your consideration.

In the previous Lecture we saw that the fourth Gospel, considered in itself alone, contains nothing directly contradicting its own testimony concerning its author. But we have already made it clear that the difference first comes to light when we place this fourth Gospel beside the others, or even present it in contrast with them. It cannot be denied that, here and there, we receive a different impression. Many a time the expression seems to come to our lips: "If this is true, then I can hardly accept the other; for Christ seems to represent himself in John differently from what he does in the synoptic

---

[1] Roger Hollard very properly writes thus on the character of Jesus Christ, in the *Revue Chrétienne*, by Edm. de Pressensé: "Christian piety is fed by our four canonical Gospels, and yet it knows but one Christ. The significance of this fact is important. In the people, as well as in a child, there is an instinct which surpasses any acuteness of the best criticism. We can say of the people what Jesus said of his sheep, — 'and a stranger will they not follow.' If, now, the view mentioned is established, and the Jesus of John is totally different from the one of the first three Gospels, we must confess that Christendom has saluted a stranger by the name of Master for more than fifteen centuries without the slightest doubt; and has regarded both the stranger and the Master worthy of the same adoration. Such a misconception would not only be without a parallel in history, but would even have history against itself!"

Gospels." Now, is it possible that he is another, or really a different Christ? I need not say a word on the importance of this question. Two conceptions inexorably excluding each other cannot be equally true. However much it would cost us to give up John, we should have to adapt ourselves to this loss; for it is not one witness for the truth, but the truth itself, that can make us free; and, as thinking Christians, we must certainly act with reference to freedom from sin, but yet not less with reference to freedom from error. You will now follow me with increased interest as I compare, at the present time, the doctrinal idea and then the historical representation of the fourth Gospel with those of the first three, with special reference to the question, whether the two sides stand in such strong contrast with each other that we shall be compelled to say: "We must accept either one or the other, but not both?" After we have reduced the diversity stated to its true limits, it will not be difficult to draw the proper conclusion, both in reference to the authenticity and credibility of this writing in general, and the rank which it is to take permanently among the sources for the history of the life of our Lord.

I. The doubt arising from the very peculiar doctrinal system of the fourth Gospel has furnished its latest opponents with a strong, and, as they think, apparently insuperable weapon. It was strikingly said not long ago: "We do not doubt the authenticity of John's Gospel because of weak and unsatisfactory evidence, nor because doubts have been raised

against the historical character of its accounts, but
because we believe that we have found in it a system which is totally at variance with that which it
must be presumed that the disciple whom Jesus
loved could and must have believed."

We are constantly hearing at our left such expressions as these: "See for yourself, that the form
in which you hear Christ speak in the first three
Gospels is infinitely different from the garb in which
he clothes his teachings in the fourth. And what
a broad abyss there is between the two in the
matter, spirit, and tendency of Christ's words! Here,
the truth is presented through the transparent me-
dium of a parable, while your ears are there greeted
by the sharp tone of excited controversial language,
carried out by our Lord in endless repetition, and
answered by his enemies with inconceivable mis-
understanding and obstinate contradictions. It appears as if the Johannean Christ not only must be
misunderstood, but that he purposely wished to be
misunderstood; his teaching is doctrinally coloured, and
the substance and centre about which everything turns,
is not the Gospel of the kingdom of God, as in the
synoptic Gospels, but his own person. Everything
depends on whether you hear in this Gospel the
preacher of repentance, or Jesus himself, or the
Apostle, speak; or, whether they all speak the same
thing in almost the same form. Is it supposable
that the elaborate discourses of Jesus, which we
constantly meet with here, were really delivered by
him in this form, and, — supposing that John is

the writer, — have been thus recorded with satisfactory fidelity? Indeed, not merely the form of the words of Jesus, as they are here presented to us, but also their import is of that kind that there is good ground for the mistrust which gives rise to our question. Still more. In the first three Gospels, you hear the voice of a simple Rabbi of Nazareth, whom we understand, become fond of, and can follow; but the Johannean Christ appears before our eyes in superterrestrial splendour, continually bearing witness to the supernatural relation in which he, and he alone, stands to the Father. He never appears as a person from the midst of Israel, but always as one who stands in opposition to Israel, and speaking of his own importance both for the believing and the unbelieving world. There, he begins to speak first at a definite time of his suffering and death; here, we hear him make mention of his tragical departure at the very beginning of his public ministry. There, the resurrection and the final judgment are portrayed in poetic colours, just as we know them to have been anticipated by the Jews, and as Jesus, — a phenomenon which we can readily understand, — conceived the same thing; but here, we hear him speak of an eternal life this side the grave; the question is not at all concerning hell, the visible Second Coming, nor the general judgment; everything is conceived in a perfectly spiritual way, but is heard, at the same time, in an altogether different circle of ideas from that in which we have elsewhere moved. In reading Matthew,

5

Mark, and Luke, the wanderer seems to be travelling over a pleasant and fruitful plain, but in reading John he ascends a mountain whose peak is lost in the clouds. Or rather, the first three Gospels remind us of a cheerful brook, whose bottom we can clearly see as it hastens onward; but John is a majestic lake, whose surface mirrors the firmament with its stars, and whose depth is altogether concealed from our vision."

If we have now declared fully and plainly what has seemed obscure to many an one on attentively reading the fourth Gospel, it cannot excite our wonder if the opponents of its authenticity advise us, on the ground of these and other animadversions, to speak in future no more of a *Johannean Christ*, but rather of a *Christian John*. But shall we all the less avoid a full explanation of these charges, or withdraw from the consideration of this question: How far do the ideas of diversity and antagonism here coincide? We promise to present to you less what is new than what is complete; and we would at the same time suggest to our opponents to avoid the continual repetition of what has been said and as often refuted. Yet we frankly place before you for examination the following remarks, as a subject for your thorough and impartial reflection.

First: Every distinguished personage, — and certainly all apply this term to the Saviour, — presents to the observer different, and more or less heterogeneous, sides and points of view, which, on superficial examination, preclude each other, but when seen closely, complement one another to a certain degree. One of Gœthe's biographers says of him, that there was hidden in him ten different persons; we discover in Luther, Augustine, and Paul, such a multiplicity and fullness of intellectual and spiritual life that it sometimes costs us an effort to discover in the very divergent exhibition of this life the same fundamental characteristics of one and the same person. How very different the Paul of the Epistle to the Romans, for example, appears from the one of the Pastoral Epistles, or the Paul of the Acts of the Apostles from the one of the Epistles in general! So much is this the case, that, if one does not look deeper and further, he will sometimes be involuntarily led to call one or the other picture unhistorical, merely through being governed by the first impression. We hear the great Apostle to the Gentiles saying on one occasion: "I desire to be present with you now, and to change my voice" (Galatians IV. 20); and we know how remarkably he succeeded in this more than once. But, on the scale of such an instrument, an infinite variety of notes can take place without any disturbance of harmony. Yet, if this is the fact in Paul, much less can it surprise us to find the same thing in Him who was more than Paul, and in whom it is much easier for us to suppose an infinite wealth of forms and expressions of life than the contrary. In the polished and thousand-faced diamond there shines one and the same light in a multiform blending of colours; and should we expect the case to be

5*

different in an infinitely higher sphere, — the spiritual and the Divine ? Even in the Christ of the
synoptic Gospels there slumbers such a depth of
self - consciousness, together with an exhibition of
such glory and with such an abundance of form,
that it can excite nobody's wonder to perceive in
him both thoughts and forms which those of his
biographers whom we have heretofore consulted
either did not make us acquainted with, or, at least,
did not do it in such a manner.

Second: It is proper to observe, that the first
three Gospels exhibit a great difference in the matter
and form of our Lord's teaching. In the Sermon on
the Mount we find here and there a striking application of metaphor, just as we find it continually in
John; but we look in vain there for parables in the
strict sense. But later, on the other hand, we see
our Lord opening his lips on the shore of the Sea
of Galilee in order to speak in a succession of parables, of which different ones, apparently on the
same day, were spoken to the same audience. And
as the period of his public instruction approaches
its termination, we hear from the top of the Mount
of Olives a prophetical and eschatological discourse
(Matthew xxiv. and xxv.), which varies in import
and tone as much from the popular parable as the
parable does from the Sermon on the Mount. Our
Lord speaks at one time as the Lawgiver of the
New Testament, at another as the friendly, popular
teacher, and at still another, as the herald of his
own Second Coming. Leaving Matthew and Mark

out of the question for a moment, we find just in that part of Luke whose great value has been acknowledged by later criticism (the account of the Last Journey to Jerusalem, chapter IX. 51 — XVIII. 14) a treasure of thoughts and doctrinal expressions whose existence we are scarcely permitted to anticipate by the first two Evangelists. The parables in Luke, — I may mention merely those of the Unjust Steward, the Rich Man and Lazarus, and the Unjust Judge and the Widow, — when placed beside those of Matthew, have such a peculiar appearance that one could almost prophesy the appearance of some critic who would venture to doubt the one or the other series. From these particulars I come to the conclusion, that Christ, who could draw out so many relatively new things from this single rich store-house, could certainly not have been so poor as not to be able to resort, if necessity required, to many another store-house more adapted to circumstances and better suited to his purpose.

Third: Another point which we would now ask you to observe. The evident difference in matter and form between the words of the Johannean and the synoptic Christ can be explained in great part by a difference of circumstances and purpose. I confess that if I should read, for example, that the farewell words in John were spoken before a mixed Galilean multitude, it would sound to me as incredible as if I heard that the Sermon on the Mount had been delivered in Solomon's Porch at Jerusalem before the unbelieving Jews. But it is well knonw

that John transports us, by his description of our
Lord, principally to Judea, while the remaining Evangelists refer us almost exclusively to Galilee. Should
it be a proof of Christ's wisdom in teaching if he
had spoken to the people in the same tone as to
the most prominent Jews, or *vice versa?* Could not,
and must not, the tone in which he here announced his joyous message to the poor and ignorant,
and that in which he there opposed the oppressors
and seducers of the people, have been different in
each case? A proof of the correctness of this observation may be found in the fact that where we
see in Matthew, for example, our Lord coming in
contact with the Jews of Jerusalem (as in chapter xv.,
in his conversation on tradition and the laws of purification with the Pharisees and Scribes who had
been sent to him, or in chapter xxIII., in his controversial discourses at the end of his labors), the language is altogether different from that before the
people who hungered after salvation, and it breathes
the same holy indignation which we find in the
castigatory words in John's Gospel. On the other
hand, we hear him in John speaking so clearly and
comprehensively, according to the necessity and circumstances of the moment, — we need only refer
to the well - known conversation with the Samaritan
woman, — that it could hardly excite our wonder
if we found a leaf of this kind in the first three
Gospels.

Fourth: From what has been said, if we tarry
at the form of Christ's words as related by John,

we must confess that we find here no parables in
the strict sense of the word.   But we can little
doubt that this form was much more adapted to
public instruction than to dialectical controversy
with the representatives of Rabbinical learning; and
still less can we doubt that in the fourth Gospel
the metaphor, — as those of the Good Shepherd
and the True Vine, — is carried so far, and is so
strikingly elaborated, that it sometimes approaches
the dramatical and historical character of the real
parable. Almost everything which criticism has objected to in the form of our Lord's words in John
has its analogies and parallels in the synoptic Evangelists, — which analogies and parallels are sometimes
remarkable, especially if we bear in mind the difference of circumstances and purpose. Complaint is
made, for example, at the length of the Johannean
discourses. But, from the Sermon on the Mount, as
presented to us by Luke (chapter VI. 17—49), it is
plain that Christ sometimes delivered also in Galilee even more extended discourses. It is held that
Christ's words sometimes repeat themselves. But
without reminding you at length that, notwithstanding a partial repetition, our Lord's speaking in John
moves on uninterruptedly, and in its flow continually
carries with it new grains of gold, we may observe, that also in Matthew, Mark, and Luke we
sometimes find two or more parables employed in
the elaboration of almost the same fundamental
thought. He who, like Strauss, can call the Holy
of Holies of Christ's High-Priestly Prayer "tedious,"

is as little competent to pronounce a correct opinion
in this department as he who places the music of
Mozart or Beethoven on a level with the intolerable
din which seems to be the pleasure of our house-
keepers when cleaning the house at certain times
of the year, but which is the very terror of about
as many quiet-loving masters of families.

Much has been said against the mysterious, paradoxical, and profoundly mystical character of some
of the statements of John. I might, perhaps, apply
here the sentiment of a celebrated man: "He who
scorns paradoxes does not love the truth;" but I
will rather ask, whether we have to seek altogether
in vain for this kind of expression in Matthew and
the two other synoptic Evangelists? Such a statement, for example, as "He that loveth his life shall
lose it, and he that hateth his life in this world
shall keep it unto life eternal," may also be read
substantially in the first Gospel (Matthew xvi. 25);
and what can sound more paradoxical then the saying which has *not* been preserved for us by John:
"For whosoever hath, to him shall be given, and he
shall have more abundance: but whosoever hath
not, from him shall be taken away even that he
hath" (Matthew xiii. 12)? It excites suspicion that
the words of our Lord in the fourth Gospel are
generally misunderstood, and that where they are
spiritually intended, they are perverted to absurdity
by literal interpretation. But also in Matthew
(chapter xvi.) and Mark (chapter viii.) we hear that
even the Disciples regarded our Lord's warning

against the leaven of the Pharisees and Sadducees
as a proof that they had taken no bread with them;
and in Matthew (chapter xxi. 45) it is communicated
as something remarkable that the chief-priests and
Pharisees understood our Lord on that occasion,
which, according to this Evangelist, must by no
means have been the case usually. I might say
more; but this is sufficient. To the eye that does
not look for contradiction and opposition, this is perfectly clear: In the synoptic Evangelists our Lord
sometimes speaks in such a Johannean way, and in
John so synoptically, that, if one absolutely adheres
to their opposition, he has scarcely any other choice
left him than to pronounce a large part of both accounts utterly unauthentic and incredible.

This will become very plain to us if we take
into more thorough consideration the contents of
Christ's declarations according to both accounts.
Without doubt, the statements of Jesus with reference to his superhuman origin and dignity are far
more numerous and forcible in the fourth Gospel
than in those we meet with in the other three. We
know full well that they are a thorn in many a
side, but we ask at the same time this question:
Where does our Lord say anything according to
one which he denies according to the other., or
where does he deny according to this account what
he asserts according to that one? Does the sceptic
suppose that by adhering to the synoptic Evangelists he is really exempted from accepting the supernatural character of Christ? Yet it is not in John

that we read that great utterance: "Where two
or three are gathered together in my name, there
am I in the midst of them" (Matthew xviii. 20);
nor: "I am with you alway, even unto the end of
the world" (Matthew xxviii. 20); nor: "If David
then call him Lord, how is he his son" (Matthew
xxii. 45); nor, — but why should I burden you with
a long succession of such declarations? That mysterious and majestic one: "All things are delivered
unto me of my Father; and no man knoweth the
Son but the Father; neither knoweth any man the
Father save the Son, and he to whomsoever the Son
will reveal him," [1] proves sufficiently that the assumption that the Christ of the first three Gospels
was a merely human Christ, bears the stamp of
evident falsehood.   The sceptics know no other
way of getting out of their difficulty here than by
applying to the scientific department the "rounding-
off" system that has been applied in our day with
good results to the political sphere; and thus maintaining with Strauss, for example, that one half of
the grand utterance, "no man knoweth the Father
but the Son," is well enough in place, but that the
other half, "no man knoweth the Son but the Father,"
was never spoken by Jesus. [2]

   This, by the way, is a critical operation which
may be applied with extraordinary results to a

----

[1] Matthew XI. 27. Compare Luke X. 22. See, also,
Matthew XXI. 37; XXII 2; XXIV. 35, and other parallel
passages.
[2] *Leben Jesu, für das deutsche Volk bearbeitet*, p. 209. 1864.

number of other objectionable passages, but, without
doubt, would finally prove to even stone-blind eyes
where dogmatism and where true science can be
found. We say, further, that men utter an evident
untruth when they assure us that the Christ of the first
three Gospels places himself on a level with all men
in order to pray with them, "Our Father;" and
perhaps also, "Forgive us our debts." [1] Formerly,
the opinion was held that Christ did not say, "Let
us pray," but, "After this manner therefore pray
Ye: Our Father," and that from his twelfth year
he made an evident difference between "*Our* Father"
and "*My* Father,"—which cannot be denied according even to the synoptic Evangelists, and therefore expresses plainly enough the consciousness of
an altogether special relation to the Infinite. If our
Lord places his purpose and majesty more strongly
in the foreground in the fourth Gospel than is the
case in the first three Gospels, it is because he
speaks in the two cases under totally different necessities and circumstances. His discourses in Galilee, which are directed to the people, exhibit a
more introductory and pedagogical character, while
his disputations with the Jews of Jerusalem are
more polemical and apologetical. Yet there, as well
as here, he declares himself to be the Son of man,
— though with supernatural origin and dignity, —
and the Son of God, but at the same time conscious
of his dependence on the Father. The claims which

[1] Keim, *Der geschichtliche Christus.* 3rd Ed. p. 39.

he makes with reference to himself are the same in both cases. If objection is made to the fact that he prophesies in John the death of his enemies in their sins, it can be said that the eight woes in Matthew, or the sentence pronounced upon the impenitent cities of Galilee (Matthew xi. 20—24), do not have a less fearful sound. A declaration, on the other hand, like that in the synoptic Gospels: "He that loveth father or mother more than me is not worthy of me" (Matthew x. 37), is just as immoderate as the direct pardon of sin is blasphemous, if he who speaks them both has no higher rank, either in his own consciousness or in the eyes of the Evangelists, than merely that of one of our fellow-men. No doubt there is a difference, but it is no other than that between the half-blown bud and the perfectly-developed flower. It has been very correctly remarked, that the synoptic christology does not merely *assume* the Johannean statements, but that it *requires* them, in order to complete it, and *vice versa*.

Nor is the case at all different with the manner in which our Lord, according to both accounts, proceeds to announce his Messianic character, his suffering, and his death. There has been great injustice in concluding from the account of the incident at Cæsarea Philippi (Matthew xvi. 13 — 17) that Jesus had neither expressly professed before this time to be the Messiah, nor had spoken of his suffering and death. An impartial reading and comparison of even the synoptic accounts alone, show us that he had earlier indicated one as well as the

other, though in a more figurative manner; [1] and thus
it cannot seem strange to us to hear our Lord speak
in John, at the very beginning of his public labors,
of the "destruction of this temple," and of "being
raised as a brazen serpent," and soon afterwards
declaring himself to the Samaritan woman as the
promised Messiah. From the first three, as well as
from the fourth Gospel, there is sufficient evidence
that, in his frank disclosures, as well as in the figurative garb of what it was necessary to say with
carefulness, he constantly kept in view the condition and necessity of the circumstances of the occasion. According to both accounts, we hear him
intimate his approaching end, at first more guard-
edly and figuratively, but subsequently, openly and
precisely. According to all four Gospels, he repeatedly prophesied his resurrection from the dead,
and thereby exhibited in the most positive manner
his Divine foreknowledge. Those who will not
accept this fact in John, must deny it in all the
Gospels alike, and ascribe only to those the right
of speaking who hold such prophecies to be a priori
impossible, and, accordingly, allow their historical
criticism to be controlled by dogmatical prejudice.
In the synoptic Gospels, as in John's, Christ's passion and death are produced by the same cause, and
are indispensable for the same purpose; there, as
here, that passion and death contribute to the glori-
fication of the Sufferer himself, and an interest in

[1] Matthew V. 11, 12; VII. 21—23; IX. 15; XII. 39 ff.;
Luke IV. 18—22. ff.

the fruit of his life and death is made dependent upon the same conditions.

If we were to supplement all that we say by a number of Scriptural proofs, there would be almost no end of quotation. You can compare the Scriptures with the Scriptures for yourselves. Permit me to direct your attention to the doctrine of eschatology, because it is here, in particular, that great weight has been laid on the difficulty in question. "In John," we hear it said, "there is not a word of the lower regions, of the resurrection of the dead, and of the subsequent judgment, as is the fact in the first three Evangelists." This is certainly the case, we answer, if this Gospel must first be subjected to a sort of military execution, and the critic lays down his rule that this or that could not have been said by the Johannean Christ because it does not fit the scheme (prepared by the critic himself) of his ideas, or if the expositor determines to cast out the obnoxious element from the Sacred Text by a dexterous stroke of his art. But if such operations as these be not welcome to you, I would then ask you this question: "What must we understand by the Johannean Christ speaking of 'an hour' in which all who are in their graves shall hear his voice; of a resurrection 'in the last day;' of a judgment appointed for this 'last day;' of a waiting 'till he comes,' and of a second coming 'to take his children to himself?' " [1] It would be indeed diffi-

---

[1] John V. 28; VI. 39, 40, 54; XII. 48; XIV. 3; XXI. 24.

-cult for us to imagine that all this means a merely
spiritual coming. I readily grant that the Resurrection, the Judgment, and the Second Coming of
our Lord at the end of the world, stand altogether
in the background in the fourth Gospel, but yet they
are by no means absent from it. On the contrary,
the idea of eternal life refers here repeatedly to a
future life; [1] while, on the other hand, there are
traces in the first three Gospels that Christ speaks
in them of life and resurrection in a more spiritual
sense. [2] And thus we come to this conclusion: The
opposition must be regarded as purely relative, but
by no means as a real contradiction. On the contrary, the apparent contradiction lies merely upon
the surface, while the coincidence lies in the depths
below.

In the same way the difference in our Lord's
doctrinal system, — so far as we can speak here
of a doctrinal system, — gives our opponents no
ground for denying the authenticity of this Gospel.
We can not, without great impropriety, doubt the
credibility of John in communicating such, and so
many, highly important statements. Must it be regarded as altogether inconceivable to meet here
with the very words of the Incarnate Word? Must
we, forsooth, suppose that John allows our Lord
to speak just as, according to his view, he could
have spoken, and possibly should have spoken? I
know that this is maintained, but we have already

1 See, for example, John IV. 14, 36.
2 See, for example, Luke IX. 58; XV. 24; XX. 38.

had occasion to see that assumption and proof are ideas not always found together. It cannot be denied that a very great coincidence exists between John's own use of language and that of Jesus in John's Gospel. This is a natural result of that inward relation in which he stood for years with our Lord, whose manner of life, thought, and speaking he had gradually appropriated. Nevertheless, we perceive a very essential difference between the use of language by the Evangelist himself and the principal persons of his history. John, for example, calls Jesus the Logos, yet Jesus never calls himself this in John's Gospel, but, as in the other Evangelists, the Son. Jesus here calls the Holy Spirit "the Comforter," as his representative with the Disciples; but John, on the contrary, calls Jesus "the Advocate" (1 John ii. 1), literally, the Paraclete, as the representative of his children before the Father. Jesus speaks of his kingdom and the kingdom of God; but John does not use this expression in his Gospel or in his Epistles when he speaks himself. Whence such a difference, if the words of our Lord in this Gospel are to be regarded as nothing more than the Evangelist's own simple mixture?

As far as the Baptist is concerned, John's record has a more majestic sound than we find the case in the first three Gospels, but yet it contains nothing which it was impossible for the last and greatest of the Prophets to explain; and at least a measure of this difficulty disappears on observing that the fourth Gospel gives an account of this record principally after the appearance at baptism, when there undoubtedly appeared to him a new and higher light, while the synoptic Evangelists, on the contrary, mention his record in an earlier period. It is not necessary for us, therefore, to deny that the Evangelist, in reporting our Saviour's words, used a certain degree of freedom. In ancient times there was not a continual effort for diplomatic and stenographic exactness on such points. The Spirit which led John to record the words of the Word was not only a Spirit of truth, but also of freedom; but it is beyond all doubt that we can regard him as a true and faithful reporter of the words of Jesus.

In order to prove this conviction to be well-grounded, we do not now appeal first and directly to the promise of the Holy Spirit, which was made by Christ and was fulfilled through him (although we could make this appeal without thereby incurring the charge of arguing in a circle), as this promise and its fulfillment are not only communicated to us by John himself, but also by the synoptic Gospels, the Acts of the Apostles, and the Epistles. [1] We would lay just as little stress upon the supposition, — which, indeed, is very reasonable, — that the Evangelist, many years previously, even before his Gospel had seen the light, had gathered together his own records of what was of such incalculable

[1] Matthew X. 19, 20; Luke XII. 11, 12; XXIV. 49; Acts I. 8. Compare John XVI. 13.

value to his own heart. We prefer to direct your
attention to the power of his love, by virtue of
which such lasting recollections as those, instead of
becoming dissipated by time, constantly became more
deep and living, and stood out in magnified prominence and clearness at the end of his life. We
may ask, whether, with this profound reverence,
— many call it an *idolatrous* one, — which the
Evangelist entertained for the Master, it is not psychologically inconceivable that he should have placed
in his mouth such promises and threats, exhorta-
tions and prayers, as he could and must have known
had never been really uttered? We present this
thought for reflection: Whether a collector, who desired to let our Lord speak in human love as God,
ever came to the thought of proving his Divine nature and origin from the fact that in the 82nd Psalm
there is once exceptionally given to men the name
of "gods" (John x. 34—36)? We lay special stress
upon the many parenthetical observations and di-
gressions of this Evangelist, which are scattered
throughout his account, now for the purpose of explanation and now for the establishing of some expression of our Lord, and we ask: Why would he
have regarded it necessary, at any time or place, to
make this distinction between his own view and the
words of our Lord if he had not been conscious
that he was giving a true and faithful report of
Christ's words?

To be brief, let me direct your attention to the
many apparently unimportant parentheses which,

being incontrovertible traces of personal observation, acquire a proportionately great importance, but which are utterly without purpose, and totally incomprehensible if we regard the whole account as an artificial composition. Take, as an example, the narrative of Christ's last evening. There the communication of the words of Jesus is interrupted by the remark, "and it was night" (chapter XIII. 30); then by the psychologically clear questions of Thomas, Philip, and Judas not Iscariot (chapter XIV. 5; XVIII. 22); further, by a declaration of the Master, "Arise, let us go hence," — which, as is plain from what directly follows, was not immediately succeeded by the outbreak, but, as is thought, by the conversation of the disciples, which explains that mysterious expression, "a little while" (chapter XVI. 16); — and finally, when they think that now everything is suddenly plain to them, by the expression of their surprise: "Lo, now speakest thou plainly, and speakest no proverb." I would like to ask an impartial judge, who had never heard of this controversy, this question: Can you not grasp with your own hands, can you not taste and feel, that here is truth and life, — such life as must be experienced, and never imitated? In fact, we can confidently maintain, as Hase does, who was a theological genius in everybody's opinion until the fatal day that he lost his scientific fame in the estimation of a certain class by his defence of John: "The strongest proofs against the fourth

6*

Gospel turn before my eyes into proofs of its Apostolic origin." [1]

In view of all that is now said, can we affirm that the words of our Lord, as communicated by the synoptic Evangelists, are essentially different in form and contents from those in John? We certainly cannot see the clear sun if we maintain this seriously for a moment. But we do not forget that the synoptic and Johannean Christ by no means appears just the same, down to the smallest particular. There is a diversity, but it is like that between the two views of a metropolis seen from the sea and from the land; the difference is apparent to the eye, but the high towers prove that we see the same city before us, though new points of view, — all of which harmonize, — present themselves constantly to the acute vision. There is such a difference as exists between a landscape which is seen at one time from a favourable point on the plain, and at another from an elevation; or such a difference as exists between the starry heavens as seen from the northern and southern hemispheres, when there are other constellations, but the magnificence is all of the same general character. There is really a difference here, but it is the natural result of what an Apostle of our Lord calls "the exceeding riches of Christ." And the same riches to which we are indebted for being able to place the Pau-

---

[1] See *Apologetisches gegen Strauss*, in Krause's *Protestantische Kirchenzeitung*, 1865; 3. Compare, further, his Letter to Baur: *Die Tübinger Schule*. Leipzig, 1855.

JOHN'S GOSPEL AS AN HISTORICAL RECORD.   85

line picture of Christ beside the synoptic and Johannean one, and which cause our Lord still to reveal himself frequently "in another form," as he did
to those two disciples who went into the country
(Mark xvi. 12), are revealed in the great diversity of words and discourses as repeated by the
different Evangelists.   These riches make it very
easy to understand how the writers could paint the
same picture on different sides without coming at
all into conflict with the truth; but it is utterly inconceivable how such a Christ as the one of the
Gospels, and particularly the one of John, could have
been a fiction of men standing so far below the
object of their adoration.   Yet, we will hereafter
speak of the Johannean portrait of Christ considered
as a whole.

II. We will still tarry a while at particular
points, and proceed to answer this question: Whether
the historical representation of the fourth Gospel,
any more than its doctrinal system, drives us to
the conclusion that it is unauthentic and incredible?
You have heard much said of the conflict in our
times between the synoptic and Johannean accounts
of the life, deeds, and fate of our Lord.   And we
may ask here, whether this conflict is really so
great that we can never think of a compromise,
much less of a permanent peace?

The *first* point where opinions diverge is this:
"The beginning of the life of Jesus," we are told,
"was purely human; he was the child of an earthly
mother; according to two accounts he was con-

ceived in a miraculous manner; but it does not
follow from anything that is further said that he
had an existence on earth before his incarnation.
The Johannean Christ, on the contrary, was possibly
not born, or perhaps had no human mother and no
physical brethren." But just the contrary is plain
from John's Gospel; for the difference lies simply
in the fact that Matthew and Luke begin with the
earthly origin of Christ, while John begins with the
heavenly, so that in John's case we see the golden
thread stretching from heaven downwards, but in the
case of the other Evangelists we see it stretching
from earth heavenwards. This difference can only
appear to be a contradiction in the eyes of him
who assumes at the very beginning that our Lord
had no other than merely an earthly origin, or,
in other words, who silently accepts as a fact what
must first be proved. But he, on the contrary, who
institutes an impartial comparison, will discover
that the one description is a postulate of the other,
and so far is this the case that each complements the
other in a satisfactory manner. The miraculous conception and birth of our Saviour, — I must here
take for granted that this is credited by the de-
fenders of the synoptic account, — permit us to believe, a priori, that he who commenced his life in
such an extraordinary manner, belonged to a higher
order of things than one simply earthly; and this
supposition becomes clearer and more certain by the
Johannean account. This account, on the other hand,
makes it highly probable that if God's Son appear

at all in the flesh, it will take place in an extraordinary manner; and we learn from Matthew and Luke that this actually so occurred. If John is silent on this miracle, it simply arises from the fact that he is pursuing quite another train of thought. Their method did not suit his object; yet an acute ear does not fail to catch an indirect, yet almost unmistakable, reference to it in the peculiar manner in which he describes the spiritual birth of God's children, with the exclusion of all carnal extraction. [1] It is no proof of John's own view, that, in John's Gospel, Philip calls our Lord, "Jesus of Nazareth, the son of Joseph" (John I. 45). He shows plainly enough that he is not of the opinion that Jesus was of Galilean descent, as we see by the noteworthy passage: "Jesus went into Galilee, for he himself testified that a prophet hath no honour in his own country" (therefore, not in Galilee, but in Judea, — John IV. 43, 44). [2] He, therefore, indirectly establishes the synoptic accounts, which, indeed, he contradicts in not a single point.

No greater difficulty is produced by a *second* point of difference, — the one concerning the duration and scene of the public labors of Jesus. The duration is not defined in the least degree by the synoptic Evangelists; and though it is plain from John that it extended over the space of about three successive years, he nevertheless tells us nothing

---

[1] John I. 13: "Which were born, not of blood, nor of the will of the flesh, nor of the will of man, but of God."
[2] Compare Van Oosterzee, *Life of Jesus*, Part. II. p. 102 ff.

which the rest deny, but merely something on which
all the others are silent. We, therefore, see clearly
that the impression that these public labors lasted
but a year and some months, — as urged by our
opponents, — is not correct, just as is frequently
the case with other impressions. As far as the
scene of the labors of Jesus is concerned, it is true
that the first three Evangelists mention Galilee almost exclusively, while John leads us chiefly to
Judea; yet he also relates how our Lord appeared
during his public ministry at Capernaum, at the
time of the second Feast of the Passover, while,
on the other hand, we must infer from the synoptic
Evangelists that he was present a number of times
in Judea and Jerusalem before he went thither to
celebrate the last Feast of the Passover. That lamentation in Matthew (chapter XXIII. 37), "O Jerusalem, Jerusalem, thou that killest the prophets and
stonest them which are sent unto thee, how often
would I have gathered thy children together, even
as a hen gathereth her chickens under her wings,
and ye would not," is sufficiently convincing on this
point, unless we hold, with Baur, that no personal
ministration of Jesus among the inhabitants of the
metropolis is meant, or, with Strauss, that these
were not the real words of Jesus. But if our Lord
was in Jerusalem only at the last Feast of the
Passover, who will explain to me the fact that
many inhabitants of Judea and Jerusalem gathered
about him in the beginning (Matthew IV. 25); that
he entered the house of Mary and Martha, as an

acquainted guest (Luke x. 38—42); that he found in Joseph of Arimathea a disciple who had his own sepulchre in Jerusalem, and most probably dwelt there (Luke XXIII. 50—53); and that he had friends there, and in the neighbourhood, for whom one word was sufficient to place fully at his disposal an ass for his entrance, and a room for the celebration of the Passover (Matthew XXI. 3; XXVI. 18)? All these facts, gathered merely from the first three Gospels, prove that our Lord did not go to Jerusalem for the first time shortly before his death, and thus they confirm indirectly, yet for this reason the more strongly, the Johannean account. He who reflects very carefully upon this point will clearly see, that if our Lord regarded himself at the beginning of his labors as the Messiah of Israel, his entrance into Jerusalem must not be the end but the very beginning of his ministry, just as John narrates. And he who has the least conception of the exalted symbolism of Christ's deeds, will certainly see, with us, the great propriety of his beginning and ending his public ministry by the purification of the desecrated temple. And thus the contradiction in the present instance is merely an imaginary one.

In the *third* place, there is no positive contradiction in reference to Christ's conduct toward his friends and enemies. The calling of the first Apostles, we are told, is described by the synoptic Evangelists in a totally different manner from that of John. But what prevents us from supposing that the latter, who, in his Gospel (in a certain sense

the Genesis of the New Testament), goes as far back
as possible to the very beginning of things, describes
in his first chapter the first meeting of our Lord
with the five, who follow him in a preliminary way
at first, but whose subsequent call to real apostle-
ship is described by all the synoptic Evangelists?
The characters of the principal persons, at least,
are the same in both accounts. If you take, for
example, Peter and Mary, according to the account
of John and that of the synoptic Evangelists, you
will receive from both the same impression, though
at one time favourable and at another less so. The
family at Bethany, as we become acquainted with
it in John (chapter xi.), corresponds perfectly, —
at least, so far as the character of the two sisters
is concerned, — to the small but masterly picture
drawn by Luke at the close of his 10th chapter,
yet without the mention of anything more than the
name of the place where they lived. We sometimes
see in John, indeed, new persons appear in action
before us, — Nathanael and Nicodemus, for example,
— but should we therefore look upon them with
suspicion, and maintain with immoderate dogmatism
that these are not historical figures that we are
dealing with, but invented types of some tendency
of thought? If this is the case, I propose that every
one who writes history be implored never to mention a single new name in his account, lest he should
lose his credit for consideration. Nicodemus, for example, certainly does not appear to be a mythical
phantom; in all three cases where we meet with

him, he speaks and acts in such a way that no
psychologist, but only a critic of a certain stamp,
will deny his actual existence. We see him not
merely come, but exist, grow, ripen into a disciple
of our Lord, and be characterized, withal, by a
psychological truth which can only be the real
expression of historical reality. Is he a type, then
he is a type of many people of that and of a later
period. But it is said that, for this reason, he is
not a historical person, just as if one character ex-
cludes the other, and as if the John who is described as a historical person might not at the same
time have been a type also. This is the same arbitrary arrayal of idea in opposition to reality, and
of religious truth in opposition to historical fact,
which, from Lessing's day down to ours, has become a source of many misconstructions and mis-
fortunes in our Dutch theology.

Nor can any objection be raised against the fact
that, according to John, the Jews were quite early
full of murderous thoughts against Jesus, while, according to the first three Evangelists, these plans
came to light at a later period. These latter say
nothing of the earlier stay of our Lord at Jerusalem,
for they had no cause to describe the increasing
intensity of the conflict of parties. What they tell
us concerning the previous conduct of the prominent
Jews toward Jesus gives us really no ground for
supposing that John has painted them too darkly.
On the contrary, the eight "woes" which Matthew
describes as breaking forth over these whited sepul-

chres are doubly intelligible if all that is true which
John relates of their increasing enmity toward the
Master. Such an eye as his looks keenly at hatred
in the germ; and the fearful enmity at the end,
such as the synoptic Evangelists describe it, could
have been, from the very nature of the case, the
kindling of a fire which had long been smouldering
under the ashes, and. gradually burst into a flame.
Great injustice is done to John by maintaining
that he idealizes the Samaritans and Gentiles, and
elevates them at the expense of the Jews. But also
in the synoptic Gospels the better side of the Samaritans appears in contrast with the bitter enmity of
the Jews (Luke x. 33; xvii. 16). According to all
four Evangelists, Pilate is weak and destitute of
character. Though Jesus says (only in John) that
the Jews had "the greater sin" than Pilate (John
xix. 11), yet this excuse is at the same time a
warning and an indirect charge. And if John had
really designed the elevation of the Gentiles above
the Jews, how could he have been so silent concerning the centurion at the cross?

It has been regarded objectionable, in the *fourth*
place, that John says nothing of many particulars
in the life and works of our Lord which appear in
the foreground in the first three Gospels. We will
hereafter speak of the causes of this phenomenon,
when we come to discuss the composition and purpose of his writing. Meanwhile, we will here suggest, that we cannot be too careful in drawing conclusions from one's silence instead of from his words.

John nowhere speaks, for example, of the healing
of persons possessed with devils, nor of the healing
of the leprous and the lunatic. But have we, therefore, a right to assert that he is silent for doctrinal
reasons? Can we not just as well imagine that
such diseases were of more common occurrence in
Galilee than in Jerusalem, and was it the appointed
duty of an Evangelist who relates but six miracles
to give an account of at least one of each variety?
John is also silent on the institution of Baptism and
the Lord's Supper. But we find in his Gospel the
idea that constitutes the real essence of both these
symbolical solemnities; namely, the being born of
water and of the Spirit, and the living fellowship
with our Lord, as symbolically represented in the
eating of the bread and the drinking of the wine
(John III. 5; VI. 51). One must certainly have read
this Gospel with very peculiar eyes if he can draw
from its silence the conclusion that the author, in
contradiction of the whole Christian Church of his
period, denied or opposed either the existence of
these two sacraments or their right to exist. It is
very plain that it was not his peculiar office to
portray the glory of the Incarnate Word in special
prominent parts, — as, for example, miracles, baptism, or the transfiguration on Mount Tabor, — but
rather to describe it in its progressive spiritual revelation, in opposition to the darkness of the world.
It seems to me that his silence on more than one
miracle, which has caused so much offence to sceptical criticism, must much rather serve as an im-

portant recommendation of him than as an objection
to him. How little such silence gives us the right
to infer his ignorance, and then the non-existence
of a fact, is easily shown by observing that John,
who is silent on the struggle of Christ's soul in
Gethsemane, has nevertheless immortalized that expression of our Lord, "Now is my soul troubled"
(John XII. 27), as well as that other one, "The cup
which my Father hath given me, shall I not drink it?"
(John XVIII. 11). By this double declaration John
shows that his Christ, as well as that of the first
three Gospels, can also grieve and pray. In the
whole history of the suffering and death of our
Lord, the words and characteristics that are mentioned in both accounts so naturally unite that one
harmonious picture stands before our eyes. It is
impossible for any one to doubt that John describes
Christ's physical resurrection who has impartially
read his account of the visit of the two disciples
to Christ's sepulchre, and of his subsequent appearance, which Thomas witnessed. Though John declares that our Lord suddenly stood in their midst
while the doors were closed, this only proves that
the Risen One appeared in a glorified body, but by
no means that the narrator denies the corporealness
of his renewed body or of his appearance itself.
And though, in conclusion, John does not speak of
the miracle of the ascension, he only shares this
silence with Matthew. He shows none the less
plainly on this account that he, too, regarded the
exaltation of our Lord as a visible occurrence.

And now we come, *finally*, to that special difficulty which, as has been recently supposed, has. a far more unfavourable bearing than all others on the authenticity of John's Gospel. We refer to the difference between him and the synoptic Evangelists concerning the day of Christ's death. "According to the first three Gospels," we are told, "our Lord ate the Passover at the usual time, on the evening of the 14th Nisan, and that he therefore suffered death on the cross on the 15th. According to John, on the contrary, the Jews must eat the Passover on the evening of the day of his death, and therefore the first real day of the feast was not until the following day. Now this is a point in which the evidence of John is diametrically opposite to that of the other Evangelists; from all external and internal grounds, the synoptic Evangelists are right, and the writer of the fourth Gospel, having a special purpose to serve, has unmistakably represented the affair differently from what was originally the fact."

We will speak hereafter of this special purpose; for the present, we will say only a few words as clearly as possible on the phenomenon itself. It belongs to those questions in the department of historical criticism on which science has not yet spoken its last word. I will only give you my view here, but you may find it more elaborately developed elsewhere. I firmly believe that this difficulty, too, can and must be perfectly removed. We should regard such a discrepancy simply impossible even if we were obliged to take a much

lower view than we are justified in doing concerning the historical reliability of the Evangelists, or
their accurate acquaintance with the history of our
Lord. According to all four Gospels, as we think,
our Lord died on the 15th Nisan, after he had
eaten the Passover lamb with his disciples on the
previous evening, which was the legal time. Though
John seems to contradict this when he relates
(chapter xviii. 28), that "the Jews went not into
the judgment - hall lest they should be defiled, but
that they might eat the Passover," yet this last expression need not necessarily mean the Passover
lamb, but the meal of the Passover sacrifice, which
began at noon of the same day; and when John
says that our Lord was crucified on the "preparation - day of the passover" (chapter xix. 14), we
should have in mind the preparation - day before
the Passover Sabbath, which preparation - day was
also the first day of the Passover itself. We are
aware that there are some exegetical difficulties
connected with this construction, but they are far
less than those into which we should be led by
adopting any other construction. If, as is asserted,
our effort to discover harmony in the present instance is nothing less than unscientific bungling,
we can certainly receive this charge with composure when we remember that we are in the company of such men as Wieseler, Tholuck, and
Hengstenberg. [1]

[1] Compare my *Life of Jesus*, Part III., in loco, and the
literature there cited; also an Article, *Pascha, christliche und*

But granted just for a moment, though we only do it for the sake of argument, that an irreconcilable contradiction exists here, we must hold that the synoptic Evangelists have in this respect followed a less reliable account than the one used by John. Jesus was not, therefore, crucified on the first day of the Passover but on the preparation-day of the Passover, therefore, on a week-day, just as would seem to be the case from some evidences in the synoptic account. We need only call to mind Simon, who returned from the field, and the purchase and preparation of spices by the women, together with other particulars. Until within a few years ago, such men as Réville and Colani really acknowledged the superiority of John, in consequence of this and other grounds, since the wind which was blowing from Tübingen had not yet fully swelled the sails of their ship; and as trustworthy a scholar as Bleek has acknowledged the correctness of this view. But just this very objection to the fourth Gospel is thus turned into an argument in its favour, yea, into a guarantee of its authenticity, whose great importance is self-evident to every impartial person. It is clear that this statement could have been made by no obscure person, and by no diplomatical partisan; and in view of all we have said, we may frankly declare that only an Apostle, and none other than the Apostle John, could have made it.

Pascha-Streitigkeiten, by G. E. Steitz, in Herzog's *Real-Encyclop.*, Vol. XI. p. 149 ff.; and a treatise by L. Paul in the *Theol. Studien und Kritiken*, 1866, Vol. II. p. 362 ff.

7

Nor has any one the slightest ground for forging
a weapon against the authenticity of the fourth
Gospel from the controversy which was carried on
in the Christian Church of the second century concerning the proper time of the celebration of the
Passover. The brief time allotted us affords as
little opportunity for relating the history of this controversy as for following modern skeptical criticism
in all the serpentine windings which it has made, in
order, by its learning and unmistakable acuteness,
to convert this difficulty on the Passover into a
fearful engine of war against the fourth Gospel. It
is asserted that this Gospel was written for the
sake of opposing the so-called Quartodecimani, a
narrow Judaistic party of Christians of Asia Minor,
who, like the Jews, still celebrated the Passover on
the 14th Nisan, and defended this custom by an
appeal to John and his fellow - Apostles. Let us
leave out of consideration for a moment the question
whether a whole Gospel like this would have been
proper and necessary for their secret purpose, since
a simple description of the most prominent events
which occurred on the last evening and day of
Christ's life would have been perfectly sufficient to
answer the demands of their controversy. But who
does not clearly see how even the ground for such
a supposition is removed if it be true that our Lord
was crucified, — just as we find to be the case in the
fourth Gospel, — not on the 14th, but on the 15th
Nisan? If John did celebrate the Feast of the Passover on the 14th Nisan with the Christians of Asia

Minor, he did it, most likely, not in memory of the
real moment of the death of Jesus, but in memory
of the Jewish Passover, which, as now the true
Passover Lamb was slain, must have gained all the
greater importance in his affection, as it was now
connected with his own remembrance of the memorable institution of the Lord's Supper and the Great
Example symbolized in it. This coincides perfectly
with the character of an apostle of the circumcision,
— which character he had in common with Cephas
and James, — and it also harmonizes exactly with
the relatively great respect for Jewish customs
which the Christian Council at Jerusalem connected with the day. Thus John's conduct harmonizes perfectly with his own Gospel, and this, in
turn, with the other three. How could it ever have
occurred that the Evangelists openly contradicted
each other on such a point as the real day of the
death of our Lord, which was necessarily known
very early and universally?

We have felt it proper to say this much on a
point concerning which whole volumes have been
written, with the most varied conclusions, none of
which claim to present an interpretation perfectly
free from difficulty, but the one which is attended
with the least. We must add one remark, however,
in reference to this whole difference in the statement of the day of our Lord's death and of the
controversy on the Passover prevailing in the early
Church. But granted, for the sake of argument,
though we by no means make any concession here,

7*

that it is not possible to gain any perfect evidence
on this matter, and that the difficulty continues to
exist in full strength. Then the very serious question arises, whether this one objection can outweigh
the many decisive grounds which declare the authenticity of this Apostolic writing? On this question, it seems to me, no truly impartial person can
vacillate one moment in uncertainty. Well now,
let us once suppose that the authenticity of John
amounts to a hypothesis, which we will allow for
a moment to stand in opposition to the hypothesis
of a later composition; we then have this as our
result: There is everything in favour of the first hypothesis, while against it there is but a single phenomenon to which we would have to place a mark
of interrogation. Tell me, can this one interro-
gation-mark destroy the force of all arguments?
Should not one strong light on one dark point be
perfectly sufficient, in this mysterious affair, to convert this apparent or real conflict into the most
beautiful harmony? If nothing else we have said be
satisfactory, may not our answer here, as in many
similar cases, be this: "I know of no solution that
really satisfies me perfectly, but I confidently believe that there is one which will be reached hereafter?" For my part, I doubt very decidedly whether
one is in the right way to this solution by contem-
plating this Gospel in the light of modern criticism.
However, as the matter now stands, we can by no
means derive from this mysterious phenomenon any
proof against the Johannean origin of the fourth

Gospel, from the simple fact that *this writing was never referred to in the second century, or later, by a single adherent of this narrow-hearted and limited tendency, for the direct combating of which this Gospel is alleged to have been written.* How can this be explained if there is not ground for being convinced of its Apostolic origin, whether we will or not? Why did no one in the second century take the slightest notice of this strongly polemic tendency of John's Gospel, — a tendency which has occupied so splendid a place of honour among the new discoveries of the nineteenth century? As such was not the case, should not this whole polemical tendency be placed where it belongs, — in the department of the imagination and of hypercriticism?

Grouping together all that we have said, we can affirm without a blush that we enjoy the enviable privilege of seeing extremely little of this "screaming contradiction." We have seen that, with the exception of one mysterious point, the difference between the historical accounts of the fourth Gospel and those of the three others is as easily harmonized as the difference in the manner of Christ's teaching as presented to us in the two cases. Thus the greater part of the accumulated difficulties dissolve into merely apparent differences, and an ex- . cellent theologian has very properly said that apparent differences are only "motes on Christ's regal robe." We can by no means regard those which we have observed as spots in the crown of the fourth Evangelist; and if we are asked, what can

be inferred from the diversity in John's Gospel?, we
would reduce our answer to this brief form: That
diversity proves nothing against its authenticity,
but, if well examined, pronounces directly in its
favour.

The diversity proves nothing against the authenticity of the fourth Gospel for the very reason that
it can be explained by its *plan and purpose*. The
writer has plainly declared the object which he had
in view (chapter xx. 31): "But these [things] are
written, that ye might believe that Jesus is the
Christ, the Son of God; and that believing ye might
have life through his name." According to his own
testimony, therefore, he was not impelled to write
by any petty party-interest; his ideal was an infinitely higher one. He would set forth the truth
in all its full splendour, in order to strengthen the
faith of Christians; he would do this didactically
and not polemically; yet we may confidently say,
that his design was indirectly apologetic against
the error whose invasion from different sides he had
himself witnessed. Yet was it actually requisite
that he should describe the whole history of our
Lord's life without a single omission? He wrote for
Christians who had already long been acquainted
with the principal substance of Apostolical information as recorded in the synoptic Gospels, and he
must therefore have been also acquainted with their
contents. He would by no means refute these contents, but add much that they do not furnish. He
would not displace the ideas possessed until his

time, nor (as has been maintained very unjusti-
fiably) supply their place by others, — he would
gain his object by completing the true representation
of his predecessors through the aid of a new writing.
The great importance of this point requires that
we should look at it somewhat more closely. It
must appear very improbable to every one, *a priori*,
that an Apostle who composed a Gospel twenty-
five or thirty years after the other Evangelists,
should ignore or attempt to refute the work of his
predecessors; in that case, our Lord's first witnesses
would have to be looked at with real Tübingen
eyes, and pronounced fanatical partisans. But the
matter of the fourth Gospel is utterly unintelligible
if the writer was not himself acquainted with the
contents of the first three, and did not suppose them
also known by others. He speaks of the Baptist,
without describing his appearance; of the complete
circle of the twelve Apostles, without describing
their call; and of Bethany as the dwelling-place of
Mary and Martha (chapter XI. 2), without having
scarcely mentioned the two sisters previously. While
Matthew makes the public labours of Christ commence about the same time with the captivity of
John the Baptist, the fourth Evangelist, on the contrary, merely makes this remarkable statement
(chapter III. 24), as a mere passing suggestion:
"For John was not yet cast into prison;" and he
also communicates some particulars of the history
of the preceding days and weeks, which the rest of
the Evangelists pass over in silence. Matthew and

Mark give an account of the anointing at Bethany,
but John first mentions the name of Mary, and in
this way causes the fulfillment of the prophecy of
our Lord, — just as it is stated by the other Evangelists, — "that what this woman had done should
be told in the whole world for a memorial of her."
He first makes us acquainted with the name of
Malchus, with the event connected with Annas, and
with a number of particulars in the history of the
death and resurrection of our Lord.

By one word John calls back to life recollections that would have been in danger of being lost
for ever had it not been for his written bequest.
It is plain that the fourth Gospel is nothing more
nor less than a rich legacy bequeathed to the
world after the collected accounts of the first three
Evangelists had already been domesticated in the
Church. Do I say too much when I affirm that this
Gospel also furnishes a real report of the oldest
tradition of the Church? And we have not a single
reason for distrusting it on this important point.
The fragment of the canon in Muratori, that priceless document of the second century, declares that
John wrote in answer to the express application of
his fellow-disciples and bishops. Hieronymus, the
Church Father, relates about the same thing; and
Clement of Alexandria communicates expressly as a
"tradition of the oldest presbyters, that John, having
seen that the external, and, as it were, corporeal
part of the events in our Lord's life was already
written by the synoptic Evangelists, felt himself

compelled to write a spiritual Gospel." [1] In fact, it must excite our astonishment, if not suspicion, to read at the present time very acute explanations of the origin, design, plan, and groundwork of the fourth Gospel, in which such explanations as are given on the orthodox side are simply passed over in silence as if they had never been made. It is certainly natural to suppose that what is held to be only a tradition derived from the second century is just as able to present us with the truth as can the critical conjectures of the nineteenth century, which cannot appeal to a single authority. Nothing prevents us from concluding that John, with a full appreciation of everything communicated by others, felt himself inspired to add from his own treasury that which had made the deepest impression upon his own mind and heart. And as he did this, why should we subject his testimony to suspicion, as it bears upon its very face the character of its peculiar adaptation?

But do not suppose that we ascribe to the fourth Gospel no higher character than that of a supplement to the other three. Such a harmonious unity as this could never have arisen from a mere conglomeration of all kinds of additions. John's Gospel

---

1 Compare Van Oosterzee, *Life of Jesus*, New Ed., Vol. V. p. 144; and Augustine, the beginning of his *Tract* XXXVI, on the Gospel of John: "It is not without reason that he relates in his own Gospel that he had leaned on his Lord's breast at supper. He therefore drank from that breast in secret, but he gave forth to the world what he had drunk in private."

is, in our opinion, a masterpiece in the most sublime sense of the word. As a stone thrown into
the water produces widening circles, and as the
theme of a piece of music constantly returns in
richer variations, so it is with the fundamental truth
declared in John's Gospel. We believe that we can
hear in an expression of the first chapter this fundamental truth, — the text of the whole sermon of
this Gospel: "And the light shineth in darkness;
and the darkness comprehended it not." Some one
has not unjustly called this Gospel a "painting of
a sunrise;" the higher the sun rises the more
violently does the fog boil up; and the more directly
the fog strikes us in the face, the more glorious
does the splendour of the king of day appear before
us. An elaborate survey of the groundwork and
plan of this writing is not necessary for the purpose which we here have in mind; it is enough to
say, that the Evangelist's object could have been
none else than to portray Christ as the Light and
Life in its increasing conflict with, and in its grand
victory over, the unbelieving world. This definite
purpose, we readily confess, exerted an unmistakable
influence upon his selection, arrangement, and grouping of facts. To the portrait of Christ made by his
predecessors, John adds with great predilection such
features as can best contribute to place that portrait
in the most sublime light before the eyes of his
readers. To mention one example, it is certainly
not accidental that he should begin with the divinity
of the Word and close with that confession of

Thomas which sounds like the echo of that beginning. We lay special stress upon the point that the intentional representation of persons and facts in a special light proves nothing whatever against their strictly historical character. What is arranged symmetrically and antithetically, to a certain degree, can also be truly historical. Strauss somewhere calls the fourth Evangelist the "Corregio of Sacred History," and as we look at the exquisite blending of light and shade in his unapproachable picture, we willingly endorse the term. But the historical painter who knows how to place his principal figures in a full light, but paints others in the dark background, has not necessarily given in these figures the creations of his own glowing imagination.

We return to the point where we began. The peculiarity of the fourth Gospel, which is perfectly explicable when we look at its groundwork and purpose, does not prove anything against its Apostolic origin. We must express ourselves more strongly: If the diversity between John and his predecessors be well considered, it becomes a strong proof of the authenticity of his account. Do you not feel its power yourself? Any one who in writing would smuggle in his own wares under the Johannean flag, would certainly have to be very careful never to come into even apparent contradiction to the first three Gospels. He who by crafty premeditation would invest himself with the appearance and manner of an Apostle, must take the greatest pains to utter an echo of the Apostolic witnesses, but never a note that is not in perfect harmony with them. If, therefore, the diversity of doctrinal idea and historical representation between the first three Gospels and the fourth still seems strange, then I may say that this diversity is perfectly inexplicable if we are here dealing with an anonymous author. But all the difficulty will disappear if we accept the fact that this is the work of an Apostle, who occupies a perfectly independent position beside the three other Evangelists, yet whose testimony he continues, enlarges, and completes.

We might conclude here, but having advanced so far in the defence of this Gospel, we cannot postpone making a little sally in order to answer this question: "What is the use of adhering to this 'odd' Gospel, as Renan calls it, after it is proved that it never could have been written by John?" You know the answer of modern criticism, that we have here a writing produced by a certain tendency; that is, a writing prepared with the fixed purpose of disseminating in broader circles the ideas of a narrow church-party, and of accomplishing this end as well as possible by making use of an historical representation with a romantic colouring. It is further said that the author was not an eye-witness, but a cunning partisan of a later period; that he did not ask, whether that really happened which he related, but whether it could subserve the interests of his own party? Further, his special aim is said to have been to oppose the celebration of the Passover practiced by a certain Judaistical party of the second century, and, by a gentle method, to effect an introduction into the Church of the views of a certain Gnostic school, — according to some the Marcionitic, and according to others the Valentinian.

I will only notice these general charges without going into particulars; I shall not attack persons, but opinions and principles. But I openly ask every one who has the capacity of distinguishing truth from mere fiction, whether the author of the fourth Gospel has ever made on him the impression of having been a sly Jesuit, with whom the end sanctifies the means? Does not that fresh, frank, and subjective element which pervades the entire account of John give us reason for thinking exactly the opposite to diplomatic and sectarian deliberation? Yea, does not this Gospel contain much which stands in direct contradiction to this alleged origin and tendency? It is said to be a ripened fruit on the soil of an improved Gnostic tendency, but it is directly the opposite of the fundamental views of the Gnosticism of the second century. Gnosticism was anti-Jewish, and was distinguished by its profound contempt of the Old Testament. But here I hear our Lord expressly declare that "salvation cometh of the Jews;" I see that he faithfully attended the Jewish festivals at Jerusalem, and even those which the people were not obliged to attend. I notice that he continually alludes to the Old Testament, which John quotes almost as frequently as Matthew. Gnosticism prejudices the

true humanity of our Lord; but, as we shall subsequently be convinced, the fourth Gospel acknowledges his true humanity, and maintains it with
emphasis. Gnosticism attached great value to the
baptism of our Lord; but in the fourth Gospel this
baptism is mentioned much less elaborately than
even in the first three Gospels. One might almost
say, in fact, that such an author has just as little
spiritual affinity with the Gnostics as a flower of
Paradise with a thistle. [1] It is asserted that it was
a part of the writer's scheme to prove the superiority of John to Peter; that it was a plan so
shrewdly devised that it could remain in concealment for eighteen centuries, but that now it is so
evident that even many of the smaller peculiarities
can be seen. "See, for example [oh, what wise
forethought!], that the author takes good care that
the people should know how John ran more quickly
than Peter to the empty sepulchre" (chapter xx. 4)!
What a pity that even in the following chapter
(xxi. 7) he permits Peter to be present with the
risen Jesus sooner than John! And how does it
square with this plan, that he who would place
Peter in the background has preserved for us that
glorious confession, at the end of the 6th chapter,
which Peter expresses in the name of the twelve

---

[1] Ebrard does not state the case too strongly when
he says, p. 736: "That, in order to triumphantly oppose the
authenticity of John's Gospel, the whole history of the
Church, and literature of the first two Christian centuries,
must be piled up and then turned bottom upwards."

Apostles? In fact, this anonymous author knows
very well how to choose means for reaching exactly the contrary to what he designs. And the
Church is said to be indebted for this grand Gospel
to such miserable and petty rivalries! One might
just as well assert, on a beautiful day, that the
earth owes the splendour of its sunlight to a fortu-
nate concurrence with the borrowed light of the
moon. But enough; we must say with De Pressensé, that "we will not reply to such arguments,
for they are devoid of the very elements of common
appreciation; we will leave such insinuations for
conscience to take care of." [1]

Or if it be still held that John's Gospel is an
imposture, let us ask: How is it possible that such
an imposture as it is here assumed to be, was not
discovered and punished? This partisan writing is
said to have opposed another party, which was
quite shrewd in the discovery of mystification. Has
the party been asleep, or allowed itself to be out-
witted even down to its very last man? It really
will not do to convert all the Church Fathers of
the second century, who continued the work of the
Apostles and who weathered the violent gale of
Gnosticism, either into fellow-criminals or into dupes.
There is much said about counterfeit writings that
are alleged to have been circulated during the first
centuries of the Christian era under the name of
illustrious men and even of the Apostles, but the

[1] *Jesus Christ*, etc. p. 224.

whole literature of the early Christian Church can furnish no parallel to such a writing, circulated under such a name, and with such great success. The imitation of truth in the present instance would have been so masterly that the most skillful counterfeiter of manuscripts or bank-notes might well take lessons of this great "unknown author."

But supposing the abuse of the Apostle's name to have been discovered, could the offence have remained unpunished? There are examples before us that clearly and definitely lead us to expect exactly the contrary. Tertullian, the Church Father, reports that a presbyter of Asia Minor prepared and circulated a work under the name of the Apostle Paul. [1] When summoned to answer for his conduct, he protested that he had done so through admiration and love of Paul. But nothing could help him, — he was removed from his office. Such was the way in which the spirit of truth decided in this instance, and would not the same spirit have been able or willing to draw a sharp line of demarcation between truth and imposture if John had not written his Gospel?

The fourth Gospel unauthentic and forged! The application of these terms to it in accounting for its origin may seem to you to be new, but I must destroy this illusion, for this is an old method of attacking it. I will not now revert to the forgotten

---

[1] Compare *Tertull. de Bapt.* v. 18; and H. W. J. Thiersch, *Versuch einer Herstellung des histor. Standpunkts.* Erlangen, 1845. p. 338.

Lützelberger, who attacked the authenticity of John, in 1840, and after allowing his imagination to be his spokesman, surprised us by the information that John's Gospel was written by a Samaritan, who went to Edessa with his parents on the outbreak of the Jewish war, when a boy of between eight and twelve years of age, and who then became a Christian, a bishop under the instruction of the Apostle Andrew, and, finally, the author of the fourth Gospel! Our first reading and acquaintance with this book, which used to be mentioned in the same breath with Strauss, still amuses us, as if it had only happened yesterday. Yet we will leave the dead to bury their dead.

Let me remind you of Faustus the Manichæan, who, as long ago as the fifth century, forged a weapon against the credibility of the Gospels on the score of their mutual discrepancies. We may judge this writing from the following extract: "We may properly listen to, and rationally examine, writings which have such little harmony as these, but after we have carefully examined everything, and made deliberate comparisons, we question whether Christ could have said much that is contained here. Ever so many words were slipped in among the declarations of our Lord at an early period, which, notwithstanding they bear his name, do not at all accord with his faith. As we have repeatedly shown, they were neither said by Christ nor recorded by his Apostles, but were gathered up from conflicting

8

reports and opinions by some nondescript half-Jews long after these men were dead." [1]

Does it not really seem that many a critic of this character in the nineteenth century had really gone to school to the Manichæan of the fifth century? And as we look at such hypotheses on the origin of the fourth Gospel, is extensive learning, or even a long argument, necessary to elicit from us the exclamation of indignity and pain: "Such hypotheses are impossible?" It is almost inconceivable that those who would draw us into such adventurous methods do not observe that they would lead us from the sphere of the remarkable to that of the preposterous. Some critics call our faith mere imagination, and assert that we poor apologists swallow camels. Continuing the figure, we might almost ask whether our opponents do not even swallow whole caravans of such animals without suffering the least indigestion?

But this matter is too serious for pleasantry, and we do not wish to run the danger of meriting the rebuke of "paying the devil too many sorry compliments for his scientific seriousness."

This much we firmly hold: That such desperate measures as we have considered would not be resorted to in order to overthrow the power of evidences that decide in favour of John if there was not a disposition to avoid, at any price, the really great stone of offence, — Miracles. Our next Lecture

---

[1] Augustine, *Contra Faustum*, Lib. XXXIII. Cap. 2 and 3.

will be devoted to a discussion of this subject. No
statement of special evidences, and no solution of
particular difficulties, will be sufficient for any one
so long as he shares, either secretly or avowedly,
Rousseau's request: "Take away from me these
miracles of your Gospel!" The subject of the third
Lecture being John's account of the miracles of
Christ, we here leave the lowly mountain-valley,
and will there ascend the lofty Alpine peak of the
Gospel History.

III.

JOHN'S ACCOUNT OF CHRIST'S MIRACLES.

"I have all respect for the connection of things, but I cannot help thinking of Samson, who did not injure the connection (bar) of the gate, and, as is well known, carried the whole gate to the top of the hill." — MATTHIAS CLAUDIUS.

> Behold this eagle, proud of flight,
> Piercing the clouds to clearer light,
> Above all witnesses of God.
> No one e'er saw with such keen eye,
> What's promised and what's now passed by,
> And what is yet to be disclosed. [1]

In view of all that we have hitherto said on the fourth Gospel, we do not hesitate a moment longer to repeat with increased emphasis this hymn of praise, composed in the Middle Ages in honour of John. The strongest and most convincing external and internal proofs of the authenticity of his account being now established, the unmistakable dif-

[1] *Volat avis sine meta*, etc.

ference between him and the first three Evangelists does not preclude their higher unity, and the beginnings and endings of all the lines which John has further extended are clearly perceptible in his predecessors. Indeed, Da Costa, an apologist of our own country, could ask with perfect right: "If any one doubt whether the fourth Gospel, because of its special and peculiar composition, belongs to the authentic Gospels, is it not just as if one doubted whether the head belongs to the body, just because it has a different shape from the remaining members and portions of the body?" Thus, we can now remain no longer uncertain as to the special rank we should attribute to John among the witnesses of our Lord, whose written records have been preserved to us by God's goodness. But this is not saying, that, in following the synoptic Evangelists, we are misled to follow those who, with partiality and ingratitude, arbitrarily elevate one witness of the truth above another. Not to leave the figure mentioned above, we would just as little dispense with the head, a foot, or a hand, all of which belong to the body; for we believe that the true salvation of faith and of science is not acquired by arbitrary mutilation, but by the careful keeping together of what belongs together. Yet we candidly assert, that, though the first three Evangelists communicate many important matters concerning the life of our Lord, it is impossible to obtain a complete, connected, and practical biography of Jesus if we do not invoke the aid of John. Numberless special

points treated by them need the very light which
he communicates. He traces a multitude of new
lines in the picture of Christ sketched by the other
Evangelists. He shows us from the standpoint of
his individual tuition just that which he has in
common with them; and this detracts no more
from historical truth than the sunbeam changes the
water, or even the direction of the brook itself,
when it falls in manifold reflection of colours on the
surface of the stream, and even lets us see its bottom. However, not to mention other things, how
could we come to chronological certainty on certain
special matters in the life of Jesus if we did not
have the light which John gives? No wonder that
the indispensableness of his testimony for our
knowledge of Christ has been recognized, even in
our day, by the very ones whom nobody would
venture to reckon in the so-called narrow tendency.
A few years ago, even some of the "modern theologians" declared John to be the principal source
for the biography of our Saviour. [1] Leaving other
writers of this class out of the question, Ernest
Renan, who has less of John's spirit than all the
new critics, and whose opinion of this Gospel is so
unfair in other respects, has given such a witness

---

[1] Compare C. C. J. Bunsen, *Bibelwerk*, *Vorwort*, Vol. I. —
"If John's Gospel is not the historical account of an eye-
witness, but only a myth, then there is no historical Christ;
and without a historical Christ, all the faith of the Christian
Church is a delusion; all Christian confession, hypocrisy or
deception; the Christian reverence for God an imposition;
and the Reformation, finally, a crime or a madness."

in favour of its relative indispensableness as may
well furnish many of our opponents with food for
reflection. [1]

In view of all this, we may now ask with increased interest: What is the reason that the Gospel
of John is still a stumbling-stone to so many, even
though a satisfactory answer may be given to most
of the objections urged against the particulars of its
contents? I do not know how to state this reason
better than in the words of the celebrated head of
the most recent critical school: "The principal argument for the later origin of the Gospels will ever
continue to be this: all of them together, and each
one of itself, represents so much of the life of
Christ in a way in which it was impossible really
to occur." [2] This expression, with praiseworthy
frankness, names just the most delicate point of
critical inquiry, and it is scarcely uttered before we
hear on all sides the cry: "If we look at the matter
closely, it is far more probable that all the Gospels
are unauthentic than that a miracle ever occurred!"
Perhaps you are aware of the witty mockery with
which Goethe, in the past century, exposed to the
gaze of his contemporaries the well-known opponent
of Christianity, Dr. Carl Frederick Bahrdt, the author
of the Most Recent Revelations of God. Bahrdt is
sitting at his desk, when the four Evangelists ap-

---

[1] *Vie de Jesus*, *Introduction*, p. xxxiii. (1st Ed.). *Les
Apotres*, *Introduction*, pp. ix, x.
[2] Baur, *Kritische Untersuchungen über die drei ersten Evangelien*, p. 530.

pear before him, who have been persecuted on every
hand, and have come to him for refuge. They meet
with a friendly reception, and are even invited into
the society of other guests; but they must first lay
off their old costume, and clothe themselves according to the most recent fashion. Luckily enough,
there are suits at hand; but, very strangely, not
one of them wishes to submit to this metamorphosis.
One after the other steals away, and John the first
of all; they would rather be persecuted than be un-
distinguishable, and the disappointed host does not
know what better to do than avenge himself on
their writings. And no wonder, for he had just
placed on paper a declaration of what he would
have done: "Thus I would have spoken if I had
been Christ!"

Though the manner of contesting the highest and
dearest truths of Christianity afterwards became
much more refined and genteel, the principle here
indelicately expressed, — that of substituting a
purely individual opinion for revealed truth, — is
still essentially the same. When the actual explanation of the Gospel history was carried to the
grave, as it was said, amid the derisive shouts of
science, the mythical explanation tried its utmost;
and when it became plain that the "innocently invented legend" existed only in the fancy of Strauss
and kindred spirits, the force of consistency required
the party to speak of an intentional fiction in the
interest of the parties, into which, as it is asserted,
the Church of the first and second centuries was

wretchedly rent. We are allowed to say, that the
Evangelists, especially the fourth, who were regarded
only as pious fanatics twenty or thirty years ago,
are now promoted to the rank of tolerably cunning
impostors; and, continuing further with John alone,
the miracles which he recounts are sufficient to cast
doubt on every serious claim that he may present
to the name of an historical writer. Even a short
time ago his Gospel was regarded as authentic, but
the sceptics privately sought either to explain the
offensive passages in a Rationalistic sense, or to
banish them from the sacred text as interpolations.
Now such men no longer scruple to make the Lord
say and do "incredible things," but, for this very
reason, they deny persistently that it was written
by the Apostle John, the favourite disciple of our
Lord.   Thus the opposing party point out for us
the very course which we must now further take.
The Johannean account of the miracles of our Lord
will employ our entire attention during the present
Lecture. We will first consider this account in and
of itself, and see whether, granting for a moment
the possibility of miracles, it bears traces of forgery
or of inward credibility. We shall then find occasion, very naturally, to discuss more generally
the question of miracles in connection with the Gospel
history,

    I. When we speak of the Johannean account
of miracles we mean specially the doings of our
Lord, which, according to the statement of this
Evangelist, took place through his extraordinary

power; and we will lay aside for a moment both the proofs of his higher knowledge furnished by this Gospel and the miraculous events that were interwoven with his entire career on earth, as, for example, the voice from heaven shortly before his death, or the resurrection of his body. We therefore have in mind the following: The Water changed into Wine (chapter II. 1—11); The Healing of the Nobleman's Son at Capernaum (chapter IV. 45—54) (granted, though it might seem somewhat unsafe, that this miracle was not only proclaimed by our Lord but was directly performed by him); The Healing of the Impotent Man at the Pool of Bethesda (chapter v. 1—15); The Miraculous Feeding of Five Thousand, which is followed by Christ's Walking on the Sea (chapter VI. 1—15); The Opening of the Eyes of One Born Blind (chapter IX.); and The Raising of Lazarus (chapter XI.). We thus have six or seven miracles, of which only one, The Miraculous Feeding of Five Thousand, is also described by the other Evangelists, while the remaining ones are communicated to us exclusively by the fourth Gospel.

If we now look attentively at these Johannean narratives of Christ's miracles, we see, first of all, that they belong, without exception, to the same department in which, according to the first three Gospels, we find our Lord miraculously operating. In John's Gospel, too, inanimate Nature hears His mighty voice; Sickness also flees here at His look; and Death is compelled to surrender its prey to His possession. Yet, with a similarity in manner, we also perceive a difference of degree. The miraculous power of the Saviour is glorified not only in restoring a sick man, but one who has been sick for thirty-eight years; not only in one who was blind, but in one who was born blind; and not only in one who was dead, but one who had lain in the grave four days. The negative school have found in this higher degree of the miraculous in the fourth Gospel an unquestionable trace of embellishment and invention; and, of course, if the impossibility of miracles and the unauthenticity of John's Gospel be once proved, there is good ground for regarding the account of such grand miracles with distrust. But if, on the other hand, we regard miracles abstractly as possible, and the accounts of miracles in the synoptic Gospels be once conceded, we can admit, with at least the same ground, that he who in the one department could perform the relatively lower class would not find it impossible to perform the greater class. Then we can also admit that John, who, as we have seen, knew and enlarged the synoptic accounts, describes with special fondness those works of our Lord which had not been recorded by his predecessors, yet seemed to him especially adapted for reaching the end which he had in view in the composition of his own Gospel. Hence, to use the mildest form of expression, there is one possibility against another. We must look more closely in order to see where the truth lies. For the present, I merely remark that a narrator who communicates far less miracles than one of his predecessors, and repeatedly enables us to see that our Lord performed many more miracles than he has specifically recorded, [1] does not awaken any particular suspicion of exaggeration or of a mania for miracles. John, on the contrary, here displays a relative sobriety which, I repeat, ought in a certain measure to gain him favour in the eyes of those in our day who deny miracles. But, as a matter of course, however few they are in quantity, their quality is, and ever will be, of such a character that his account, at least on this point, must be utterly incredible to many. We unite unhesitatingly with our opponents in saying that, when possible, the Johannean narratives of miracles far excel in grandeur those narrated by the synoptic Evangelists, and manifest a character of incomparable majesty, which, if they be once sufficiently attested, warrants us in speaking here of nothing less than a divine miraculous power.

Our second general remark is, that the point of view from which John looks at the miracles of Christ corresponds perfectly with his declared purpose in writing his Gospel.

When he writes (chapter xx. 31), "That ye might believe that Jesus is the Christ, the Son of God," he regards an account of certain miracles as one of the requisites for him to reach this end. They are to him "signs," that is, facts which,

---

[1] John II. 23; IV. 35; VII. 31, and elsewhere.

however much they are comprised within the realm
of sense, are yet peculiarly designed to bring home
to the mind the anticipation of a higher truth, and
to give it a clear view of this truth. As such, they
are also revelations of the glory of the incarnate
Word, and are especially adapted to strengthen the
faith of him who regards them with a proper state
of mind (chapter II. 11). According to the declaration of Jesus himself in John (chapter v. 36),
they constitute a portion of God's works, which He
performs on earth, and which must bear witness
that the Father hath sent him. We can scarcely
believe our ears when we hear it said that, "Jesus,
according to the synoptic Evangelists, does not perform such works to prove his divine mission," and
that, therefore, we here meet with an evident contradiction between them and John. [1] If this be true,
then it is, perhaps, not miracles in the strict sense
to which our Lord appeals in them when he says:
"Go and show John those things which ye do hear
and see: the blind receive their sight, and the lame
walk, the lepers are cleansed, and the deaf hear,
the dead are raised up, and the poor have the
Gospel preached to them" (Matthew XI. 2 — 5).
Or has Christ's declaration suddenly become unauthentic: "If the mighty works which were done
in you, had been done in Tyre and Sidon, they
would have repented long ago in sackcloth and
ashes" (Matthew XI. 21; compare also Matthew XII. 28)?

[1] See Scholten, *Evangelium Johannis*, pp. 232, 233.

This much is certain: He who candidly asserts that the Christ of the synoptic Gospels attaches no special weight to his miracles, and nowhere appeals to these attestations of his Divine mission, will have to tear out the 11th chapter from Matthew's Gospel. Yet, this is not one of those sections whose authenticity has been questioned by the most recent negative criticism.

The following rejoinder is equally unfortunate: "Miracles occur in the first three Gospels to show kindness to afflicted people, but in John, on the contrary, they are written to reveal the glory of Jesus." Now any one who does not look at the matter superficially can see at a glance that one of these elements does not preclude the other. On the one hand, should not the kind deeds of our Lord serve to reveal him as the one who should come; and, on the other, does he not reveal his glory by these very good deeds, which he performs with a loving heart? In both instances, it is perfectly plain that what Jesus *does*, serves to declare what he *is*: in both cases compassionate sympathy is the fundamental cause of miracles, and their purpose is to prove his heavenly mission, and, at the same time, the revelation of his heavenly glory.

We have been likewise very unsuccessful in finding an irreconcilable contradiction in the fact that miracles are brought by the synoptic Evangelists into the most intimate relation to the faith of the diseased person, while, in the fourth Evangelist, the only factor of the miracle is the omnipotence of the Son of God. Do not the synoptic Evangelists also prove that omnipotence is the real factor of all miraculous signs, which connect with faith and reveal it? And do we nòt hear our Lord asking also in John, before the performance of his grandest miracle: "Said I not unto thee, that, if thou wouldest believe, thou shouldest see the glory of God" (chapter XI. 40)? In neither case is the miracle caused by faith in and of itself, but only by the power proceeding from Jesus; in all the Gospels, faith is now silently supposed, and now the expressly required, condition on which the miracle is performed, — the requisite without which the recipient would be insusceptible of experiencing the beneficent power of the Worker of miracles. According to both John and the synoptic Evangelists, our Lord generally performs his miracles where there is a pressing necessity for his help, and where it is earnestly desired and confidently waited for. [1] According to both, he appeals to these facts in proof that faith in him is very reasonable (corresponding to the requirements of the highest reason), and that unbelief, on the other hand, is utterly inexcusable. [2] According to both, finally, he plainly shows that the faith which is merely established on his miracles is decided by him to be a lower order of faith; and, on this account, he repels a desire for miracles far more than he satisfies or fosters it.

[1] John II. 3, 4; V. 6; XI. 21—27.
[2] Matthew XI. 2—6; compare John V. 36. Matthew XI. 20—24; compare John X. 32; XV. 24.

In a word, the difference between the two accounts
is merely superficial here, too, while the harmony
lies concealed in the depths below, and the sphere
of miracles, rightly considered, is the same in both
cases.

Our third preliminary remark is, that if, in all
respects, there be no essential difference between
John and the remaining writers, we must employ
the same method of exposition in explaining them
all, and, where this Evangelist does not show that
he wishes to be understood otherwise, we are in
duty bound to regard his accounts of miracles as
accounts of facts, which he would have us understand as having really occurred. The question as
to the reality of their occurrence does not here come
into consideration; but we must know, before anything else, what the narrator himself intends us to
understand by them. No impartial one can doubt
that John intends to tell us of real facts, the deeds
of our Lord himself; and these, therefore, must be
explained grammatically and historically, just as his
words. There was a time when it could be said
that the truth of these miracles was self-evident;
but certain critics have arisen in the most recent
times who entertain quite a different view. In order
to get rid of believing miracles at all hazards, it
has been thought necessary to apply the so-called
allegorical explanation of the Scriptures to these
accounts. Certain sceptical writers, proceeding from
the very correct remark that the Evangelist John
represents these miracles as signs of the glory of

Jesus, have asserted that the signs here recounted were originally the unhistorical dress of religious ideas, and that the Evangelist merely recorded them to make an ideal truth intelligible in a concrete form. Thus the narrative of the miracle at the Marriage at Cana is made to symbolize the thought that Jesus transforms life according to the law into life according to the spirit, in which the former is declared to be represented by the symbol of water, and the latter by that of wine. In the same way the miracle at the Pool of Bethesda is made to represent Jesus as the Renewer of the enervated moral life of sinful humanity, or, according to another notion, the one who had been infirm thirty-eight years is a type of the morally infirm Israel, and, — who would have thought it, — the five porches full of impotent folk are a symbol of the insufficiency of Judaism for the spiritual restoration of the sick. In the same way, the walking of Jesus on the Sea of Galilee symbolizes the thought of Jesus calmly proceeding over the great sea of the world, while believers never have any rest on these tempestuous waves of the sea if Jesus is not with them. But this is enough to show us the real drift of this method. If we allow ourselves to be influenced by those who represent it, we must hold, that when the Evangelist speaks of these and similar miracles, he would not have us understand them literally but figuratively. To get at his meaning, we are told that we must call to our aid such allegorical interpretation as Paul once made use of, in

the 4th chapter of Galatians, when he proves, by a
method in vogue in his day, that the name Agar
indicates Mount Sinai, in Arabia. Thus, it is
said, there also lies in these accounts a deeper
sense, with which the narrator had to deal exclusively, and whose discovery involves us in all
manner of exegetical and critical difficulties, which
would be utterly insurmountable if the writer had
designed to give an historical account of real occur-
rences.

What shall we say of this view, which is just
now defended by the very ones who, a few years
ago, could hardly find words to express their profound contempt for such a "pious game"? We can
only suppress the question with difficulty: Whether
the highly-praised progress of science in our day
does not consist simply in relapsing into the peculiarities of Cocceian typology, and whether the systematic opponents of all authority really imagine
that people are going to take their own word when
they proclaim such views? To mention again the
name of the most celebrated poetic herald of the
modern view of the world, if Gœthe should arise
from the dead he would find ample material and
occasion for repeating his ironical rule to a certain
class of Scriptural expositors:
>"Be fresh and sprightly in your exposition;
>And what you can't explain, prop something under!"

It is, indeed, humiliating to see how easily unbelief
can degenerate into superstition, and Rationalism
into Mysticism. Does it not seem that the human

mind is eternally condemned to fall from one extreme to the other? For years the facts remained untouched, yet there was neither eye nor ear for the idea contained in them. But at present, there can hardly words enough be found for extolling the glory of the idea; but do not imagine for a moment that the narrative containing the idea is the report of a real fact! It is insipid materialism on the one side, even in the department of exegetics and criticism, while, on the other, we have a spiritualism which decomposes and volatilizes everything. Who will decide which of the two has inflicted the greater injury on the cause of truth? Indeed, it is hard to keep clear of being satirical when we find so much caprice clothed in the garb of science. The case would be different if the Evangelist would only give us the slightest intimation, as Paul does in Galatians IV. 24, that he intends what he says to be understood in the way already mentioned; but since he does not do this, what right has any one to attribute to the author purposes of which we have no proof that he ever thought for a moment? Was the Christian Church stricken for whole centuries with an inexplicable blindness, in being as little able to trace out this "profoundness" as to imagine the existence of such secret thoughts? Is not the door here thrown wide open to all kinds of ingenious and insipid notions, and does not this view substitute one *ipse dixit* for another? To mention only a few points, where do we find in the New Testament that water is used in opposition to wine

9*

as the symbol of the lower life under the law? Do
we not find that the highest life, which is salvation
in Christ, is constantly represented by the symbol
of living water? Where on earth can you get any
right for regarding the five husbands which John
says the Samaritan woman had had, as the symbol
of the five false gods of the Samaritans, while
Israel's God, which they at that time worshipped,
was not strictly theirs also? What ground have
we for regarding the one who had been impotent
for thirty-eight years as an unhistorical type of
morally helpless Israel, and, perhaps, his body as
a symbol of the rest which he sought in vain?
You may well exclaim, with a smile, half in pity
and half in vexation: "In this way you can make
what you please out of anything," — and you have
a perfect right to say so.

In reply to all this, do we really deny that.
John's accounts of miracles contain higher ideas?
If we were to say this, we should be just as partial
as those whom we contradict in the utmost sincerity; indeed, we would be doing worse, for we
would be placing ourselves in opposition to John
himself. There is no doubt, for example, that he
communicates the account of the Miraculous Feeding
of the Multitude as a sign that Jesus, according to
his own words, is really the Bread of Life; the
Healing of the One Born Blind, that he is the Light
of the World; and the Raising of Lazarus, that he
is the Resurrection and the Life. Evidently, John
deals more fully than the other Evangelists with

the words of our Lord, by which he throws light
on his miracles, and gives us as clear a view of a
particular side of his character as of the miracle
alone. But we may lay down this proposition with
a good scientific conscience: He does not present
the truth of the words which he reports in the mirror
of fictitious history, but in that of real fact. Fact
and idea are related to each other just as the body
and the soul, which can no more be identified than
they can be arbitrarily sundered. The fact is the
corporeal idea, and the idea is the soul of the fact.
If I should explain this truth by one example, I
would say, that if the truth of the miracle at Cana
is proved, and the purpose of its performance made
clear, then we are at liberty to find also in it
á posteriori the expression of the thought, which is
true in and of itself, that Jesus creates the higher
from the lower, and transforms life under the law
to life according to the spirit of the Gospel. Other
thoughts of similar beauty may, perhaps, be drawn
from the historical narrative for our edifying application. Much depends on the perception and taste,
which are more influenced by a certain spiritual
discernment than by definite hermeneutical rules.
But to assert unhesitatingly, that, because we find
certain things here and there, therefore "the Evangelists designed to say strictly this and nothing but
this," and to adhere to this opinion, even though
he does not give us any intimation of such a purpose, and, which is much worse, to conclude that
the truth thus discovered is not contained in the

narrative of a real fact, but is concealed in the
finely-spun web of romantic poetry, — surely, the ab-
horrence of miracles must indeed be a very obstinate
and severe evil when it compels its victims to perform such perilous operations! The case is simply
this: — That we are only allowed by our opponents
to choose fact or symbol, while we, clearly convinced of the injustice of the alternative, insist upon
answering: Fact and symbol, symbol and fact, at
the same time.

Unquestionably, the accounts of miracles contained in the fourth Gospel, however grand the
thoughts also symbolized in them, lay claim to being
regarded and treated as miraculous facts which
really occurred. But now the great question arises:
If we leave miracles out of the question for a moment, do these narratives, as such, bear traces in
their details of improbability and invention, or, do
they not bear the impress of credibility and fidelity
even in their finest shades?

We shall be able to answer this question if we
subject every account of a miracle to a close, though
brief, treatment. — The Miracle at the Marriage at
Cana (chapter II. 1 — 11). — We need not yet
fancy, with Renan, that our Lord took pleasure in
attending such wedding - feasts, — as this was
a favourite place of refreshment to him from time to
time, — in order to find it somewhat strange that
he should perform his "first sign" just at a wedding. I assure you that no one would have expected this as the first sign of the Son of man.

May we not add here, that just this surprise is far
more calculated to weaken the supposition of invention than to strengthen it; and that a Gnostic-
Christian romance, — as Bruno Bauer called this
Gospel twenty-five years ago, and as it is held
to-day by many negative theologians in Holland,
— would have been more plausibly introduced in
another and apparently less exceptional manner. This
exceptional character disappears, however, at least
partially, when we remark that the miracle occurred
at the transitional period from the private to the
public life of our Lord, in those first days after his
return from the wilderness where he was tempted,
whose history the first three Evangelists pass over
in total silence. [1] Of the personal recollections

---

1 [Trench says: "'This beginning of miracles' is as truly
an introduction to all other miracles which Christ did, as
the Parable of the Sower is an introduction to all other
parables which he spoke (Mark IV. 31). No other miracle
would have had so much in it of prophecy, would have
served as so fit an inauguration to the whole future work
of the Son of God. For that work might be characterized
throughout as an ennobling of the common and a trans-
muting of the mean — a turning of the water of earth into
the wine of heaven. . . . . . We need not wonder to find
the Lord of life at that festival; for he came to sanctify
all life, its times of joy, as its times of sorrow; and all experience tells us, that it is times of gladness, such as this
was now, which especially need such a sanctifying power,
such a presence of the Lord. In times of sorrow, the sense
of God's presence comes more naturally out; in these it is
in danger to be forgotten. He was there, and by his presence there struck the key-note to the whole future tenor
of his ministry. He should not be as another Baptist, to
withdraw himself from the common paths of men, a preacher
in the wilderness; but his should be at once a harder and
a higher task, to mingle with and purify the common life

which John had of his earlier intercourse with the Master, he communicates one particular, which was so indelibly impressed upon his heart because it had been to him, and also to the small circle who had similar feelings, the first strengthening of their faith. It is a scene from the boundary - line between his domestic and public life, somewhat the same fact among the miracles of Christ as Luke's account of the declarations of Jesus when twelve years old is among the words of Christ. It is the public appearance of what had hitherto been concealed; and as in Luke there is the transition from boyhood to youth, so here is there a transition from the period of preparation to the period of the fulfillment, which had long been patiently awaited. How psychologically clear is it that Mary, in her long years of silence and patient waiting, expects and would even occasion something grand, though she herself does not know what![1] But how natural and appropriate that our Lord should suggest

of men, to witness for and bring out the glory which was hidden in its every relation. And it is not perhaps without its significance, that this should have been specially *a marriage*, which he adorned and beautified with his presence and first miracle that he ever wrought?" *Notes on the Miracles of Our Lord* (Am. Ed.), pp. 83, 85. — J. F. H.]

[1] [Dr. Whedon, an American commentator, says: "Whoever doubted about the miraculous birth of Jesus, his mother certainly could not. No eyes like hers would, in his growth, have understood his miraculous development. Nor is it natural to suppose, that at this moment she did not understand that he had left home to pass through the preparation for his full Messianic office. She must therefore have known that the time for his divine manifestation had arrived. In the perplexity of the present moment she turns to him, as

to her, with friendly seriousness, to occupy the place which was now more becoming than ever to the mother of the Messiah! Only he who goes no further than the mere sound of the words can see in them anything harsh and disrespectful; he who listens more carefully will here perceive the same respect, but also the same independence, which, according to the other Gospels, [1] our Lord ever observed toward his mother, and will much rather see in this undesigned coincidence a proof of the truth of the Johannean account.

When Jesus speaks of his "hour," which had not yet come, it is plain from the connection that he can hardly refer to anything else than time. Neither does the hour come (how much like God!) until Mary has testified her faith and subjection by the words: "Whatsoever he saith unto you, do it." Finally, the hour comes, and, as though our Lord would acknowledge the reception of the six new guests, he changes into good wine the water con-

to a divine aid, hopeful that he could afford relief, even if it required a supernatural power. ...... The Protestant Church rightly interprets the language as informing the mother, that over the exercise of his official functions neither the authority of his human parent, nor the influence of his blood relations or private friends, has any right of control or interference. As in the temptation, Jesus had established the principle that miracles must not be performed for his own low self-interest, so now, he declares that no fleshly relationship must expect to derive profit of a worldly nature from its connection with him." *Commentary on Luke and John,* p. 242. — J. F. H.]

[1] John II. 4; XIX. 26; compare Matthew XII. 46 — 50; Luke II. 49; XI. 27, 28.

tained in the six stone water-pots standing outside.
Now I will not ask you, whether so much mildness,
united with such tenderness, does not rather merit
the name of a miracle of love rather than a "miracle of luxury," but will simply direct your attention to another point. Granted for a moment that
this account, leaving its purpose out of the question,
is fictitious, do you not think that the inventor
would have been at least careful to place in a
clearer and stronger light the time, the manner,
and the impression of the miracle? But, as you
must have already observed, the miracle is here
rather silently presupposed than narrated; it takes
place outside and not inside of the hall; it is not
established by the bridegroom, but by the governor
of the feast, in language which indicates his surprise and at the same time his ignorance. The miracle appears as though covered by a transparent
veil, so that one must even conjecture whether *all*
the water has been changed into wine. There is
not a word said of the impression produced by it
on the guests, nor even on Mary; neither is a word
said about the Performer of the miracle, which would
have directed attention to the peculiar higher purpose of the act itself. Judge for yourselves whether
the maxim, that "people do not invent after this
fashion," may not be applied here with perfect propriety!

The Healing of the Nobleman's Son at Capernaum was a second miracle at Cana, after the first
Passover, during the public ministry of our Lord.

It was performed by Jesus at a distance, whether
we may regard it as at that moment performed, or
only announced as indubitably certain, and really
occurring after this announcement (chapter IV. 45—54).
It is asserted that this narrative is designed by the
fourth Gospel to characterize a faith which, not
being established on mere words, but on the vision
of a sensuous sign, is disapproved as such by Jesus.
Certainly, no one denies that such a faith as this
contrasts very unfavourably with that of the Samaritans already mentioned. But it is just as certain
that no one can understand why this description
could not have been drawn from reality whose confession of faith on this point is comprised in the
couplet:

"Hans does not ask: 'Be the miracle great or small?'
But: 'Can there be such things as miracles at all?'"

According to the first three Evangelists, there
were Jews enough who sought miracles, and it is
just as natural that our Lord should oppose this
perversity as he should finally not refuse the sup-
plicated aid of sufferers. Who does not observe
the paternal heart in that tone of anxiety of soul
with which the nobleman replies to Christ's well-
merited reproach: "Sir, come down ere my child
die?" Who does not feel the Saviour's compassionate heart pulsating in the declaration immediately
following: "Go thy way; thy son liveth?" Who
cannot understand that the blissful sight immediately
moves the surprised father and all his family to
believe? The man believed the word that Jesus

had spoken unto him; but if the narrator had designed to expose ingeniously the worthlessness of
faith in miracles, he should at least have left out
the conclusion of this striking narrative, or given
it quite a different direction. He could then have
represented Jesus as being compelled to put the
Jews' love of miracles to the blush by inexorably
refusing the desired sign; but, in the present instance, he performs a still greater one. The "Go
thy way" of our Lord, the hasty meeting of the
excited servants, and inquiry after the hour of re-
covery, — indeed, everything mentioned in this narrative, would be so utterly aimless and even inappropriate unless we here had before us the reality
drawn from life and personal experience.

   Do we find the case different in the Healing of
the Impotent Man "which had an infirmity thirty
and eight years," — a miracle which, according
to John, was performed at Jerusalem on the Sabbath day (John v. 1—16)? As a miracle performed
on the Sabbath, it takes its place in a series of a
number of similar ones mentioned by the first three
Evangelists, though Luke is the only one who communicates the scarcely less surprising healing of a
disease of eighteen years standing. [1]   There is no
discoverable trace of an allegorical meaning of the
Impotency, of the Five Porches, and of the Pool,
except merely in the imagination of the negative
critics, who will rather surrender themselves to the

---

[1] Mark III. 1—6; Luke XIII. 10—17; XIV. 1—6.

mercy of a worn-out exegetical method than of an
irrational faith in miracles, thus comforming to the
rule, that, "of two evils, choose the less." What
John relates of the disposition and conduct of the
impotent man is, psychologically, just as probable
as what he immediately afterwards relates concerning the deportment and feelings of the Jews. Verily,
John's account represents the true state of the case,
and if it had a design to perpetuate the knowledge
of something else than a miraculous deed, the object of all these individual features and ornaments
in the background of his picture is utterly inexplicable. All that we here read about our Lord, the
question of his solicitous love, the majestic manner
in which he performs his miracle, his considerateness
in withdrawing from the multitude, and the earnest
warning, which takes special necessities into account,
with which he finally crowns his demonstrated benefi-
cence, stand here so perfectly according to his
spirit, as we discover it also in the other Gospels,
that what is related is worthy of him in every respect.

We might even wonder at finding such a revelation of his glory merely mentioned in John if we
had not been reminded, in due time, that it belongs
specially to the circle of miracles performed in the
neighbourhood of Jerusalem, and that, with such an
abundance of the signs and miracles of our Lord,
of which all the Evangelists make mention, no one
ever thought of giving an elaborate account of them. [1]

1 Matthew IV. 24; VIII. 16; IX. 35; John XXI. 25, and
many other passages.

John, who has merely indicated by a single word
the miracles by which Jesus first excited attention
(chapter II. 23), describes the one before us more
elaborately, because it was on this occasion that the
Jews first conceived their plans of murder (chapter v.
16, 18); and so far, therefore, it constituted the
initial point of the growing conflict between light
and darkness, which he now had to portray more
in detail. Yet, however great was the enmity called
forth ,by this miracle performed on the Sabbath day,
we can perceive that our Lord, on the following
Feast of the Tabernacles, very positively refers to
this as the first stone of offence (chapter VII. 21—24).
John felt all the more influenced to relate this event,
because it gave him a welcome opportunity to communicate that vigorous discourse in which our Lord
defends his labours on the Sabbath, and he mentions far greater works performed by him as the
Renewer of spiritual life. However, to assert that
therefore the account of the miracle is only pre-
mised, without any historical ground, in order to
illustrate this idea, is a hypothesis that is applicable
anywhere else sooner than in the department of
serious, thorough, and impartial science. In fact, it
makes a painful impression to see the leaders of
science, so-called, who have been able to stand their
ground with splendour on dizzy hieghts, descend to
such a hopeless abyss.

Neither can we pronounce a more favourable judgment when we perceive at how low a price the
negative school gets rid of the miracle of Christ's

Miraculous Feeding of the Multitude, which is followed by his Walking on the Sea. This is the only one which John has in common with the synoptic Evangelists, and this occurs very probably because it transpired at the time of the second Passover, during the public ministry of Jesus, though not at Jerusalem, and, in connection with the discourse succeeding it, produced the beginning of a dissension among the disciples, by which the final decision was immediately prepared and accelerated. In speaking of the miraculous feeding of the multitude, we would neither repeat all the difficulties which this account presents to the apologist from an orthodox point of view, nor all the subterfuges which men on natural and naturalistic standpoints have employed to avoid the only correct explanation. We would only state, that this miracle is one of the best authenticated in the whole of sacred history. It is communicated by all the four Evangelists with an elaborateness and transparency which admit of no doubt as to its real meaning, and, notwithstanding the difference in accessory circumstances, confirm the same principal fact. Further, we should, above all, not forget that the miracle itself is of a character which it is impossible to attribute to invention; it is not merely performed, but it is also afterwards spoken of by our Lord and his Disciples; [1] and there must have occurred at this time some sign which excited just the aston-

1 Matthew XVI. 5—12; Mark VIII. 14—21.

ishment described by John, because we can only explain by such an extraordinary circumstance the unbounded enthusiasm of the people, which was soon afterwards succeeded by a very perceptible coolness, when it became evident that Jesus would not be the Messiah in the sense of the worldly-minded Jews. [1]

We do not express ourselves too strongly when we say, that, once admitting the possibility of miracles, there is not one, with the exception of the resurrection of our Lord, which is attested and confirmed in so many ways as just this miracle of feeding the multitude. Under such circumstances, you would think that at least the historical reality of the event would be acknowledged. But no, in spite of all the warrant we have for this narrative, it is utterly incredible! And why? Because "Jesus himself, in the 30th and following verses, censured the desire for a visible miracle, as that of manna, and, therefore, could hardly have performed the miracle of feeding a multitude." [2] Indeed! Then how did the multitude ever conceive the thought of desiring such an astounding sign as that of getting manna from heaven, if nothing at all had occurred to suggest this idea to them? According to my view, the wish for a repetition of the miracle performed by Moses is perfectly clear if a miraculous feeding of the multitude on the preceding day had been really witnessed, and which could very easily excite the

1 John VI. 15, 16; compare vers. 66 ff.
2 Scholten, *Evangelium Johannis*, p. 230.

insatiable thirst for miracles to still higher demands? But, on the contrary, no one can understand what could suddenly call forth the strange desire for heavenly bread if ordinary bread had been merely distributed in the usual manner. Just because our Lord had performed such an astonishing miracle on the previous day, he now had the best right for censuring an inordinate desire for miracles.

According to the accounts of all the Evangelists, Christ, in his all-powerful love, performed the miracle of feeding the multitude with five loaves, not that the wishes of the people might be satisfied, but that their temporary want might be supplied. While John says of Jesus, that, "He himself knew what he would do" (verse 6), this clear knowledge does not preclude that compassion which Matthew and Mark so prominently extol. In the mention of the great concourse of people, and of much grass being in the place, you again perceive without difficulty the eye-witness, and had it been the writer's purpose to portray a Christ who performs miracles solely "to reveal his own glory" (just as if this were in conflict with his performing miracles "through love"), I doubt whether he would have told us at the conclusion how the Saviour withdrew from the enraptured multitude to sacred solitude. At least, no thaumaturgist, who performs miracles for exhibition, acts in this way in order to rear a memorial monument to his own greatness. Indeed, this miracle proclaims in a striking manner the great truth that Christ is the Bread of Life; yet, for this very

10

reason, the declaration has such an elevated sound
because it is, so to speak, the account of an incomparable matter of fact. We, too, learn with admiration that Jesus satisfies the wants of the world
with apparently small means, yet without exhaust-
ing the supply, yea, even having a surplus. But,
on the other hand, this thought has not called forth
the narrative, but the miraculous deed shows us this
truth, as in a clear mirror, · which is further confirmed by the experience of all ages.

We next come to the Healing of the One Born
Blind, which is narrated in the 9th chapter. We
are now assured by the negative school that it was
invented to show that Jesus is the Light of the
world. Invented! It is known that Renan declared
himself ready to believe a miracle in case it be examined and established by a committee especially
nominated and authorized beforehand for that purpose. Should we not be almost tempted to speak
of a holy irony of history, which has already fulfilled this arbitrary demand many centuries before
it was uttered? For, in truth, an examination is
here conducted by the most acute and hostile eyes;
the witnesses are called; opinions are heard; and
the various possibilities are weighed against each
other as though on gold-scales, — and what is the
result? It is this: While the miraculous deed remains incomprehensible, the invention of the account
of the miracle must be regarded as utterly inconceivable. Yes, inconceivable; for, by assuming the
opposite, what is the use of that whole supply of

details, which did not stand in the slightest relation
to the principal thought: "Jesus, the Light of the
world?" I know what your answer will be when
I ask you, whether you regard these particulars as
invented: The astonishment of the neighbours; the
diversity of opinions; the dissension of the Pharisees; the cunning and forbearance of the parents;
the immovable calmness, the increasing frankness,
and, I was almost going to say, the knavish confidence, of the one born blind in presenting the
knowledge of his experience as of equal weight
with the knowledge of the Pharisees; and that
humble confession of his faith in the attentive and
condescending love of our Lord? As a matter of
course, the healing of the one born blind is regarded
by the Evangelist as the visible representation of
the truth that Jesus is the Light of the world; but
this truth has so much weight in his eyes just because it was not merely uttered, but preached, by
a grand event. We are no more surprised that the
restored blind man was cast out by the Jews than
when we hear him confessing, after this event, that
Christ is the Son of God. To speak frankly, it
would excite our wonder more if one or the other
of these circumstances had not been mentioned. We
cannot discover the slightest trace of a fixed purpose of inventing and reporting such particulars,
without regard to the reality of their occurrence.
However, if we have symbolism and allegory here,
why do we not also have them in the clay and
spittle, and in the neighbours and parents? The

10*

148

conclusion is manifestly in favour of the truth of the
account; and let it be remembered that we are not
here discussing the question of good taste and sound
understanding. In fact, as we look at the critical
objections that are presented with the most important air imaginable, we can sometimes hardly re-
frain from repeating the well-known question: "Are
these men serious, or jesting?"

Finally, we should now pay attention to the
crown of all the Johannean accounts of miracles,
— The Raising of Lazarus, the striking revelation
of the truth that Jesus is, in the most exalted sense,
the Resurrection and the Life. There is no need
of proving that we read this truth here in sacred
hieroglyphics; but it is absurd to suppose that the
whole narrative was merely invented to bring out
this truth clearly; indeed, it is almost inconceivable
that a period, which, like ours, entertains and cher-
ishes a desire for the tangible, has neither eye
nor heart enough for the heavenly reality that can
be tasted and felt, so to speak, in almost every
line of this inimitable statement. Do you not discover history in that mention of the anointing by
Mary (chapter XI. 2), even before it is afterwards
described; in that description of the family at Bethany, and of the different states of mind of the
sisters, which is so unintentionally confirmed by the
account at the end of the 10th chapter of Luke; and
in the delineation of Christ's emotion, of the feelings
of his enemies, and of the sickness, death, and resurrection of Lazarus himself?

But Lazarus himself, we are told, is a mere fiction, and owes his name accidentally to the well-known Parable of the Rich Man and Lazarus! As, namely, Abraham declares in Luke that the Rich Man's brethren would not repent even though Lazarus rose from the dead, the fourth Evangelist is declared to have made Lazarus really rise from the dead, without the Jews being converted, in order thus to impress upon the parable the stamp of a higher truth! Truly, it has been justly said: "If this is the way in which criticism is conducted, then I no longer know by what means we can be taught to distinguish truth from fiction." [1] What can now be said, in conclusion, in favour of the monstrous conjecture of an accidental coincidence of names? I present another conjecture in opposition to it: In the well-known parable, our Lord, with an involuntary allusion, and one which he alone understood, gave the name of Lazarus to one of the principal characters. This is the more natural as .it can be proved chronologically that he had uttered that parable just on one of the two days which he

---

[1] See Cramer, *Bydragen*, etc., Vol. I. p. 276. Uhlhorn, in his four *Vorträge über die moderne Darstellung des Lebens Jesu*, p. 94 (Hanover, 1866), expresses himself still more strongly when he says: "Then this is speculation! I really do not know which to admire most, the productiveness of the pseudo-John, who created such a history out of merely isolated hints, or the acuteness of the critics who know how to trace out the origin of this account after the world had been in ignorance of it for eighteen hundred years, or, finally, the credulousness of those who regard such a discovery as possible."

spent at some distance from Bethany, filled as he
was with the thought of the sickness and death of
the brother of Mary and Martha. [1]   Placing one
conjecture against the other, I believe that the latter
admits of a stronger defence than the former. But,
leaving both out of the question, I beg that the
Gospel history be not stretched upon the Procrustean
bed of such an unwarranted supposition as the one
advanced by the negative critics! One would have
the same right to-morrow to assert that the account
of the stay, and of the hospitable reception, of our
Lord in a Samaritan city (John IV. 40—42) arose
from the parable in Luke (Luke x. 30—37), that a
merciful Samaritan poured oil and wine into the
wounds of a badly-treated Israelite. Now just as
much can be said for this conjecture as for the
other one that we have mentioned, — which is
simply nothing.

But if miracles are possible, why superscribe
over this chapter in particular the words: "An ar-
tistically-devised Fable?"   As Jesus, by the word
of his power, raised to life two other dead persons,
who are mentioned by the synoptic Gospels, — and
no one has ever proved the contrary, — it could
not be too great or surprising a task for the same
power to raise from the dead Lazarus, who had
lain in the grave.   The manner in which Christ
first puts faith to the test and afterwards rewards
it, harmonizes perfectly with the conduct which we

Comp. my *Life of Jesus* (Dutch Ed.), Vol. II. p. 728.

see him observing both previously and subsequently.
We find even the figure of death as a sleep (verse 11)
in the other Evangelists also (for example, Matthew
ix. 24; Mark v. 39). It has yet to be proved by
our opponents that the Evangelist allows two days
to elapse after Christ had received news of the
sickness, just to show that the miracle should be a
greater one! Our Lord could have had unknown
reasons which did not permit him to go immediately, and he would undoubtedly employ this necessary postponement for the discipline of his weeping
friends, the sisters, in patient and believing trust.
The conversation of our Lord with Martha before
the performance of the miracle (verses 23—27), is
attended with just as little insurmountable difficulty.
Certainly, if that great utterance: "I am the resurrection and the life," was designed to mean only
that Jesus is the source of all spiritual life, then
the logical connection between this utterance and
the previous one: "Thy brother shall [bodily] rise
again," can hardly be proved. Yet the difficulty
disappears when we suppose that our Lord, in order
to throw more light upon, and strengthen, this prophecy, calls himself the Resurrection and the Life
in the widest sense of the terms, so that, while the
spiritual resurrection is not excluded, the bodily one
is chiefly meant. Our Lord by no means intends
them to expect a spiritual resurrection instead of
the bodily raising which they hoped, but would
awaken in her the thought, that whosoever liveth
and believeth in him, though he were dead, shall

yet really live, and therefore can be called back by
him to this life at any moment.

The greatest historical objection ever raised
against this miracle is the silence of the synoptic
Gospels on an event which, like this one, is so
majestic in itself and so decisive in its consequences. And, indeed, we do not disguise the fact
that this phenomenon is somewhat surprising. [1]
More than one supposition, with different degrees
of probability, can be adduced in explanation of this
circumstance. But, granted that not one of the conjectures can be satisfactorily demonstrated, and that
we could not give to the question: "Why are the
synoptic Gospels silent here?", any other answer
than: "We do not know, What is your opinion?",
would this of itself warrant us in regarding a narrative with distrust which bears upon its very face
so many unmistakable evidences of truth and reality? Verily, if the narrative stood altogether
alone in the Johannean account, and in that of the
other Evangelists; if no informer mentioned anything of similar character about Jesus; and if at least

[1] ["To the popular view, and to the eye of modern
science, the raising of the dead appears the greatest of
miracles; but to a true spiritual view the casting out and
controlling demons may be far greater. The former is a
mastery of passive or willing human nature; the latter is a
mastery of hostile powers. But the reality of the present
miracle is unconsciously attested by all the Evangelists;
since they all describe a sudden popular excitement in favour of Jesus which can be solved only by some such fact;
an excitement which soon reacted, and resulted in his crucifixion." Whedon, *Commentary on Luke and John*, p. 332.
— J. F. H.]

the rise of such a forgery might be explained in
an acceptable manner, there would then be some
excuse for a certain degree of doubt. But the fact
really is, that, though the silence of the other
Evangelists be surprising, invention by this one is
utterly inconceivable. For if Lazarus was really
not raised, what are we to suppose? One of two
things: The narrative must have either *some* or *no*
historical ground. If it have some historical ground,
then what is it? Is it, as Renan has supposed, a
feigned death, a dramatic deception, in which Jesus
was at once both spectator and actor? You certainly turn away with horror and disgust at such
shameless frivolousness in casting that which is holy
to the dogs. Or, has it no historical ground? Then,
as Réville holds, is the whole narrative a sort of
allegory or legend, intended to teach us how Jesus
awakened from their spiritual sleep of death the
outcasts of Jewish society, as then constituted,
whom he loved, and whose lot he deplored. Truly,
he who endorses such a view without any shadow
of proof expects too much of the credulity of his
readers. [1] The miracle is incomprehensible, but this
fiction is as incomprehensible as the mystification
designed to supply it. But what is the use of
speaking more on this point? I can now understand why Spinoza declared that he was ready to
believe in Jesus if he could only concede this miracle. But he could not do this, for it was not the

---

[1] "He calculates strangely on the stupidity of his hearers
who feeds them with such nonsense." *Godet.*

narrative itself, but his philosophical system, which
impeded his faith.

II. His philosophical system, we say, and not
the historical accounts, was an impediment to his
faith. This assertion naturally leads us from this
narrow sphere to a wider one. There is no doubt
that the great majority of the purely historical objections raised to every particular account of miracles can be met by quite a satisfactory answer.
But it becomes clearer every day that these objections constitute only the curtain behind which an
infinitely greater doubt lies concealed. Strauss has
somewhere said, that, however venerable and harmonious the witnesses for the apostolic origin of the
Gospels might be, he would even then not believe
their contents. Do you ask: "Why would he not?"
He gives us his own answer: "Everything that would
make Jesus a supernatural being is well-meant,
and, to a certain degree, is perhaps beneficent; but
if it continue permanent, it becomes an injurious
delusion, which is now more corrupting than ever
before." In other words, we should reject a miracle itself, even though attested by a still greater
number of harmonizing witnesses. There is no need
of proving that he here only sincerely expresses
just what we hear openly proclaimed and accepted
with gladness. ¹ We hear the cry from different

¹ Zeller, the most vigorous champion of the Tübingen School
since the death of Baur, says, in his *Vorträge und Abhand-
lungen geschichtlichen Inhalts*, 1865, p. 491, that, with his con-
genial friend, he could not admit the reality of such an

sides: "Miracles are inconceivable!" Another says: "They are undemonstrable!" A third exclaims: "They are at least destitute of importance!" You cannot expect me to discuss these questions at length. The *pros* and *cons* have been repeatedly weighed and met, so that it will probably suffice merely to present you a brief summary of the arguments; for it is better to say something additional than, by injudicious silence, to leave what we have said incomplete and unsatisfactory. We will conclude the present Lecture by a brief examination of the three objections already mentioned, which are offered not merely against the Johannean account of Christ's miracles, but against the accounts of all the Evangelists. [1]

"Miracles are inconceivable." This is the first expression which many now use in casting aside the accounts informing us that water was changed into wine, that bread and fish were miraculously increased, that a man who was born blind was healed, and that a dead man was raised to life.

event as the resurrection of Christ, "no matter how strongly it might be attested."

[1] In view of the utter impossibility of here treating properly the question of miracles, I refer the reader to the literature furnished in my *Life of Jesus* (Dutch Ed.), Pt. I. pp. 257, 311; Pt. II. p. 32 ff.; also especially to the excellent treatise by Professor Zöckler, of Greifswald University, *On the Importance of Miracles in Nature and History*, published in the apological periodical, *Der Beweis des Glaubens*, 1866, pp. 65 — 85; and to the monograph of F. L. Steinmeyer, *Die Wunderthaten des Herrn in Bezug auf die neueste Kritik* (Berlin, 1866), which imparts much important matter, particularly on the Raising of Lazarus, on pp. 197 — 210.

The modern negative spirit has placed itself within
a few years — or, I might say, months, — on a
height where it sees the question of miracles so far
beneath that it does not any longer regard it worthy
of its notice. It seems like a razed fortification,
by which the victorious general leads his troops,
and behind whose fragments only a few solitary
soldiers lie concealed. What a pity it is that the
general is compelled to take the road leading by
this ruin, and that the supposed invalids are so
bold and incorrigible as now and then to fire a
gun, and not always in the air! We are not the
only ones who imagine that the magnanimity practised by this and that one in passing out of the
way of this question does not indicate strength, but
weakness, and is rather a proof of the tactics than
of the conscientiousness of our opponents. This
much is certain: That at least the empirical philosopher has no right to assert dogmatically that miracles are impossible. For this assertion in the department of empirical philosophy is nothing less
than a purely dogmatical declaration. Empirical
philosophy pays attention to what occurs everywhere in nature; but when it undertakes to decide
on what can or cannot happen, it treads upon the
department of speculative philosophy, which the
devotees of empirical philosophy are in the habit
of avoiding as a territory full of vapour and fog.
The poet's castigation applies very well in their
case:

"Of what do such rough brooms
Leave behind them a trace?
Men now haste to deny
What only just took place!"

I need hardly remind you of the utter destitu-
tion of support, at least on the empirical standpoint, for the declaration that what does not take
place to-day could not have taken place yesterday.
It is no wonder that the term, "Miracles are impossible," is here gradually pronounced with an ever
descending voice, however loud it may still reëcho
in many hearts. Only he can say that miracles are
impossible who is ignorant of the existence of another and higher order of things than those to which
the usual course of affairs refers us. The denial
of miracles is, really, the denial of the supernatural.
There is a conception of miracles which does not
permit him who enjoys it to hesitate for a moment
at the word "impossible." If we look at miracles
as a purely arbitrary interference of God with the
existing order of things, as an infraction of that
order of nature whose definiteness and regularity
very justly excite our greatest admiration, and, in
a word, regard them as absolutely contrary to nature, and therefore assuredly contrary to God, it is
not then so difficult to banish faith and miracles to
the realm of old wives' fables by a single stroke
of the pen. But if we carefully consider the matter,
it is pure compassion to combat such an opinion of
miracles, because it is no longer defended by any
thoughtful mind.

The case is altogether different when miracles
are regarded as not in conflict with all nature, but
only with that which we are acquainted with; as a
momentary deviation from the usual order of things
at the sign of an almighty, wise and holy Will;
and as a special revelation of Him who reaches, by
both ordinary and extraordinary ways, the end that
compels our respect. Now is such a miracle as this
possible? This question must be answered in different ways, according to our different ideas of God.
If I occupy a deistic point of view, and regard God
not merely as distinct from, but also sundered from,
the world, — as One who lets the universe keep in
motion, according to its own laws, just like the
works of a watch, then I cannot conceive a miracle to be possible unless there is a total change
in God's relation to the world. If I be a pantheist
or naturalist, and therefore deny the existence of a
personal God, who is elevated as Spirit above the
cosmos, it is self-evident that I must, at all hazards,
explain everything as the purely natural product of
finite causes, and that when I see something which
I cannot comprehend, the most that I should do is
to stand still in astonishment, but never make the
confession that this was really a miracle.

But if, on the other hand, I take the Christian
theistic view of God, and therefore acknowledge
Him to be a living and personal God, who, though
infinitely exalted above the world, is nevertheless in
continual and direct relation to it; who is not only
the Eternal Power by which all things are supported,

but the Holy Will by which everything is governed, and is by no means confined to the laws which he has ordained for the creature that is dependent upon Him, — if this be my point of view, I cannot seriously question at least the possibility of the occurrence of miracles. This possibility of a miracle occurring in a particular case must be settled by historical and critical inquiry; but the word "inconceivable" can only be repeated in case our God, to speak with Henry Heine, is a God who is "pantheistically laced-up" and who does not reveal himself in the universe, — he has no self, because he is nobody, only a something, — but is gradually revealed in the thinking mind. But if our God really has self-consciousness and freedom (and how could he be the Absolute Spirit without these), then we must necessarily distinguish between the laws of nature and the will of God, as the former are determined by the latter. In our opinion, the so-called monistic theism, which acknowledges the personality of God on the one hand, and, on the other, denies miracles, is only a happy inconsistency, which does more honor to the heart than the understanding of those who hold it, and must necessarily lead either backward to a worn-out system of Deism, or forward to hopeless pantheism. A miracle is really nothing else than the revelation of the almighty freedom of Almighty Love, which, by its special interference with natural laws, restores the moral order which was disturbed by man in consequence of the sinful abuse of the freedom which God had given him. Neither God's unchangeableness nor wisdom is in this way injured in the slightest degree; the occurrence of miracles is not an injury but an advantage to the eternal order of the world, which was at first moral but was afterwards destroyed by sin. Thus, the question of the con- ceivableness of miracles is, in other words, this question: "Is it conceivable that God should interfere for the redemption and restoration of a race cor- rupted and made miserable by sin?"

Do you suppose miracles to be impossible? Very well; then, in that case, there is also no special saving revelation of God, and no real revealing act of God, but only a merely subjective process of God towards revelation. Then there is also no more answer to prayer than the excitement and elevation which the one who prays communicates to himself by "spiritual gymnastics," as it has been properly called, and in which, intercession for others may be called the climax of all folly. Then we cannot conceive of conversion, at least as the intro- duction of an inward principle of life, and as the beginning of a new life in truth, but at most only as the purely natural development of our inherent goodness. Then there is also no independent gov- ernment of the world, · but only an eternally im- movable order of the world; and there is also no creation of all things from nothing, at the beginning of time, by an Almighty Will. The denial of mir- acles must of itself lead to the absurdity of a so- called eternal creation, and this again to a theory of the merely natural development of one thing from another, of man from the monkey, of organic from inorganic matter, and this, perhaps, from the atom, and the atom — from what? Here we stand precisely at the same point where philosophy, in its tender childhood, and the systematic opponent of miracles are struck blind when they come to discuss the first of all questions. Truly, the theory of an unbending connection of causes in the natural and moral world, where there is not left a finger-breadth for the freedom of the eternally living and operating God, avenges itself with fearful severity. The end of this denial will be, that the bells will toll simultaneously the burial hour for religion and philosophy, for they did exist, but are no more. Even morality itself is not safe, and I can perfectly understand how not only such a learned man as Richard Rothe sees no difficulty in such proofs of divine omnipotence, [1] but that there are so many besides him, who, now regarding religion as the prime necessity for man, and Christianity as the special saving revelation for the sinner, will not allow themselves to be robbed of their faith in miracles at any lower price than they would require to part with their faith in a living God, without

---

[1] The profound and acute Professor Rothe, of Heidelberg University, in his excellent work entitled *Zur Dogmatik*, p. 66 ff., has presented a deduction and vindication of faith in miracles on a Christian and theistic standpoint, which cannot be recommended too heartily, especially to those who continually assert that no "thinking" and "conscientious" man adheres any longer to miracles.

11

whose personal participation they could not live, and without whose grace they could not die in peace.

But some one, perhaps, sighs: "I would accept miracles if they could only be proved." Allow me to ask this question in reply: "What do you understand by proof?" Do you desire a mathematical proof in the department of history and religion? Or do you desire that the one who performs miracles be duly attested before a committee nominated by, or composed of, such men as Strauss and Renan? But a juggler, who was compelled to maintain himself in this way, would certainly be anything else than an ambassador of God, a messenger of truth and of life. Would not many a member of this court constantly increase its requirements, and would a conviction arrived at on such wise have anything in common with religious faith? Belief in miracles, as you will readily grant, is not merely to acknowledge that, for example, a dead man rose on a certain day at a certain place, but that God, either immediately or by the instrumentality of his servants, there and at that time raised this dead person. In other words, true faith in miracles is also a religious faith. But such a faith can be awakened, strengthened, and justified on rational and moral grounds, though it can never be demonstrated in such a way as will leave no avenue of escape for him who does not grant the premisses, and evades the consequences at all hazards. It is sufficient that miracles, like the sun, are revealed in a certain peculiar splendour to the single eye and the receptive heart.

But perhaps some one asserts that we are not acquainted with all the laws of nature, and that, therefore, while we are able to prove that something was unusual, we cannot prove that it was a miraculous deed of God. But we know enough of the laws of nature to be able to say, that, for example, it is impossible to explain by the usual course of nature the miracles which John relates. The accounts of miracles contained in the Gospels are of such a character that we cannot hesitate to say: "How strange, how wonderful!" They are, moreover, usually connected with language which compels us to see in the miracle also the sign of a higher operation; and they are the revelation of One who, in a moral respect, awakens and merits our confidence. According to the words of Jesus himself, there is no doubt that false miracles could and did occur (Matthew xxiv. 24), and nowhere has more gigantic deception been practised, or been more successful, than in this mysterious realm. Therefore, faith in miracles is always a wonderful faith; hence the necessity of increased care in seeing what, and on what ground, we should accept anything as miraculous; and hence we cannot evade the question, as to whether or not there are signs by which we can distinguish true miracles from false ones. But as the existence of counterfeit money is rather a proof for than against the original existence of real money, so does just the pretended miracle

11*

all the more induce and justify the presumption
that also real miracles must have occasionally occurred. Whether this was really the case in the
sphere where we are guided by the hand of the
Evangelists, is a question that can only be properly
answered by impartial historical criticism, which
must be distinguished from dogmatical and philosophical criticism. You do not require us to
guarantee in a pefectly satisfactory manner, and in
a few moments, the credibility of even only a
portion of the Gospel accounts of miracles. But if
you desire that we should mark out in general
outline the way in which, according to our notion,
this proof can be always attempted with good results, according to the necessities of the present
time, your suggestion is just as welcome to me as
it can be of interest to you.

In order to reach the end in question, I regard
it necessary to begin with Christianity as a phenomenon related to the whole history of the world
and reformatory of the world. No one can deny
that with this Christianity there came into the world
a new moral and religious power, which has totally
changed its previous aspect. . He who thoroughly
and impartially studies history will see, with continually increasing clearness, that it is impossible
to regard this Christianity as the merely natural
result. of the Jewish or heathen religion of the day,
or as the result of the philosophical thought of
previous centuries; and no one has ever yet succeeded in giving a merely natural interpretation of

the monotheistic peculiarity of the Children of Israel, from whom Christianity sprang. Thus, we are justified in arriving at the presumption that we are dealing with the fruit of a special revelation, and this presumption is strengthened if, in the first two centuries after Christ (not to speak of later miracles), we meet also with various phenomena, even in the natural sphere of life, which perceptibly vary from what we are taught by our ordinary daily experience. [1] The miracles of the post-Apostolic age are as the waning twilight of a sun which has set, but is not quenched and is far from being forgotten. The most credible witnesses of this period refer to an earlier one, as an age of more numerous and dazzling miraculous deeds. Thus Quadratus, for example, a Christian apologetical writer at the beginning of the second century, a fragment of whose work has been preserved by Eusebius, the Church Father, relates, that even at his day there were many of the sick still alive who had been healed by Jesus, and that there were then living those who had been raised by him from the dead. [2]

As we go steadily backwards from this company into the vestibule of the Apostolic Age, the few Epistles which the most negative criticism has found itself compelled to leave in our possession will suffice to show that the earliest Christian period was

---

[1] Compare Tholuck's essay on *The Miracles of the Catholic Church*, etc., *Vermischte Schriften*, Vol. I., especially pp. 28 — 49.

[2] See my *Life of Jesus*, Vol. II. p. 309.

a scene of miracles. "He therefore that ministereth
to you the Spirit, and worketh miracles among you,"
were words which the Apostle regarded amply sufficient to put the Galatians to extreme shame; [1] and
he himself, the great Apostle of reasonable service
and of sound understanding, could declare to his ad-
versaries in Corinth, that "the signs of an Apostle
were wrought among you in all patience, in signs,
and wonders, and mighty deeds" (2 Corinthians
XII. 12), so that, in this respect also, he was not
a whit less than one of the chief Apostles. The
various extraordinary gifts that were manifested in
this same Corinth are universally known. Miracles
were not only the signature of the Church but the
seal of fellowship of the most distinguished Apostles,
and particularly of Paul. This same Paul has performed and experienced miracles. He appeals to
visions and revelations, by which he had received
communications which he positively and consciously
distinguishes from his own perception and opinion. [2]
He is himself a moral miracle, when we compare
his life as a Christian with his previous life; he is
a miracle whose solution he gives us himself when
he tells us that he has seen the Christ who had
died, and who had been persecuted by him. On
historical and psychological grounds, it is as preposterous to regard self-deception in his case as

[1] Galatians III. 5; compare 1 Corinthians XII. 9; Hebrews II. 4.
[2] 1 Corinthians VII. 10, 12, 40; 1 Thessalonians IV. 15,
and other passages.

imposture by others. [1] Only a few years after this same Paul's conversion, he proclaimed in Corinth what he repeats somewhat later in an Epistle to the same Church, that Christ died, was buried, "rose again the third day," and appeared to a number of his friends. The manner in which he makes this declaration renders it impossible for any impartial expositor to look at the fact in any other light than as a bodily resurrection and coming forth from the grave.

As a witness of this miraculous event, Paul stands with all the other Apostles. Every one of them was a personal security for the fact, and, so far as we are able to see, from the very first day when Christianity appeared in the world. Their faith, and the faith of the entire early Church, is utterly inexplicable if it is not established on facts. It is impossible that witnesses so numerous and of such a character could have taken a visionary view of what they neither believed nor expected; hunger can desire bread, but it cannot create it. Even scepticism has been compelled to make the following confession: "It is only the Miracle of the Resurrection that can dissipate the doubts which threaten unavoidably to banish faith itself to

---

[1] In view of all that has been recently asserted and misconceived by our opponents, we refer the reader to the excellent essay by Professor Schultz, of Königsberg University, published in *Der Beweis des Glaubens* (1866, pp. 33—49), entitled: *Das Zeugniss des Apostels Paulus von der Auferstehung des Herrn, gegenüber den Ansichten von Schenkel und Strauss.*

the eternal night of death." [1] Jesus must therefore
really have risen, as is declared by Paul, together
with all the Apostles, and as is also particularly
declared by John, whom, from all that has been
said, we must admit to be a credible witness on
the life of Jesus.

There is no doubt that John gives an account
of a bodily resurrection of the deceased Saviour.
Let him who thinks that he can destroy this irref-
utable testimony, do it; but do not compel the
Apostle to relate what he really does not. We
have already observed, that everything which he
communicates about the empty grave, the linen
clothes found there, the visit to the grave by himself, Peter, Mary Magdalene and others, would
have been as devoid of purpose and as superfluous
as you can conceive, if he had not perfectly agreed
with the remaining Apostles on the fact of Christ's
bodily resurrection. How would an author who
believed that Jesus did not bodily rise from the
grave, ever have conceived the notion of attribut-
ing to him the words addressed to Thomas: "Reach
hither thy finger, and behold my hands; and reach
hither thy hand, and thrust it into my side; and
be not faithless, but believing?" Still more. Would
the same author ever have mentioned the different

1 Baur, *Das Christenthum der drei ersten Jahrhunderte*,
p. 39. — On the ground and importance of faith in the resurrection of our Lord, compare the Fourth Lecture, entitled,
The Son of Man, in F. Coulin's excellent work, *Conferences
sur l'humanité du Christ*, p. 141 ff. 1866.

appearances of the Risen One among the *signs* performed by him (chapter xx. 30) if they had not possessed in his view a miraculous character, that is, had not borne the mark of an actual bodily resurrection? A Christ who, like all other men, continues dead in body, but lives immortally in spirit, and plays the ghost after his death (to use an expression of Strauss against Schenkel), is certainly not the Christ portrayed in the fourth Gospel. [1]

As we have thus ascended to the highest peak in the mountain - range of miracles, — the bodily resurrection of our Lord, — we have gained a solid point of support whence the hotly contested territory can again be gradually possessed. Yet we now have the actual revelation of a higher order of things, a supernatural power, whose presence and operation we are not justified *a priori* in regarding as inconceivable. But now Christ himself stands before our eyes in a light where it is possible, and even probable, that he could thus have conquered death, and was able to control the power of the material world. The miracle which takes place in him makes it very easy to suppose that he could perform deeds which infinitely surpass the universal power of man. The account of his life furnished us by reliable witnesses declares plainly that this really was the case.

---

[1] Compare his quizzical treatment of Schenkel's notion (which has been shrewdly ignored by a. certain school), in his controversial work, *Die Halben und die Ganzen*, p. 57 ff. Berlin, 1865.

As for the credibility of the single accounts, it is not difficult to start questions of greater or less importance concerning some of them as soon as they are isolated. But how speedily does everything assume quite a different light when we look at the miraculous deeds of our Lord by the aid of his own declarations concerning himself, and when we look from this centre to all the points of the sacred circle!

Then it usually follows, that what may justly awaken distrust when considered alone bears the impress of beauty, truth, and significance when taken in this connection and associated with this Person. And then when we come to particulars, and see how many delicate psychological characteristics of the truth are furnished by these accounts of Christ's miracles; how inseparable is the bond between the words and deeds of our Lord in the fourth Gospel, as well as in all the rest; how great a difference can be proved between the canonical and the apocryphal accounts of the miracles of Jesus; and what a difference there is between his signs and those of others, whether real or pretended performers of miracles, — I shall mention merely Apollonius of Tyana, Mohammed, and others, — need I tell you in advance the result of such a candid and conscientious inquiry? I believe that I have already anticipated it, and have no more thought of reviving the trivial objection, that we must in that case accept also all the later accounts of miracles, for example, those of the Romish Church. As for the

latter, you will have observed that we do not belong to the class who hold that the miraculous gift
was unconditionally withdrawn at the death of the
last Apostle. We will subject the accounts of subsequent miraculous deeds to as impartial investigation as those furnished by sacred history; and if we
can find that the external and internal grounds in
the former are just as satisfactory, we shall be just
as willing to acknowledge it. But if it follow that
later accounts of miracles were only simulated in
many instances, we will never admit that such a
castle in the air be dignified to the rank of an
arsenal, from which there can be taken spurious
weapons for battering down the impregnable fortress
of the Gospel history of miracles.

What further objection can be raised to our
claiming the name of disciples of orthodox science
on the ground of our firm belief in miracles? As
a matter of course, our knowledge of nature has
been immeasurably extended within eighteen hundred
years, but it has not yet led us to believe that
Christ and Christianity can be satisfactorily explained without appeal to a higher interposition.
Though we are now better acquainted with nature
than men of an earlier day were, and though we
must confess that these things have happened, yet
this is another ground for seeing in the accounts
of Christ's miracles nothing less than the finger of
God. The Evangelists were, it is true, simple-
hearted men, and not suspicious critics; but they
had a better knowledge than a certain class of the

critics of our day, — they had a sacred sense of truth. It were impossible for him who places Jesus as high as they, and bows as reverently before him as they, to imagine such foolish things about him as a deviser of miracles, and to tell such un-blushing falsehoods, as those who oppose them would falsely attribute to them. We take their testimony in deciding as historical proof that which we cannot deny without becoming involved in in-finitely greater difficulties than follow from a firm belief in miracles. Criticism — of course, we ac-knowledge its right; but the criticism that we are contending with is not truly free, but absolutely bound; for it is not ruled by philosophical prin-ciples, but by philosophical prejudices. And as long as God gives me a voice to speak, I will raise it in protesting against this illicit mixture of true history and false philosophy.

Let us now group together what we have said in detail. By opposing the miracles narrated in the Gospel history, we would have to accept much greater miracles, and even absurdities. Neverthe-less, we will make a reply, though the objection of our enemies is hardly worth the trouble. "The whole question of miracles," it is said, "is, after all, of but little importance. Why contend longer about things which, having happened so many cent-uries ago, cannot contribute anything to the general satisfaction of men? Jesus is the same to me that he was before, whether I believe that he arose bodily from the dead, or not; and my salvation is

not endangered even though I doubt that water
was once changed into wine, or that the eyes of
a man born blind were opened." What reply shall
we make to such reasoning as this, in which, as I
often think, truth and error are perhaps unconsciously united, and are therefore doubly dangerous?
Miracles without importance! It does seem to me
that the very ones who make this assertion do not
believe what they say. Almost every page of John's
Gospel proves, with perfect clearness, that they were
of great importance in his estimation. [1] We learn
from Christ's own declarations, recorded by John
as well as by the synoptic Evangelists, that He
also attributed great importance to them.

It is remarkable with what unsuspecting frankness those who deny miracles attempt to persuade
themselves and us, that, when they thus despise
our Lord's miracles, they have him on their side,
holding that he never regarded such deeds of any
special value. Because our Lord had said that
signs would be done in his name by false prophets,
did he not also positively say: "The same works
that I do [among which are his miracles also], bear
witness of me, that the Father hath sent me;" and
again: "Go and show John again those things which
ye do hear and see;" and again: "But if I do,
though ye believe not me, believe the works; that
ye may know, and believe, that the Father is in

[1] John I. 50; II. 11; III. 2; IV. 29; V. 36; X. 25;
XX. 30, 31.

174 JOHN'S ACCOUNT OF CHRIST'S MIRACLES.

me, and I in him?"[1] If Jesus more than once reproached the people for their lusting after miracles, can we conclude that it is a matter of small importance for God to bear witness to the Gospel of his Son, by signs, and wonders, and deeds? I grant that the impression of miracles cannot be so powerful upon us as upon the contemporaries of our Lord, but their importance has not diminished in the slightest. How can it be possible that these things should really happen, and occur with direct reference to our salvation, and be authenticated in such an incontestable way, and yet should permanently be remarkable only as enigmatical antiquities? The correctness of this view is at least improbable, and it is not substantiated by the experience of many persons of early and later times who have been led to Christ by these miracles in the fullest sense.

As a matter of course, historical faith in miracles cannot of itself save any one. Who has ever asserted such an absurdity? But without humble faith in Jesus Christ as the Son of God, who was given for our offences and was raised for our justification, and as the One who was able to do just such miracles as the Gospel relates, we can not and shall not be saved. The expression: "I believe in Christ, whether he perform miracles or not," is very superficial, and indicates rather a certain good-natured and optimistic state of mind than thorough

[1] Matthew XXIV. 24; compare XI. 2—6, 20—24; John V. 36; X. 37, 38.

reflection. One may believe in Jesus, as some imagine him, and continue in this faith, even though he let go miracles; but, without miracles, would one direct his attention to Him, be led to Him, and fall at His feet? The expression: "Jesus remains the same to me whether I believe in miracles or not," amounts to about as much as, — speaking plainly, — he is only the Socrates of Israel, the Ideal of humanity, the religious Genius. No doubt, with such a Jesus as this it would be a matter of no importance whether or not if, together with the many strange and grand things that he did, he occasionally healed the sick, or took a few steps on the surface of the sea.

But is it necessary to adduce any further proof that this Jesus is that of the whole Christian Church, or of the Reformers and Martyrs, or of the Evangelists and Apostles? The acknowledgment of his divine miraculous power, which was glorified in numerous deeds, is naturally and inwardly connected with this last-named, and only saving faith. It is not quite correct to say: "We do not believe in Jesus because of his miracles, but for Jesus' sake we also believe in his miracles." The first part of this declaration is as true as the second, and one does not preclude the other. If we look at Jesus in the light of his own statements, it is not difficult for us to accept his miracles also. But, on the other hand, an appeal to these miracles, united with other proofs, justifies our most holy faith, and the Christian's contemplation of them

constantly strengthens this faith. Thus, on the one
hand, they remain the unsuspected attestation of his
great mission; and, on the other, they are the sufficient revelations of the glory of his exalted Person,
the beams of the Sun of the spiritual world, which
dazzle our eyes, but are more natural to the Sun
himself than would be the absence of such signs
from such a phenomenon. But here, as you observe, our consideration of the* question of miracles
reaches a point where it passes over into another
inquiry: "What do you mean by the Apostolic, and
especially the Johannean, Christ?" We shall devote
the following Lecture, which is the last and by no
means least important of our series, to the investigation of this question. For the present, we cannot
comprise all that we have said in a better way than
in the poetical language of a genial theological
friend:

"Goodness is such a foreland; godly deeds are hills;
And faith's efforts in God's strength the lower mountain height;
But in Christ's miracles the Alpine world begins,
O'er which his resurrection-peak sheds dazzling light." [1]

[1] Dr. John P. Lange.

IV.

THE JOHANNEAN CHRIST.

"Even the attacks of recent negative criticism, with its astounding exegetical operations and divinations, — in which it bears the seeds of its own ruin, — will pass away without effect; and though they are dealt against John's Gospel with extraordinary energy, and with a great show of learning and acuteness, as we might naturally expect, they will nevertheless not be able to pluck a single feather from the mighty wing of this Eagle."

H. A. W. Meyer.

A memorable hour arrived in the history of a youth belonging to an honourable family in France, during the second half of the sixteenth century. Though scarcely fifteen years of age, he had been led by blind guides to unbelief and the denial of God's existence; and the serpent's teeth, sown on the unguarded field, had already begun to produce their destructive harvest. His godly father, who was deeply concerned for the salvation of his son's

178 THE JOHANNEAN CHRIST.

soul, placed a New Testament in his room, and offered the silent prayer that he might "take and read it." It really came to pass that the son did take it up at a leisure moment. His eye rested accidentally upon a passage which, according to his own words, so affected him that he "suddenly felt the divinity of the subject, and, together with the majesty, also the power of the words that so infinitely surpassed the flow of all human eloquence." "My whole body was convulsed," he continues, "my soul was confounded, and I have been so affected this whole day that I have scarcely been conscious of my own identity."

In later years he looked back upon this hour as the decisive turning-point of his life; and he walked until death in the way which was at that time opened before him. It was not quite twenty-five years after this remarkable event, that he was preaching the Gospel of the Reformation at Antwerp, while the light from the blaze of the funeral pile which was consuming his companions in faith shone against the windows of the hall where he preached. And when the pestilence that raged in Leyden, in the year 1602, numbered him among its victims, it was universally acknowledged and lamented that a shining light in the ecclesiastical and scholastic heavens had set. This young man was our celebrated countryman, Professor Francis Junius; that Bible-leaf bore the inscription of "The Gospel According to St. John;" and the passage which he read was the beginning of the familiar First Chapter:

"In the beginning was the Word, and the Word was with God, and the Word was God." [1] "In the beginning was the Word." Francis Junius was certainly not the only one who, at that time and afterwards, has felt the majestic force of this declaration; perhaps there is one herè and there in this audience who can speak of a similar impression, though in a less degree. But do you not also believe that these individuals are confronted by a far greater number who, instead of reëchoing this witness of John, regard it as a contradiction? I believe that the prevailing tendency of the times on this point is not expressed in the above confession of Francis Junius, but, rather, in the well-known scene from Gœthe's Faust, a moment before Faust hears the voice of Mephistopheles. As Faust stands upon the boundary-line between Heaven and Hell, he once more takes up the original text of the New Testament, to translate it anew; but at the very first sentence: "In the beginning was the Word," he stands motionless, in painful perplexity. He exclaims: "I cannot value the Word so highly; I must translate it by something else." So he now writes: "In the beginning was the *Thought*;" but yet this does not sound quite right. He then writes: "In the beginning was the *Power*;" but even that does

---

[1] See an account of this interesting occurrence given by Francis Junius himself in his *Autobiography*, lately introduced at the beginning of his *Opera*, Geneva, 1813, and also published by J. A. Fabricius, *Delectus Argumentorum, etc.*, pp. 352—354. Hamburg, 1725.

not satisfy his mind. Finally, he takes advice, and writes: "In the beginning was the *Act.*"

His desire for what was tangible concealed from his vision the highest idea; Scripture had to accommodate itself to him, or he would not bow before it; and you know the end of a way which began on this wise. O that, in this respect, Faust had never been anything else than simply the product of a creative imagination!

What has given occasion to the dissension between negative criticism and the Johannean Christ, and in what way has it gained such dimensions in the most recent time? I am not surprised that, as you cast a retrospective glance upon the course of our inquiry, you should repeat this question with the sense of painful surprise. Nevertheless, you can hardly conceive of a more complete harmony of external and internal proofs than those which can be adduced in favour of the fourth Gospel. However relatively great the difference may be between this and the first three Gospels, the idea of an irreconcilable contradiction on cardinal points is not to be mentioned for a moment. Even the miracles related here present no more serious difficulty than that which can be offered against the entire department of Scriptural miracles by those who deny the supernatural altogether.

If, under all these circumstances, we direct attention to the numberless subterfuges which our opponents employ to escape the power of demonstration, we need hardly hesitate to repeat the

prophecy of one of the most excellent Scriptural
expositors of our times: that "negative criticism, in
spite of all its array of learning and acuteness,
will not be able to pluck a single feather from the
mighty wing of this Eagle." [1] And yet the attack
is constantly commenced anew, and those who
make it obstinately refuse to give their opponents
a better name than "warriors for the lost cause."
In this case, the cause of opposition must lie deeper,
and in quite a different department from the one in
which we have hitherto moved. Behind this controversy there must lie concealed other antipathies than
those which we have already become acquainted
with.

What can they be? Let us look to one of the
most talented champions of the modern sceptical
tendency for an answer. "We need," declares Colani, "a living, true, and human Christ. This generation, which the Spirit from on high animates
more than it did the subjects of Constantine or the
people living at the time of the Thirty Years' War;
this generation, which, it must not be forgotten, is
the child of eighteen hundred years of Christian
development, wishes as its Master a truly historical
person, and not one who belongs to the misty department of theological abstraction. It wishes as
its Saviour a hero who did not gain victories
without a conflict. It will not believe in him until,
like Thomas, it has placed its finger in the marks

[1] H. A. W. Meyer.

of the nails, and its hand in the wounds of his
heart; that is, until it shall have felt the scars
which the daily conflict of spiritual life has left
behind in the soul of the Son of man." [1]

"The synoptical Christ," we hear asserted, "may
answer to this inquiry, but it is utterly impossible
for the Johannean Christ to do it; whatever he
is, he is not flesh of our flesh, and bone of our
bone." "The denial of the authenticity of the fourth
Gospel," the objector continues, "may be subject to
great difficulties, but they cannot at all come into
consideration when we compare them with the difficulties which, well-meaning but helpless apologist,
you have hitherto been unable to solve. For, see,
it is not this or that particular of his history, but
it is the principal character himself, with whom I
cannot harmonize; I would have to forget everything which I have learned, through so much labour
and conflict, by the light of modern sceptical views.
The frame may be never so splendid, and the mirror
as clear as possible, after so many centuries, but
the form which I behold in this glass is obscured
by a mist which my eyes cannot penetrate. I can
have respect for an excellent religious man, but as
to bowing before an incarnate God, who dies and
rises again, — pardon me if I say that I am a
little too old, and have thought, and heard, and
read a little too much, to do such a thing!" Do
you not recognize this tone? Indeed, I might almost

---

[1] F. Colani, *Jésus-Christ et les Croyances Messianiques de
son Temps*, p. 169. Strasburg, 1864.

ask, have you not heard it reëchoing now and then even from some hidden corner of your own heart, where you scarcely dared to look? If so, you cannot regard as improper the topic to which I request your attention at this time, and which I design to be the climax of all that I have said.

As I have previously observed, the Johannean miracles become perfectly clear, to a certain degree, when we regard them as the natural beams of more than an earthly sun which, in Christ, shed its lustre upon the world. Yet the transition from the beams to the sun itself is not merely easy, but it is also natural, and even unavoidable. In my opinion, and certainly in yours also, the present course of lectures would be destitute of a very essential element if I neglected to direct your attention more specially to the Johannean Christ, who, regarded minutely in the light, is both the object and the centre of this conflict. For everything which we have previously said concentrates here, and it is only from this centre that the whole truth in this department can be arrived at. I will no more attempt to portray the glory of John's picture than I would rashly attempt to draw aside the veil which conceals some of its colours from us. Yet I will present to you the idea of Christ which we meet with in this Gospel, and try to place it in its true light, in opposition to the incorrect sceptical view. Yet you will not think it amiss that, in this last Lecture, I should enter a somewhat wider field, in order that we may treat some of the vital questions which the consideration of this picture of Christ naturally calls up in our minds. If I can thus succeed in holding up before you this picture in the form in which the Apostle has painted it and beheld it, I may regard my object as accomplished, and can pray that the blessing of Heaven may rest on what has been said.

"Who art thou?" According to the sacred account (John viii. 25), this question was asked our Lord by the Jews of Jerusalem. We would repeat the question, though in a totally different sense; and would direct our view with increased attention to the person of Him whose works lead us, in view of what we have already considered, to expect so much that is glorious and transcendent. But, we have scarcely asked the question before. we begin to listen to a stream of complaints, which we just now begin to understand.

"The Johannean Christ," we are told, "is merely a supernatural being, whom we do not see gradually appearing like every other historical character, but standing suddenly before our eyes as a heavenly phenomenon. Like the Minerva of heathen mythology, who came into existence full-grown and heavily-armed from the head of the father of gods and of men, so does this Christ appear at once on the scene of history in all his full grandeur as the Son of God, who designs to communicate to the world what he had long before seen and heard in heaven. By virtue of his immeasurable knowledge, he exhausts at once the mysteries of the heart, the future, Deity, and humanity. Even at the outset,

he sees the end of his career; and he is sure of
his victory before he begins his struggle. He has
no temptation, no conflict, and no human development; he does not grow, but is perfect from the
beginning to the end. In body, he is a man; but
what is he in spirit and heart? We discover in
John's Gospel but little or nothing of all the truly
human thoughts and sensations which make the
synoptical image of Christ so attractive to our view.
The Johannean Christ is exalted above all human
emotion. Though he walks among the Jews, he
speaks to them of 'their' and 'your' law, just as if
he were not bound to it in the slightest measure.
He lives on earth, but it is as one who spends but
a short time here, that he may return again to his
Father. He places himself on a level with this
Father, and lays claim to an honour which can only
be ascribed to the Father. In a word, the Ego,
which here continually stands in the foreground, is
not human, but merely apparently human, who
utters unheard-of things concerning himself. Even
when he prays we hear him say 'we' and 'us', as
had never before been said by human lips; this
Christ strictly prays and returns thanks, not expressly for his own sake, but (he once said it himself) 'because of the people who stand by.' Finally,
he is himself the object of religious adoration, and
allows himself to be saluted by Thomas with: 'My
Lord and my God!' But why say anything more
of this Johannean Christ? He who stands before
us in such a light certainly deserves any name

sooner than that of a truly historical person. And for this very reason he cannot be our Christ; we cannot comprehend him, love him, nor follow him; indeed, we cannot truly admire him, for the picture stands too high in the` air."

Now what shall we reply to these numerous objections without repeating something that we have already said, or transgressing too far the limits which we have laid down for ourselves? Forsooth, if these words contained nothing but the pure truth, we, too, would hesitate to follow John as our guide to a correct understanding of Christ. Permit me to give you my view of this way of treating a question. It does not seem to be utterly without foundation; if it were, we would not find it necessary to take it seriously into consideration at all, for error is only permanently dangerous because of the small quantity of truth that may underlie it; but these objections are in the highest degree unfair, exaggerated, and partial. Truth and error are here mingled in such fine proportions that, in the present case, a proper distinction is absolutely requisite for a proper understanding. Let us, in making our reply, see what we frankly must and can admit with perfect readiness. That which will be afterwards left us will then be of double value.

First of all, we hold it indubitably sure that the Christ whom John enables us to hear and behold, must be more than human both in origin and character. We are glad to see this fact acknowledged by those who previously opposed it boldly; and,

while some learned critics still hold that the declarations in John must be referred to the ordinary
capacity of a purely human knowledge, we must
regard such a procedure as a result of either the
complete or partial rationalistic desires of the
heart. [1] In reply to this, we unhesitatingly exclaim,
whether such critics are willing to hear us or not:
"No, — This Christ shines before us in more than
human splendour! He appears before our eyes not
as a merely human ambassador of God, but as a
being of higher rank. He asserts not merely a
moral, but.a supernatural, union with the Father.
It is a unity of power and of will which can only
be explained by the unity of nature. According to
his own declaration, it was not simply in the
counsel and foreknowledge of God, but personally,
— that is, with self-consciousness and self-volition,
— he existed with the Father before Abraham, and
even before the world was."

His knowledge leaves far behind it all the general human perception of God's nature and of individual men, however fully developed this perception
may be; and his purity does not bear the slightest
trace of the unequal conflict which we must constantly carry on. We are perfectly justified in repeating the assertion, that no man ever spoke like

1 We have in mind especially here, in addition to the
previously mentioned work of Weizsäcker, Professor W. Beyschlag's *Christologie des Neuen Testamentes.* Berlin, 1866.
The reader may also compare an article by O. Pfleiderer,
on *The Johannean Theology,* in the *Zeitschrift für wissenschaft-
liche Theologie,* by Hilgenfeld, 1866, No. III.

this One; and an acute apologist did not miss the
mark when he made the following declaration:
"The deepest foundation for the almost fanatical
obstinacy with which the pioneers of this critical
tendency refuse to recognize the authenticity of this
Gospel, is, in reality, nothing less than the fact that
this Gospel testifies more decidedly and abundantly
of the true divinity of Christ than the remaining
ones." [1] But just these two terms, "decidedly" and
"abundantly," lead us at once to a second remark,
— that John by no means stands alone in his
description of our Lord's person. If. the fourth
Gospel had never existed, a glance at the other
writings of the New Testament would show us that
even the most diverse writers perfectly harmonize
in recognizing the supernatural character and dignity
of our Lord. We have already made reference to
the testimony which Jesus gives of himself in Matthew, Mark, and Luke, but the material is so abundant that we do not run any risk of repeating
ourselves if we return to this important point. We
may say to our opponents: "You object to the Johannean Christ. Very well, let us leave John's
portrait of Christ out of the question for awhile,
that we may see what kind of a Christ the remaining parts of the Holy Scriptures bear witness to;
but, above all, what is the picture drawn by his
own language." May I ask you what you think of

---

[1] O. Zöckler, *Die Evangelien-Kritik*, etc., p. 33. Darmstadt, 1865.

a Christ who exalts himself above all previous la-
borers, as the son of the householder having a vine-
yard (Matthew xxi. 33); who, in the authority of
his sojourn on earth, compares himself with a
nobleman who travels for awhile in a foreign land,
that he may receive for himself a kingdom, and
then return (Luke xix. 12); who speaks of his
angels, and is aware of having authority over le-
gions of them, as their Lord and Master (Matthew
xiii. 41; xxvi. 53); and who, after his resurrection,
permits himself to be worshipped on a mountain in
Galilee, and immediately afterwards declares that
all power is given to him, not only on earth, but
also in heaven, and that baptism in the name of
the Son must be administered at the same time in
the name of the Father and the Holy Ghost (Matthew xxviii. 17—19)? Do his words have a human
sound when he calls himself the temple (Matthew
xii. 6); when he describes the sin against the Son
of man, in distinction from that against the Holy
Ghost, as the climax of pardonable sins (Matthew
xii. 32); and when he makes eternal salvation or
misery directly dependent upon the confession or
denial of his person (Matthew x. 32, 33)? Or, are
all these passages unauthentic, interpolated by some
later writers, and to be referred to the category of
the sins of some pretended revisor of the oldest
Gospel accounts? A person would have to be stone-
blind if he could not see the real tendency of such
a would-be criticism; and the expression of the
learned Lücke is of special application here: "Where

purely subjective caprice begins, all criticism comes to an end." [1]

But we hear our enemies, whom we would much rather salute as brethren, shouting out from their camp: "My Christ is that of the Sermon on the Mount." Indeed! After all, does it not satisfy such critics to see that the same Christ who places his lowly Apostles on the same level with the persecuted Prophets, therefore places himself higher than any of them; who adjudges to himself the right of being saluted with "Lord, Lord;" who does not himself appear before Gods judgment bar at the head of all humanity, but decides the destiny of all as their only Judge, and by whom each one who would inherit eternal life must be acknowledged as his servant; and who soon afterwards promises the most abundant reward to every one who will give to the thirsty a drop of cold water, not merely in His name, but in the name of one of His least disciples? [2]

Need we add more? How many expressions of our Lord, which a Christian heart did not doubt until two or three years ago, must be subjected to suspicion, before everything is discarded which, according to the changing opinions of these negative theologians of the nineteenth century, it was impossible that this amiable Rabbi of the first century could think or say? I go further. I refer to Paul, who, as is demonstrable, presented essentially the

[1] *Comment. Evang. Johannis*, Vol. I. p. 104.
[2] Matthew V. 12; VII. 21—23; X. 42.

same testimony as John concerning our Lord, though
he did it twenty-five or thirty years before John; to
the Epistle to the Hebrews, where, years before the
destruction of Jerusalem, the truly divine nature of
the High Priest of our profession is so expressly
attested with his truly human nature that this
Epistle sometimes appears to be an unintentional
commentary on the words of our Lord himself in
John; and to the whole cloud of witnesses for the
truth during the Apostolic Age down to the unknown
Ananias of Damascus, who, in speaking of Christ's
believers, describes their peculiar character with this
single touch: "that call on *His* name" (Acts IX. 14).
Now what conception of Christ's person, I ask you,
must be presupposed by this calling on the name
of One crucified by Israelites, as all of them had
originally been, and by godly Israelites, as this
Ananias was?

I have hitherto confined myself merely to the
New Testament, not having taken a step in the Old
Testament, whither this same Ananias invites me.
And yet I find in the Old Testament that the picture
of the Messiah is already painted in such strong
colours, that Israel's minstrels and prophets must be
called the most extravagant men if the same picture
did not stand before their eyes in all its supernatural splendour. Judge for yourselves whether these
titles of dignity do not sound much too high for
one who was merely anointed by man: "Wonderful,
Counsellor, The mighty God, The everlasting Father,
The Prince of Peace" (Isaiah IX. 6). Can you have

in mind merely the most religious of all religious
men when you read of a Princely Scion "whose
goings forth have been from of old, from everlasting"
(Micah v. 2); when, in the last of the Prophets,
you see the expectation of the Messiah joined with
the idea of the "messenger of the covenant" (Mal-
achi III. 1); and when, in the visions of Daniel
(Daniel VII. 13), you see one coming with the
clouds of heaven "like the Son of man," — an expression which was taken from this passage and
used by our Lord and which, to the acute ear,
contains a significant presupposition of something
supernatural? [1]

But enough. I understand as clearly as I sincerely lament, the inability of those occupying a
negative standpoint to reconcile themselves to the
idea of a supernatural Christ. But I declare it
very unfair to make John alone, or chiefly, responsible for an obligation in which, at all events, he
is united with so many Apostles and Prophets. You
can hardly hesitate to say that the question here
does not depend upon "everything or nothing," but
is one of degree; and he who would wage a further
warfare against John because he has presented us
with a supernatural picture of Christ, should be at
least consistent in his action, and, if I may so express myself, boldly tear half of the leaves out of

---

[1] In the expression *Son of man*, there is a reference to
an antithesis, and we see the force of it when we remember
that he so frequently called himself the *Son of God*. See
C. F. Schmid, *Bibl. Theol. des Neuen Testamentes*, Vol. I. p. 159.

the Bible. But if he employ this energetic measure,
he will find that the remaining half will be only
the more incomprehensible and incredible.

However, suppose we take for granted, for a
moment, that the Johannean Christ exhibits a merely
superhuman character. Now the greatest charge we
have to bring against those whom we must contradict in our very heart, is their continual arraying
in antithesis those parts of John's Gospel which are
most intimately united. We hear them say, that "in
the first three Gospels we have a Christ who is
truly human, but nothing more than human; but
in the fourth Gospel, on the contrary, we have
a Christ who is truly divine, and human only in
appearance." Now this contrast, we observe, in the
third place, is to the highest degree unfair. If our
words did not have too strong a sound, we might
say that the Christ of John's Gospel is not less
human, but just as much so, and, if possible, more
so, than of either of the other Gospels.

We know that it is objected, that John merely
represents Christ as the Logos in a human body,
and that this Evangelist is therefore by no means
free from the leaven of the Docetæ, a sect of the
first century which denied the proper humanity of
our Lord. We are hardly able to express our great
surprise that such a view can be laid to the charge
of an Apostle who regarded the spirit of Antichrist
as the denial of the very truth that Jesus Christ
really became flesh (1 John IV. 2 f.). We emphatically ask: Where does Christ, as he speaks and

13

acts in John's Gospel, give occasion for such a severe charge? It certainly cannot be where, in humble simplicity, he calls himself "a man that hath told them the truth" (John VIII. 40); or where he expresses on the cross the most tender and devoted care for his mother; or where he is heard to complain: "Now is my soul troubled" (John XII. 27). Even admitting that the last-named passage indicates the lower life of his soul, it is nevertheless certain that John, who has preserved the expression, elsewhere informs us that our Lord was "troubled in spirit" (John XIII. 21). This certainly indicates a really. human circumstance, which occurs this time in the very highest department of his inward life.

But we hear it also asserted, that "the Johannean Christ is highly exalted above all human emotion." In reply to this, I must ask: What ground have you for drawing this conclusion? Is it because he takes part, at a wedding, in the joy of a young married couple; or, burning with holy zeal, because he scourges the defilers of the temple; or, weary and thirsty, because he sits down beside a well of water; or because he does not touch the food which his Disciples brought soon afterwards, since his soul was satiated with the higher enjoyments of life; or because he looks with hearty sympathy at a man who had been diseased for thirty-eight years; or because, having scarcely escaped the impending stoning of the exasperated Jews, his heart sympathized with the sufferings of one who had

been born blind; or because he rejoiced on account
of the Disciples, that he did not go to Bethany; or
because he wept tears, the evidence of the purest
humanity, at the grave of a friend whom he designed soon to raise from the dead? Now it is
true that we read in John xi. 33. that our Lord,
as he looked at the weeping Mary and the Jews
accompanying her, "groaned in the spirit, and was
troubled;" and this emotion, we are told, is here
described in a way that does not indicate sympathy,
but passion, — such a wrath as this Gospel attributes to even God himself.

But even allowing this to be true, what becomes
of the verse which soon follows: "Jesus wept?" In
such a heart as his was, was there not at the same
time room for wrath on the one hand, and for compassion on the other? And was not that a truly
human sensation of our Lord when, as we read in
Mark (chapter iii. 5), "he had looked around about
on them [his enemies] with anger, being grieved
for the hardness of their hearts?" Remarkable
indeed! It used to be the case that when people
read in the Scriptures about God's wrath, even a
little child could say that this is a so-called "hu-
manizing" expression. But now-a-days, when we
see in Jesus traces, of wrath and indignation, it is
said that they are more a proof *against* than *for*
his proper humanity, as people also speak of a
wrath of God; and thus the theopathic Christ is made
a substitute for an anthropopathic God. However,
this is not the first time that the opponents of mir-

13*

acles would compel us to believe very miraculous
things at their mere *ipse dixit.* Yet absurdity
reaches its climax, perhaps, in the strange assertion
that "the Logos was angry because any one should
dare to weep over a dead person in the presence
of Him, the Prince of Life. It was not therefore
a human emotion, but a divine displeasure at a
human feeling, which expressed itself in such an
inappropriate manner!" What a good fancy, however. But there is only one little measure that
must be employed in order to remove every impediment out of the way. Is not the 35th verse:
"Jesus wept," the shortest in the entire Bible? It
has been declared unauthentic, and that the author
consequently represented his Logos as standing with
dry eyes, without a human heart, at the grave of
Lazarus! Now one or the other of these things
must be admitted. Either such an artist as this inventor could not have committed such an egregious
error as to make the Logos weep, or, allowing this
touching narrative to be really historical, he must have
believed nothing less than the true humanity of our
Lord, — and thus the proposition opposed by us
falls to the ground. [1]

No indeed; the Christ of the fourth Gospel was
not ashamed to call his Disciples, *brethren;* [2] and
although taking his origin from above, he regarded

---

[1] Compare Bonifas, *Sur l'humanité de Jesus-Christ, selon
l'Evang. de St. Jean,* in the *Bulletin Théol.* of the *Revue
Chrétienne.* December, 1864.
[2] John XX. 17; compare Hebrews II. 11.

CHRIST'S DIVINITY REVEALED IN HIS HUMANITY. 197

nothing truly human as foreign to himself. We even see the divinity revealed in him unfolding itself in a truly human way; he reveals himself as the Son of God, but as the one who took upon himself our nature, in body, soul, and spirit. Do you desire any further proof? Not only according to John, but according to the first three Evangelists, his knowledge of what is concealed is wonderful; but we meet occasionally with a single remark, which the writer seems to make almost involuntarily, that this knowledge, notwithstanding all its majesty, does not cease to possess a human character. In Mark, for example, he inquires, on the road near Jerusalem, whether there is any fruit on the figtree; and in John we hear him asking about Lazarus: "Where have ye laid him?"; and that he has the grave shown to him, — all of which could never have been sheer dissimulation. [1]

[1] Mark XI. 13; John XI. 34.

[Dr. Van Oosterzee, it will be seen, unites with the most prominent living evangelical theologians of the Continent in holding that Christ voluntarily subjected his Divine nature to a partial renunciation (*Verzicht*), in consequence of its union with humanity. This view, when carefully examined, will be found to be at variance with the Decree of the Council of Chalcedon, of the fifth century, which holds, that in Christ there is *one person;* in the unity of person, *two natures,* the divine and the human; and that there is no *change,* or *mixture,* or *confusion of these two natures,* but that each retains its own distinguishing properties. The Athanasian Creed says, "perfect God and perfect man." It is only by accepting the completeness of each nature in Christ, the non-divinity of his humanity, and the non-humanity of his divinity, and the perfect union of both in one person, that, as it seems to us, we stand upon really firm ground. As for Christ's divinity, his *possession* of it

His holiness is spotless, but even this is developed in a human way, in the midst of disappointment, conflict, and temptation. Is it urged that, for the Christ of the fourth Gospel, there was no development, no baptism, no conflict, no temptation,

was not limited in the slightest degree, and the few passages that indicate his limited knowledge must be referred solely to his human nature. The only direct Scriptural declaration that Christ did not know the future is Mark XIII. 32: "But of that day and that hour knoweth no man, no, not the angels which are in heaven, neither the Son, but the Father." But even this passage admits of explanations perfectly consistent with Christ's omniscience. The reading, "neither the Son," is not regarded genuine by some of the most orthodox and learned Biblical scholars; further, the word "knoweth" has a sense of the Hebrew *hiphil*, which denotes in verbs of action, when the act passes over to another: *I make another to know, I declare.* This is its meaning in 1 Corinthians II. 2: "For I determined not to know any thing among you, save Jesus Christ, and him crucified." It is unnecessary to repeat all the passages in proof of Christ's perfect omniscience, but we may take as specimens: "For Jesus *knew from the beginning* who they were that believed not, and who should betray him" (John VI. 64); and: "For he [Jesus] *knew,* who should betray him" (John XIII. 11). The term God-man has its objections, though supported by the strong authority of Origen. Unless it be used carefully, it is liable to lead to the adoption of such a confusion of natures in Christ as really makes of them a *third,* which combines the essential qualities of both, and yet is neither humanity nor divinity in their distinct completeness. "If the divine nature in Christ had been imperfect," says Richard Watson, "it would have lost its essential character, for it is essential to Deity to be perfect and complete; if any of the essential properties of human nature had been wanting, he would have been man; if . . . the divine and human had been mixed and confounded in him, he would have been a compounded being, neither God nor man. Nothing was deficient in his humanity, nothing in his divinity, and yet he is one Christ. This is clearly the doctrine of Scripture." See *Theological Institutes,* Part 2nd. Chh. XIII., XVI. — J. F. H.]

and no sorrowful Gethsemane? This objection has
some show of correctness as long as it is forgotten
that John is not the first, or the only Evangelist,
but simply the last one, who presupposes acquaintance
with the Gospel of his predecessors on the part of
the believing Church for which he writes; and he
therefore did not need to repeat constantly what
all knew, and which no one seriously doubted. But
apart from this consideration, the objection in question is a word which has far more polish than edge.
The human development of our Lord is merely
mentioned by Luke, and only briefly, at the end of
his second chapter (Luke ii. 40 — 42); not merely
Matthew, but even Mark, that Evangelist who just
now stands so high in the favour of most of our
modern negative critics, is perfectly silent on the
point. It is, therefore, not fair to throw this stone
at John's head alone. Though he does not expressly give an account of the baptism of our Lord,
he nevertheless immortalizes a testimony of the
Baptist, in which he plainly enough refers to that
event, and proves his perfect knowledge of it
(John i. 32, 33).

We hear it complained, that in John's Gospel
there is no struggle, no temptation, no agony of soul
in Gethsemane. Indeed! Then that life in which
every step brought on some new encounter with the
powers of darkness, is declared not to have been
a life full of conflict! It is true that John does
not speak of a temptation lasting forty days, at
the beginning of the labours of Jesus. Though he

begins his account at the time when our Lord had
already been in the wilderness of temptation, I was
not aware that our negative critics ascribed such a
strictly historical character to that account as to
warrant them in regarding its absence from the
fourth Gospel as a proof of its unhistorical character. Is it not well to call to mind that temptation in the later part of the life of our Lord
which justified Luke in writing that Satan had
"departed from him for a season" (Luke IV. 13)?
But I ask, did not the Johannean Christ hear the
voice of temptation in the words of his brethren:
"Show thyself to the world" (John VII. 4); or in
the pressing forward of the multitude to make him
their king by force (John VI. 15); or in the calmness of his own soul as he thinks of his approaching hour (John XII. 16)? With all these expressions,
is there not connected the appearance of a proof
that this outward temptation might also have been
an inward one?

John, indeed, is silent on the conflict of Christ's
soul in Gethsemane; but he was at the same time
perfectly well acquainted with our Lord's prayer
uttered at that time; [1] but he reveals to us, as
from the distance, what first shook off this pain,
when he repeats Christ's feeling words: "Now is
my soul troubled," — which is a reëcho of an
earlier lamentation recorded only by Luke (chapter
XII. 50): "But I have a baptism to be baptized

---

[1] See, besides the synoptic Gospels, Hebrews V. 7—9.

with; and how am I straightened till it be accomplished!"

It is remarkable, that every new contrast which our enemies present to us only leads to the discovery of new harmonies. When we look at the picture of Christ praying, which is the most sublime scene drawn by John, we can receive no other impression than that his account is in perfect harmony with the other Evangelists. It is true that he mentions fewer individual parts of this life of prayer than are narrated by his predecessors, and particularly by Luke. Yet, when we look clearly at his Christ, we need not be uncertain as to the kind of pulsation and breathing of his spiritual life. In the words spoken at the grave of Lazarus: "Father, I thank thee that thou hast heard me" (chapter xi. 41), we hear our Lord disclose, as it were, the most profound mystery of his sacred life; he had already prayed silently before, and the miracle which he performs bears the strong impress of a manifest answer to prayer. Though he immediately adds: "I knew that thou hearest me always; but because of the people which stand by I said it," there can be no doubt of his purpose. It is not his returning thanks, but his doing it — where he had previously prayed in silence, — aloud, for the sake of the people, in order that now, after this sign, they at least might believe in his divine mission.

Truly, it requires an effort to keep one's composure when he hears this most exalted interview between the Son and the Father, at such a time, called by no other name than "a prayer for display." Or, must we call it also a prayer for display when we behold him soon afterwards perplexed as to what he should say, supplicating in a moment of profound trouble: "Father, glorify thy name!" It is unquestionably "because of the people," as he declares himself, that immediately afterwards a loud heavenly voice is heard, as though in answer to his prayer. But what do you think of such logic as concludes that he himself stood in need of neither the prayer nor the answer, and that everything was merely necessary because of the people?

But do not understand me as ignoring in our Lord's prayer in John, especially that unapproachable, peculiar, and superterrestrial element which, naturally, can no where be more strongly expressed than just where we hear God's Incarnate Son speaking directly to the Father. We see it beaming out in unapproachable glory from the High Priestly prayer that rises from his heart in the hour of his departure. It is plain, even in his majestic "Father, I will," and in that, perhaps, still more elevated "We," that the Son, however closely united with the Father, is in every respect unlimited, and independent of him. Prayer is here so much an apparent necessity of the life of our Lord that, even in that hour, he does not pray for his present and future disciples until he has besought for himself that glory which was to crown his sufferings and his conflicts. His praying in particular, not less

than his foreknowledge and his holiness, may be
called divine, but nevertheless truly human; indeed,
without longer evading the peculiarly striking term,
it may be called Divine-human, in the fullest sense
of the expression.

If I were to use a single term to give expression to the impression constantly produced in me
by John's whole picture of Christ, I do not know
a better one for the Johannean Christ than that
which the Church owes to the celebrated Origen, —
"God-man." The "I," which is here expressed, is
not merely the man Jesus, the One sent by God,
but the manifested Messiah of Israel. It is just as
little the Logos, which was supposed to appear in
human flesh without having become real and perfect
man. But it is God's own, only begotten, and
eternal Son, like his brethren in every respect but
sin; who, notwithstanding his assumption of the
lowly form of a servant, is continually conscious of
his previous existence and heavenly origin. He is
divine even when he appears most human in our
view; and he is human even when the beams of
his divine glory, as on Tabor, shine out from every
part of his tenement of clay. It is plain from his
own expression: "We know what we worship,"
that he was a true Israelite; and it is evident that
he was truly man from his first words addressed
to John and Andrew: "What seek ye?", to his last
invitation to Thomas: "Reach hither thy finger."
But he is at the same time divine, indeed, God
himself manifested in the flesh; he is the true, the

highest, the only and eternal ideal man, because
the fullness of the godhead dwelleth in him bodily.
He presents himself here to our vision as the angel
of the Apocalypse, who stands with one foot on
the sea and the other on the land. Originally a
stranger on the earth, but yet having become
an adopted child in the household, · he reaches his
hand at once to eternity and time, to the Creator
and the creature.

And yet this picture must not convey the idea
of a double consciousness. His was not a mere
juxtaposition of two heterogeneous natures; but
what was originally two-fold is here blended into
a real and incomparable unity. Christ is not in
John a child of the human family, made perfect by
merely moral unity with God, but a personality in
which divinity and humanity, originally separated
from each other, have come so closely together and
become united, that none had ever appeared like it
before, and none will ever approach it in the future.
This is the Christ of John; this is, in fact, the
Christ of all the Gospels, of the Scriptures, of the
Church of all centuries, of all ages, of the Church
militant here and of the Church triumphant in heaven.
Bow your heads then, as I bow mine, as you behold
his glory in the mirror of this Gospel!

Let me now ask you to stand silently awhile
before this image of Christ, and consider some
questions that it involuntarily propounds to us. The
first inquiry which we frankly make is this: Could
John's portrait of Christ have been invented? In

other words: Is this invention a settled matter, or at least probable; or may it even be regarded as possible?

Let us see. Is it a settled matter, then, that in the fourth Gospel we possess nothing more than an artistically invented fable? You are naturally surprised at such a question, when you think of the many proofs of its truth which we have already discovered. Yet we are justified in asking it, when we hear some of the extreme members of the negative school declare the unauthenticity of the fourth Gospel to be a settled matter, that science has established this result, and that it is from this point of view that the Church of the future has good right for adopting its unauthenticity as an article of its faith. Even now we read occasionally in popular writings, as though incidentally, that the fourth Gospel is "improperly ascribed to John," and, only two years ago, the people were told from the pulpit that this Gospel is nothing else than a poetic Messiad of the converted heathen world of the second century. [1]

I shall not speak of the more absurd epithets that have been applied to John's Gospel, but I have a perfect right to say, that I can only with difficulty keep from despairing of the real sincerity of those who obstinately deny the authenticity and credibility of the fourth Gospel in the face of such positive and strong proofs. We might almost sup-

[1] Dr. J. C. Zaalberg, *De Godsd. van Jezus*, p. 141 ff. The Hague, 1864.

pose that many who regard everything that can be said in favour of John as positively refuted, are either still ignorant of the subject, or have never investigated it earnestly and impartially, or have been influenced by special motives to deprive it of its just rights. Perhaps it is too much to expect of the present generation of opponents of John's Gospel that they will make the frank confession of Bretschneider, that "people have been in error on this point," or of Strauss, in his earlier life, that "men are in doubt on their own doubts." Such a candid confession can hardly be expected now; but the disciples of the Lord, having no interest in denying the truth, and being taught to maintain it, will know in future the faith which they hold, and in years to come will certainly be surprised, even if they are not now, that the people of our times were able to combine so much acuteness with so much prejudice and frivolity. No one can regard the fourth Gospel unauthentic who does not mix special motives with his so-called reasons. The very prince of the Evangelists, to whom the negative critics obstinately say: "We will not have this man reign over us," compels no one to heed his words, and conceals his majestic character from the eyes of all who scorn him as an impostor. [1]

[1] "We are here in a territory where the will weighs the proofs, and definitely determines their force. We ought to be satisfied with placing the fourth Gospel in a condition where no one would hesitate to receive as authentic any book of heathen antiquity. This result being obtained, the last step to take is simply to open the door for it. If we

It is by no means a settled affair that we have
before us a forgery; for such a result is not proved.
But, on looking at John's Gospel more closely, can
we consider its forgery even probable? "That depends," I am told, "on how things usually appear
to us, and what is the state of the eye, and of the
light by which, and in which, we look at the matter."
You are right, and yet I repeat my question: Is
forgery probable here, just because improbability,
according to my view, reaches such a high degree
that it almost borders on the inconceivable? Now
let me assume that this peculiar history of miracles
was invented. Then, who invented it? Was it John
himself? The thought is too absurd to delay a
moment to consider it. Was the forger some unknown Christian, philosopher, or author of the
second century? No; it is not such a character, but
John himself, that the numberless particulars of this
Gospel reveal as its author. Even supposing, with
certain critics, that the present revision of this Gospel
was the work of a friendly hand, perhaps one of
his earliest disciples or sympathizers, even then we
have reports of the words, deeds, and sufferings of
our Lord which come directly from his most con-
fidential Disciple.

I must repeat, that he who has bestowed special
attention on the literature of the second century,
and impartially compared this Gospel with it, must

would perform this decisive act, it is not sufficient for us
simply to know, — we must also have the *will*." Godet,
Examen des princip. Quest. Crit., etc., p. 54.

conclude, that it is just as inconceivable that it could have taken its rise at that time as that an Alpine rose can grow in stiff clay, or that a nightingale can unexpectedly sing a sweet song on a stormy December evening. No second example can be adduced of such anonymousness and fiction as we would have to deal with in this instance. [1] But what could have been the purpose of this invention, for there must certainly have been some object in view? Was it to popularize the author's own ideas, in the interest of a certain party, and to make Christ appear in imaginary splendour before the eyes of a younger generation? This could not be the case, for we have already seen the insurmountable difficulties that would attend such a preposterous hypothesis. For the present, we would refer you to something altogether different.

John's Gospel is the Gospel of the appearance of the Son of God in truly human flesh. But the idea of such a personal incarnation of God in the Son of his love cannot be traced before this period, either in Jewish or in Pagan religion; therefore, it must, and can be, the fruit of reality alone. [2] Very

---

[1] "If you suppose that the Johannean Christ is an invention and deception, you must at least see that the forgery would necessarily belong to a different and grander epoch of spiritual history than to the second century, which witnessed the prolix and miserable scribbling of the Gnostics and anti-Gnostics." Thiersch, *Versuch einer Herstellung des hist. Standpunkts*, p. 287.

[2] Compare, on this important point, the entire Introduction to Dorner, *Entwicklungsgeschichte der Lehre von der Person Christi*, Vol. I., and especially p. 65.

much is said of a disposition prevailing in the
second century of Christianity to glorify the Founder
of Christianity; which disposition is alleged to have
almost irresistibly driven his followers to adorn his
head with a nimbus of supernatural character, just
as if there was not prevalent the very opposite
effort to deprive the highest and most majestic One
of his original splendour. [1] It would not have been
such an easy matter to believe, and make others
believe, that some one who was known to be originally a mere man, — a despised, though amiable
man, — was nothing less than God revealed in the
flesh. In my opinion, it would have been very
difficult for any one to bring himself or any one
else to believe such a thing, unless he were compelled to submit to the irresistible force of facts
that permitted a view of no less magnitude. [2]
Something so exalted, that we who live at this day,

[1] We are reminded of the well-known couplet:
"The world loves to blacken the dazzling,
And to drag down the high to the dust."

[2] "Do you commence by supposing that humanity believed in the divinity of Christ, and formed for itself the
legend of the divine Christ? Do you speak seriously? I
cannot believe it; for the question really is, to know how
men came to believe in a divine Christ? Pray, take care;
for it is not such an easy thing for the human mind to
believe that a man is God. The striking thing here is, not
the easiness of admitting such a doctrine, but its difficulty.
Reason does not incline me at first to acknowledge that
divinity can be personified in a being who presents himself
to me in a human form. Reason, I say, anterior to all proof
of the fact, does not incline me to this belief, but, on the
contrary, resists it." I. FELIX.

14

after the lapse of so many centuries, can transport ourselves to it only with difficulty, could not be invented by a philosophical dramatist, who had no historical groundwork whatever to begin with. We therefore have here the case of an invention being far more incomprehensible than historical reality. You can decide for yourselves the proper inference to be drawn from this fact. For myself, I do not hesitate a moment to apply Lavater's expression to John's portrait of Christ: "The impossibility of inventing Christ overcomes all doubt."

Do I go too far? Then I will leave it to you to judge whether an invention, which is by no means certain, but very improbable, could have been really possible in the present instance. As a matter of course, we speak of the possibility of it in the moral sense of the word; and we may now await with some composure the decision of all who are authorized to render one, that is, of those, and only those, who possess the organ of perceiving, and, so to speak, of feeling not only the beautiful, but also the true, the good and the holy wherever they are revealed.

Standing at the end of the long and occasionally rugged way over which we have passed together, I would once more lead this class before this picture of John, and ask them whether he makes upon them the impression of a writer of romances, who writes down what he would have his readers see; or of an eye-witness, who reports what he himself had seen and experienced? I would remind them

once more of what they know about John from
history, apart from his Gospel, and again ask:
Whether it is possible to imagine (a thing which
every opponent of John's Gospel must do) that we
here find an intentional deception, practised by a
witness of our Lord, by a truthful and devoted
witness, by a hand which once wrote over the very
entrance to the Heavenly City: "And there shall in
no wise enter into it anything that defileth, neither
whatsoever worketh abominations, or maketh a lie?"
I insist upon hearing how far the thought is absurd, that the Apostle who had read most deeply
the mysteries of the Master's soul, and was subsequently illuminated by the Holy Spirit, as he looked
back upon this dazzling phenomenon should see in
him the revelation of the Word, the wisdom and
image of the Father, and should bear witness of it
in just the way that we have? Could we expect
any other than a purely historical Christ to be described by an Apostle, who, I might say, comprised
in these words the plan of a testimony which
covered years: "That which was from the beginning,
which we have heard, which we have seen with
our eyes, which we have looked upon, and our
hands have handled, of the Word of Life; for the
life was manifested, and we have seen it, and bear
witness, and show unto you that eternal life, which
was with the Father, and was manifested unto us;
that which we have seen and heard declare we
unto you, that ye also may have fellowship with

14*

us: and truly our fellowship is with the Father, and
with his Son Jesus Christ" (1 John I. 1—3).

There exists nowhere a more thorough perva-
sion of ideas and facts than just on the Johannean
standpoint; and it is exactly here that they are
alleged to stand in deadly and irreconcilable opposition to each other. Yet what is the use of speaking longer of a possibility which, as far as John's
Gospel is concerned, disappears the more rapidly
the longer we look at it?   I will lead you once
more to the Johannean Christ, that he may testify
of and for himself; and I repeat with increasing
emphasis the question: Whether the invention of
such a picture seems to you morally possible? Who
does not see that a chiefly fictitious miraculous
account of Deity manifested in a human body would
have appeared totally different, and would not have
presented a holy and supernatural character, but a
character utterly contrary to nature? But supposing
for a moment that the Evangelist, as somebody has
expressed it, designed to give a human physiog-
nomy "to the gold-mine of the Divine Logos." [1]
But admitting that the inventor would have his hero
appear in heavenly glory, would he have commenced by presenting him to us as a guest at a
wedding?   He would have him perform a miracle
at the Pool of Bethesda, but would he have him
cure merely one sick man, and then allow him to
withdraw quite unobservedly? He would have him

[1] C. H. Hase, p. 40.

open the eyes of one born blind, but would he at
the same time have made him use the instrumentality of clay made of spittle and earth? Would he
have made him raise his friend from the dead, but
also have made him weep tears of human emotion?
Would he have allowed him to be worshipped by
some Greeks, as the time approached when the Son
of man should be glorified, but almost in the very
next moment have presented him before us as
praying that the Father might "save him from this
hour?" I might adduce more examples; yet these
are enough to explain to you my purpose, and to
let you feel the force of the argument.

The Johannean picture of Christ presents many
individual features which, if each be considered
alone, come in such direct opposition to other features that they appear necessarily to preclude each
other. And yet these characteristics, which stand
out in such contrast, blend so harmoniously that
this conviction forces itself upon us with almost
irresistible power: Only Omnipotence itself could
have produced such an incomparable reality; no
human artist could have brought forth such a creation without making some mistake, or at least once
forgetting and betraying himself.

We here meet with the Saviour in the most
dissimilar situations, circumstances, and states of
mind; but he is never so divine as to be no longer
human, nor ever so human as to be no longer divine. He is never under the necessity of improving
anything, of performing it a second time, or of re-

calling it. He has never deviated from the right
course. We always find him just at the proper
moment; he is always the master of the situation,
even when he appears to be overcome; and he
always reigns even when he serves, — and when
did he not serve? I would say to every doubter
who loves the truth: Forget all that you have heard
from others, and read for yourself once more the
account of Christ's washing the disciples' feet, with
the incomparable introduction to it (chapter XIII.):
"Now before the feast of the passover, when Jesus
knew that his hour was come that he should depart
out of this world unto the Father, having loved his
own which were in the world, he loved them unto
the end. And supper being ended, the devil having
now put into the heart of Judas Iscariot, Simon's
son, to betray him; Jesus knowing that the Father
had given all things into his hands, and that he
was come from God, and went to God; he riseth
from supper, and laid aside his garments; and took
a towel, and girded himself. After that he poureth
water into a basin, and began" — to do what? —
"to wash the disciples' feet."

Invent, if you can, such a climax as this! As
for me, I seem to feel in such a narrative the
pulsations of the thankful heart of the silent eye-
witness, and as if in this one touch I saw the whole
picture of Christ, which is at once so historical and
profoundly symbolical. As we look at such features
as these, — and there are many of them, — we are
reminded of the language of Matthew Claudius:

"Andrew, did you ever hear of anything like this? One could well allow himself to be stigmatized and broken on the wheel for the mere idea of such a God-man; and he must be crazy who could ever think of deriding and scorning him. He whose heart is in the right place, lies in the dust, and praises and adores." Amen, to such words, thou true Christian in John's spirit, thou true Wandsbeck Messenger! It seems to me as if I beheld on thy honourable face the reflection of the calm spiritual glory of the Apostle John. But what else is John than a light of the Church, which borrows all its lustre from the Sun of the spiritual world, — from the historical Christ, whom he could claim as specially his own? And yet we are told that this light is, after all, nothing more than an empty fancy, conjured up in the cloudy heavens by a glowing imagination! Away with you, ye apostles of unbelief; I would not barter away the mystery of godliness for such absurdities!

I am sure that there is a certain influence which almost compels you to adopt at least a part of what we have said. But just this feeling awakens your distrust; for soon after you have listened to arguments, the understanding again asserts its prerogative, and you propound a second question, which is altogether different from the first. You ask: Is the Johannean Christ comprehensible? This question, for you may as well confess it, is the expression of a pretty decided denial. What should we say in reply to an objection which, according to the view of a certain class, seems already to decide the case permanently? Unfortunately, it is not necessary in our times to preach the Apostolical, and particularly the Johannean Christ to a heathen Festus or to a Jewish Agrippa, to hear from all sides the reproach: "Paul, thou art beside thyself." We constantly hear the following complaint from people living in Christian lands, and often from most respectable persons: "Your Gospel is contrary to reason just in proportion to the supernatural character which it possesses; and it is in vain that you demand confidence in what stands in outright opposition to the first and simplest laws of human thought. Why do you continue to repeat the witness with which John in particular proclaimed the Incarnate Word? I scarcely commence to read it before I meet with one absurdity after another. You certainly would not have us believe that God, who is a Spirit, can have a son; that this son, full of grace and truth, lived and walked on this tarnished spot of the unbounded universe; and that such a supernatural being, notwithstanding his real character, became truly man, and died as such, in order to rise immediately afterwards from the dead, and to return to the glory of the Father from whom he came. All this is a mere empty sound, and nothing more. As I read these Gospels, and especially the fourth, I sometimes feel strangely attracted, enchained, and more than half won by this Christ; but I immediately afterwards meet with so much that is surprising, offensive, and repulsive that I lay this Gospel aside without satisfaction and encouragement. I cannot hate this Son of man, but I can just as little trust in him and follow him."

How delighted I should be if all the doubters of our times were only conscious of this dissension from John's Gospel. I could then hope that Rückert's beautiful language might be fulfilled in them:

> "What the heart cannot hate,
> And yet can not let go,
> Must be loved with full soul, —
> Pray what else can it do?"

I can hope of at least those who have gone thus far that they will have the courage to stand in silence a moment, and — alas, how many avoid it to their own injury — call out their doubt from its dark hiding-place, where it stands like a giant, to the clear light. Who knows whether or not it will dwindle into a dwarf when it once appears in clear day-light? Of course, you cannot expect me to answer in a short time even the most prominent objections that are urged against the acceptance of a special saving revelation, only one of whose most important documents we are now defending. Let us confine ourselves to the fourth Gospel, — the Gospel of the Incarnate Logos. I assume that you believe, with me, in a living and personal God, who has revealed himself in nature, and still reveals himself as the highest power, wisdom, and love. But, tell me frankly, what do you then have against a Gospel whose quintessence may be comprised in

this single expression: "God sent his only begotten
Son into the world, that we might believe through
him?" Is "only begotten Son" a term offensive to
you, at least in the sense understood and implied
by the Christian Church?

But tell me, where do you get the right to regard your idea of God as the most proper expression
of the highest touch-stone of truth, and instantly
reject as absurd what you cannot comprehend?
You believe that God is love, but can you think of
love without an object; and if you cannot, can you
imagine the creation to be the highest and only object of this love, without being lost in the abyss of
Pantheism? But the highest and eternal object of
this love, the Son "sent into the world," sounds to
you absurd, as the world is so small, and God is
so incredibly great. But do you not hold that love
to be the highest which bows lowest to the humble,
the wandering, and the lost? But as the smallness
of this earth seems to be your greatest objection,
tell me how many square miles must a planet comprise in order to be large enough to be a proper
scene for the manifestation of God's love?

It is impossible for me, as you easily see, to
defend, on the present occasion, the principal contents of this Gospel, as well as its authenticity and
credibility, against every contradiction. I would
only prove, to the extent of my power, that the
questions that press themselves upon us in contem-
plating John's portrait of Christ, are not of such a
character as to compel you to part with your faith

in his name; and I would direct your special attention to the fact, that, as soon as you allow yourselves to be scared away from this faith by the incomprehensible character of this picture of Christ, your difficulties will not disappear, but increase.

Let me present you a proof of this assertion. Take, instead of this Johannean portrait of Christ, some other one which you can much better understand, and see for yourselves whether the enigma can be satisfactorily solved. Granted that the principal person in the fourth Gospel was not the incarnate Son of God, but a mere man, — sinless, holy, and perfect man. What, a perfect man, — a man utterly devoid of sin! It is contrary to all analogy, to all observation, to all the results of experience, and to our knowledge of human nature, that such a man has ever lived; a completely sinless man is inconceivable unless we admit a direct operation of God, that is, a miracle, — which the science of our day inexorably rejects.

I am, therefore, under the necessity of going one step further. The objector says: "I grant that Christ was not absolutely sinless, but that he was excellent, amiable, and religious, or even a religious Genius." I must say that this is exposed to very serious doubts; for this "excellent man" has said such things of himself as would be blasphemous if he were nothing more than man. The nature of true religion is to make men humble, and yet this man is personified pride, which is all the more intolerable because he declares that he does not derive his honour from man. This "excellent man" dwindles more and more into a mere phantom, and, if we are to accept the supposition of our opponent, · the best that we have in his place is a fanatic, or even an impostor.

This Jesus, who is regarded by so many as anything else than really God's Son; this Jesus, a few years after his crucifixion and rejection by his own people, produced upon those of his nation who feared God the impression of such an exalted and noble character that they could "call on" his name without exposing themselves to the charge of idolatry. This Christ was scarcely proclaimed to the heathen world, — a fact which is proved by the rise of Doceticism, the eldest of all the christological heresies, — before he made upon his adherents the impression that he was superhuman. This view of his person as a supernatural, divine revelation not only obtained in the Church, but actually kept it clear of every other; for centuries it afforded a new starting-point for Christian and philosophical thought on the highest and holiest questions of life; and in every step of its course it was victorious, until, — oh, happy discovery of the second half of the nineteenth century! — negative criticism came up, and declared that all this was the upshot of the literary mystification of a sect! [1] It has been objected that it is difficult to understand the Johannean Christ well; but we who defend this description of Christ

---

[1] "John's Gospel, more than any other, has passed into the flesh and blood of Christianity." KEIM.

do not assert that it can be perfectly comprehended.
I see that faith has to contend with much obscurity, but it is clear to me that unbelief loses itself in
a midnight of absurdities, while it becomes entangled
in a net of its own ungrounded hypotheses. Do
not think that we attach no importance to the prob-
lems and questions that continually present themselves to us when we examine this picture of Christ.
To name but one example, as soon as we under-
take to fathom the full depth of this one expression:
"The Word became flesh," the measuring-line falls
from our hands.

But the advantage which we have over those
who fall into the abyss of doubt is, that we have
learned to bow our heads, our hearts, and our knees
before the revealed mysteries of God, and to repeat
the grand sentiment of the great Monod: "I do not
understand, but I understand that I do not understand." [1] "Our thinking in this department only
becomes rational when we cease to think rational-
istically." [2]   And when we see by continued study
that our faith rests upon a solid foundation, we
apprehend, with the obedience of faith, the substance of what the Gospel declares to us. And
having thus commenced to found our belief on testimony well supported, we do not simply adhere
obstinately to a blind faith in authority, — God

[1] A. Monod, *Sermons*, Vol. II. p. 312: The whole of the
excellent sermon, *The Credulity of Unbelief*, is well worthy of
being read.
[2] Auberlen.

forbid! — but to press forward as far as possible from faith to understanding. It is only in this way that we are gradually permitted to understand at least something of the mystery of God's Son, though we cannot expect to fathom it completely; and, in spite of all the mysteries which we here find, we can always say with a good conscience, that this concealment is infinitely more reasonable, more acceptable, more admissible, and more worthy of God, than everything which men have attempted to put in its place. Of course, no one will ever succeed in making perfectly clear and intelligible the manner in which Deity and humanity are united in this God-man; but is not the relation between our own body and soul also a mystery in many respects? The certainty of the fact of this union is not absolutely dependent upon the clearness and correctness with which we perceive its manner; and the revelation of "The Life" was none the less majestic and exalted because it has not yet been brought within the magic circle of some fine-spun idea.

After all, what do we perfectly understand? Not to mention the visible world, what is it that we can comprehend as soon as we enter the realm of the supersensuous and the eternal? Did not the Gospel declare, many centuries ago, that "Eye hath not seen, nor ear heard, neither have entered into the heart of man the things which God hath prepared for them that love him;" and should it excite our wonder when our eyes are dazzled by the sun, which, after a long night, comes out in all its full splendour from behind the clouds? [1] Must every question of the sick man on the origin and combination of his medicine be answered before he can use it with confidence? And would you regard it worthy of your trouble to say "Lord and Master" to a Christ whom you cannot perfectly comprehend with your small understanding? Notwithstanding all that is mysterious here, do we nevertheless not have so much clearness and glory that the Christ whom we cannot understand is infinitely above one whom our minds could grasp? Though it is sometimes difficult to believe under such circumstances, I ask if it is possible not to believe at all?

But we forget too often that it is necessary to stand in the centre in order to gain a clear view of the circumference; we must have an eye for the great and harmonious whole, in order gradually to receive light on each of the particular parts. The mistake of the defective criticism of our times is, that it can separate, but not unite; that it can observe apparent contradictions, but no grand harmonies; in a word, that it cannot see the forest for the trees! Thus the atomistic intellectualism, which

---

[1] Dr. Rothe: "To me, personally, the thought of a miracle, in the literal and strict sense of the word, is not an absurdity; and instead of regarding it as a contradiction of the regular order of nature, I would not know how to explain the natural course of the history of our race without it, nor to establish fully that pragmatism of history which I require." See *Die Aufgaben des Christenthums in der Gegenwart*, p. 73. Elberfeld, 1866.

cannot ascend the mountain because it is unable to
step over the little stones lying in the path, has its
deeper cause. "What would my readers think,"
asks Tholuck, "if somebody had opposed Paul's
preaching his 'Christ crucified' by presenting examples of the difference in vinegar, of the crowing
of a cock, and of the braying of an ass; and if
the Apostle would have thought it proper to enter
into an explanation of the relation of affinity between
sour wine and vinegar, and the relation of affection
between an ass and its mother, and the like; or if
he had looked around to find one of those available
spirits who know how to fill up a gap? We think
he would have said to the contentious individual:
'Man, your hour is not yet come!'"[1] Oh, thou who
hast a hundred times asked: "Is this Christ comprehensible?", listen for once to this other question:
"Can the world dispense with Him, — dispense with
Him for ever; can I dispense with Him?"

Can he be dispensed with? I lay before you
and myself, for our serious consideration, this question concerning the Johannean Christ. In my judgment, every truth which we defend in this department is only of permanent value when it is proved
to possess vital power, or at least vitality. In order
to answer this question, it will be necessary once
more to call up before our intellectual vision this
Christ whose picture we have contemplated together;
yet not to regard him in contrast with the Christ

[1] *Glaubwürdigkeit der ev. Geschichte*, p. 461.

of Matthew, of Peter, and of Paul, — for we have
already seen that there is an unmistakable unity
between their Christ and that of John, — but with
that Christ which the negative critics of our day
would foist upon us as their Messiah, so far as
they regard a Messiah at all necessary. It is of
the greatest importance here to distinguish very
carefully between the two, so that no one can any
longer be of the opinion that the difference is merely
of form or representation.

We must frankly make this statement: The
Christ of modern criticism has almost nothing in
common, save the mere name, with Him whom the
Christian Church has confessed and adored through
so many centuries. [1] According to it, he is nothing
else than an amiable man, the only one of his
class, but neither infallible nor sinless; a friend of
women and children, and a preacher of what his
heart inspired him with more powerfully than others
had been inspired by their hearts; a worker of miracles in part in the imagination of his contemporaries, and partly by virtue of an extraordinary
coincidence of circumstances and by the happy application of merely natural forces. Though a gift
and revelation of God, he was these in no other
sense than the lily of the field is in another department. He was condemned in consequence of a
mysterious and almost incomprehensible misconception; he rose only in the eyes and imagination

[1] Compare Köllner, *Das moderne Christusbild, ein Zeichen unsrer Zeit.*

of his disciples; he was immortal, if, and so far
as all men, and especially pious men, are immortal; and he is the ruler of the world only so
far as he once gave to it an impulse, which is yet
perceptible in its vibrations. He is destitute of all
personal and immediate relation to his Church on
earth; and he does not answer the sinner who
cries to him by saying: "Heal thyself," for the very
simple reason that he does not hear the sinner
at all.

In contrast with this Christ, whose history the
critics of our day have gathered from unreliable
sources, I place before you, — as Pilate once con-
trasted the Man of Sorrows with Barabbas, — the
King, about whom the cloak of derision is placed
a second time, and ask you frankly: "Can we dispense with Him?" I direct this question to every
one of you in particular. I ask the thinking mind,
which seeks the key to the grandest phenomenon
and also the greatest enigma of modern history, —
the Christianity in the world. Can such a Christ in
miniature (if you will allow the expression) furnish
the slightest explanation, and have we in him a
sufficient cause for such a phenomenon? I address
this question with increased emphasis to the active
conscience. Do you desire anything higher than
a divine revelation that declares only the same
thing which every well-developed human consciousness can tell you? Do you need merely an ideal,
— and, perhaps, chiefly an unhistorical one, — in
which to reflect, to develope, and to elevate your-

self? As the modern Christ is exclusively a moral teacher and a pattern, is he not more unmerciful and severe than Moses, for he places before our eyes an inaccessible height, without enabling us to attain the peak aimed at? Indeed, how can he be simply a moral teacher, as the much-lauded religion of Jesus was inseparably connected with a colossal error, — faith in the supernatural?

But, above all, I address the same question to your hearts, that are longing for rest. Has not the heart such necessities as can be supplied only by the Christ of the Gospel; and can you dare to trust in him, and to follow and love him as this Gospel enjoins upon us, if he is nothing more than man? Can you dispense with him who alone brought the Gospel to us, — the Gospel not only of God's superintending care (for that would not have been necessary if our negative critics are right), but the Gospel of God's pardoning and redeeming love, which our unresting souls need, but would never have dared to expect if it had not been revealed to us by the Father himself in his Son? I here touch the point which, at the present day, is mostly overlooked, probably just because it stands so plainly before us. If the world had needed a founder of a new religion, such as Moses, Zoroaster, and so many others, it could, at all events, have been satisfied with the Christ of Renan, Strauss, Schenkel, and others. In this event, Jesus of Nazareth would be entitled to only one place in the pantheon of distinguished men; at most in the

15 *

lararium of household gods, in which a heathen emperor of the third century, Alexander Severus, placed him with others. But a voice in our hearts declares that we do not need merely a founder of a religion, but a Redeemer and Saviour; a Mediator, who reconciled in himself both matter and spirit, friend and enemy, and earth and heaven; and, in one word, a Light and Life of the world, by which the true life is not merely declared, but revealed, acquired, and restored.

Take away this Christ of John, indeed, of the whole Gospel of the Old and New Testaments, and what have you left of the entire Scriptures? Nothing more than a collection of the literary products of a mysterious people of antiquity; a disconnected succession of poetical legends, insatiable demands and groundless expectations; and a doctrine of God, a doctrine of virtue and, at the very most, a doctrine of immortality, all of which deserve any other name sooner than that of the Gospel.

Take Christ away, and what is there left to the Christian Church? If history is worth anything, it proclaims that the Church owes its origin, its extension, its reformation, and its incipient triumph to the Apostolical Christ; that no branch could permanently bear fruit which was not connected with this Vine, and that faith in a supernatural revelation of salvation was the foundation which supported the divine edifice, the bond which still unites the Christians of all confessions. What becomes of the Church if this foundation be shaken, and this bond be broken? Not to mention any other examples, the sect of Theophilanthropists, which arose at the end of the last century, may prove to you that which follows from the very necessity of the case, — that intellectualism and humanitarianism are utterly unable to establish a permanent ecclesiastical fellowship; for this can rest alone on a common faith in the saving facts revealed to us. The evidences of decline and death which are fresh in our memory, prove to what sort of excess this modern negative criticism would bring the Church of our Lord; but this truth will only be manifested with perfect clearness when the generation which now lives on the memories and traditions of a faith which it has privately or publicly denied, has disappeared from the stage of history, and its place occupied by those who are now trained into a certain kind of greatness by the milk of this new wisdom. It is in this way, by a natural development of the evil, that not only is all Christian faith in revelation lost, but also all religion of the heart, all vitality of prayer, and all hope of eternal life; and the final result of a Rationalism which, without the slightest warrant, raises the flag of the Christian name above its cargo, can be nothing else than a materialism more or less gross, with its theoretical and practical disasters to the individual, the family, society, the state, and the world.

Enlarging our circle of observation, take away this historical, Apostolical Christ, and what view is presented to us by modern society and the world?

I do not conceal my affliction of mind when I propound to you this question, at the end of the year 1866, which has inflicted such severe wounds upon us, but, at the same time, has disclosed unfathomable abysses to our vision. I do not venture to look into the future; nor do I speak of the special judgments with which God has visited, or may visit,. Christian nations that ungratefully scorn his high gift; but I merely refer you to something which no one can deny, because it stands plainly before every eye, — to the shaking of the foundation of society, the dissolution of the holiest bonds, the stupor of all moral principles of life, the supremacy of might over right, the politics of mere facts, with its demoralizing influence in all departments, and the disunion, excitement and disquiet which men have without knowing the ground for it. In a word, I point to everything which makes our modern society in so many respects a picture of splendid misery; it is burning with fever and is weak; it is diseased and delirious. I lament with you that Christianity has thus far done very little, and is now doing but little, to discharge the high calling of the Good Samaritan by pouring oil and wine into the wounds of this almost hopeless invalid. Yet I ask, at the same time, do you know any other and better remedy than this Gospel; and can our age dispense with the Apostolical Christ? Take Him from it if you will, but what will you give it as a substitute for the future? Let a child of these times, the fallen and unhappy Alfred de Musset, answer the question by the following poetical record of his cynical scepticism, in which he thus addresses the Saviour:

"No more is Thy word my law. A new age
Has come, and with it a thirst for new things;
Hope's bright picture of the future is gone,
And fear, now dethroned, has lost its power.

Time, the all-devouring worm, hath eaten
Thy holy image, hanging on the Cross;
The nails are rusty — utterly destroyed —
And nothing gives it any more support.

And yet who can refuse both gratitude
And wonder when he calmly thinks on Thee?
I am in a strait, — a stranger to faith,
And yet unable its charm to resist;
I would even kiss the earth that bore Thee,
And which Thy mortal agony hath cured.

Thy thawing power has touched the frosty earth,
And wakened it to joy it never knew;
But now it shuts its proud heart against Thee!
How can new blood the old heart penetrate?
Who can restore the innocence of youth?" [1]

Yes, how can young blood flow into the aged heart? I know of only one way, and you also know it well. Do you remember that exquisite poem, "The Golden Legend," by Longfellow, the American poet? The principal character in it is a

[1] The Dutch translation of this poem is by Professor B. ter Haar, of Utrecht, and is in the recent (3rd) collection of his Poems, p. 289. On Alfred de Musset, compare Julius Schmidt, *Geschichte der französ. Litteratur*, 2nd Part, p. 282.

young prince, who is endowed with everything which usually makes princes the objects of the world's envy. But at heart he is diseased, languid, and devoid of spirit and hope. Yet it is no wonder, for he is tormented by an obstinate affliction, which is deeply inrooted in his nature, and for which no medicine can be found. He is irretrievably lost, — and yet he may be saved. But it can only be done in one way, which can be revealed to him by a dark oracle. If any maiden can be found who will love him enough to pour out her blood voluntarily for the rescue of his life, and if the blood of this offering be drunk, the unselfish and innocent life will bestow upon him new strength, and he will be perfectly restored. The poet says: —

"Not to be cured, yet not incurable!
The only remedy that remains,
Is the blood that flows from a maiden's veins,
Who of her own free will shall die,
And give her life as the price of yours!"

You may read for yourselves in Longfellow how this apparent impossibility was accomplished, how this offering was prepared and presented in the highest sense, and the consequence of it. I now affirm, that this is a striking symbol of the disease of our age, and of its only hope. Our age is diseased, and its spiritual vitality is dying out; there is only one means of bringing new life to its heart now weak and decaying, and of arresting the fatal gnawing of the cancer at its heart. Oh, that

faith might be communicated to it again, — faith
in a love which has voluntarily presented the most
precious offering for those who were sick unto
death; that they might find the One, who, influenced
by nothing but mercy, died for their salvation, and
yet lives; and that, in this sense, they may again
be brought to "eat the flesh of the Son of man
and drink his blood." If faith in the most exalted
love cannot save this generation, tell me, what can
do it? Oh, that we could communicate this faith
to all, or to many, or even a single lacerated soul!
Yet, this can be done by no other means than
faith; and the need of it in our day is on the increase.

If you can unite with me in this sentiment, you
cannot long hesitate to answer the last question
which I will lay before you. How can our age be
brought anew to the Johannean, the Apostolical
Christ? I need not here state my reasons for the
presupposition which gives rise to this question.
I fear that the rent between so-called modern
knowledge and Apostolical Christianity was never
so general and so deep as at the present day. The
voices against the historical Christ that were heard
resounding from the philosophical schools during
the latter half of the eighteenth century, now reëcho
from Christian pulpits and in the lecture-rooms of
theological professors. There is now preached to
hundreds of congregations something that is called
by the name of Gospel, by believing which we are
firmly convinced that it is impossible to be saved;

and the doctrines of the Apostles are opposed with increasing defiance under the uplifted banner of the Reformation. There is scarcely a single fundamental fact of sacred history which has not been already referred to the department of fiction; and he who dares to utter a lament at this state of things is told, for the calmness of his soul, that nothing essential has been taken from him, and that he cannot be thankful enough for the inestimable kindness. We even see those who formerly enjoyed a very different conviction now hurrying with alarming rapidity down the steep path of negation, as though they would prove the truth of the words: "Whosoever hath not, from him shall be taken away even that he hath."

In a word, the negative critics swear allegiance to a Christianity, and preach it up to others, for which it is utterly inconceivable why they desire special pleas, with and above other religions, as even the intelligent Jew cannot deny that this Rabbi, Joshua Ben Joseph of Nazareth, was an excellent moralist, and should be honored and listened to as a religious genius. Meanwhile, the awful truth of these other words stands out before us: "Whosoever denieth the Son, the same hath not the Father" (1 John II. 23); and many a one who believes no longer in a living God, and regards religion merely as the poetry of conscience, is afraid of ghosts. I often feel very sad when I look in silent solitude at the world so sadly unchristianized, and

my lips sometimes involuntarily utter the touching
lament in the hymn of Novalis:

> "Prompted by love,
> How much Thou hast done!
> Now past away,
> And thought of by none!" [1]

We ask with a shudder: "Shall this century
hasten to its close before a new heathenism, which
in many respects is inferior to the ancient, establish
its home in Europe, and is the man already born
whose pen shall describe the downfall of Christianity
and of the Reformed Church of the Netherlands?
No, indeed; the evil is not gone thus far, and God
forbid that we should ever live to see such a calam-
ity! In view of the many gloomy pictures before
us, we would not close our eyes to the numerous
hopeful indications of our excited age; and it is
necessary for us to maintain that hope in which
Novalis, just quoted, sang, that,

> "The day will come when my brethren
> Will again look heavenwards."

The bold and unblushing appearance of the
spirit of denial in our day has its advantages. As,
according to Shakespeare's well-known expression,
"Yes and No are no good theology," so is this
theology evidently declining, and it has in many
respects become easier to choose between Yes and

[1] See the excellent hymn: "Though all be unfaithful,"
in the *Evang. Liederschatz*, by A. Knapp. No. 2067.

No. Many are beginning to feel more earnestly the value of the Scriptural treasure the more they see it in danger; and, in opposition to the violent assailants, the number of those workmen are constantly increasing who, like the Jews on the walls of Jerusalem, are building with one hand and holding the sword with the other. We believe in the Holy Spirit, and are therefore sure that the attempt "to drive the pale phantom of the God-man of John's speculation from the faith of the Church" will surely fail. As long as the spirit of truth does not totally disappear from the Church, it will not suffer itself to be persuaded to renounce gladly the greatest and most important part of the Gospels' in order to come to Jesus himself.

Under such circumstances, what grounds have we for losing the hope that many a one who is now our opponent will shortly become our friend; that there is here and there one who will forsake the Sisyphean labor of opposing such a demonstrative power; and that here and there the future defender is slumbering in the enemy? John's Gospel has, for many, a repulsive and, at the same time, an attractive power; and the Johannean Christ still walks uninjured and unimpeded, as he once did through his opponents who threatened to stone him; and he is still protected by a better guard than his weak friends. It is impossible for us to suppose that he has already spoken his last words to this generation.

You may ask: How is that abyss to be filled

up, which, in our day, separates so many from him and his Gospel? I cannot do better than to give you an answer in three expressions. First, we must *increase our self-knowledge*, which can bring us, and many with us, to a deeper knowledge of our sins, and, at the same time, show us that it is impossible for us to obtain eternal peace through such a miserable Gospel as the negative critics would inflict upon us, instead of the one that is well-known and well-established. Second, *our study of the Holy Scriptures, and particularly of the Gospels, must be more thorough.* Which one of you, possessing a priceless gem, would allow himself to be told that he has for years been ornamenting himself with a false stone, without using every means at his command to test its purity and brilliancy? But this spiritual Gospel sheds on you a more dazzling light than the most brilliant diamond. Bring your treasure calmly to the test! We do not fear to try the sacred cause which we defend; our only fear is, that it be not sufficiently tested, or tested in the wrong way. Many a one who does not believe anything, takes the authority of others for rejecting everything, and will not any longer listen to or read anything that may be advanced in favour of the Gospel. I implore you not to follow the example of such lamentable prejudice, but search for yourselves the Scriptures, which contain more traces of inward truth than the most experienced person can prove to you. Your faith must be your personal and independent possession, and, if it be necessary, you must have it even at the expense of severe conflict.

If you have this faith, the chief way for gaining the prize set before you is, third, by a more *faithful and unflinching confession.* We would, indeed, be unmitigated fools if we believed that the propositions of false science can be refuted by this means alone. We cannot overlook the fact, that the conceited contempt with which many, — who swear by their science, and probably the last edition of their own compendium of it, — look down upon a bold and sincere confession of faith, betrays as great a measure of intolerable pride as of secret fear. It is not the critical searching for hypotheses, but the well-grounded testimony of faith, that shall and will conquer the world. People of the Lord, persevere in this testimony, every one according to his own capacity, and especially you whom God has endowed above others with the gift and calling to do it! Will not every evidence of decrease and coldness and weakness in your testimony be regarded as an indubitable sign that those in the Church who were faithful to their confession have lost courage and faith in their doctrines? Woe to us if weariness, or obscurity in our words and deeds, should give occasion to our opponents to forge such weapons out of our lamentable course! Happy will we be, ye learned and unlearned, if, in these days of apostasy and conflict, we merit the praise which the same John whom we have considered, has recorded: "Thou holdest fast my name, and hast not

denied my faith." There is no more beautiful epi-
taph for a confessor of Christ than that which was
inscribed on the tombstone of another John, — John
Knox: — "Here lies a man who never feared the
face of man."

It is such a testimony as this that I have attempted to deliver to you, as we have looked at
the signs and necessities of the present day. May
He graciously forgive all that is weak and defective
who knows that we do not seek our own, but His
honor! May the true and the good that are in it
be blest for the strengthening of your faith, and,
above all, for the glory of His name! I am grate-
ful to you for the cheerful interest with which you
have followed me to the close. Sometimes I was
compelled to tax your attention and indulgence, but
you have agreed with me that the cause required
it as but few causes can.

And now let me ask: Who shall speak the last
word in this conflict? You well know who speaks
the last word of all in every conflict for His truth.
May He maintain it in your hearts when my voice
speaks no longer; and may He preserve it when
we have ceased to meet together! I commenced
this lecture with the beginning of John's Gospel.
I close with the last words of the Apocalypse,
which I now apply specially to the fourth Gospel.
They are words of testimony, of the Gospel, and
of the Advent in this period of Advent, — in this
great Advent of the ages: "I Jesus have sent mine
angel to testify unto you these things in the churches.

I am the root and offspring of David, and the bright
and morning star. And the Spirit and the bride
say, Come. And let him that heareth say, Come.
And let him that is athirst come. And whosoever
will, let him take the water of life freely ... He
which testifieth these things saith, Surely I come
quickly: Amen. Even so, come, Lord Jesus. The
grace of our Lord Jesus Christ be with you all.
Amen."

APOLOGETICAL LITERATURE

ON

JOHN'S GOSPEL.

 ♦ ————————

SCHLECKER, F. W.—Versuch einer Widerlegung der Einwendungen gegen die Aechtheit d. Evang. Johannis.
Rostock, 1802.

VAN GRIETHUYSEN, W. H.—Pro evangelii Joannei authentia dissertatio crit.-theol.   Haderwyk, 1806.

BORGER, E. A.—De constanti et æquabili Jesu Chr. indole, doctrina ac docendi ratione s. commentationes de evangelii Joh. c. Matth., Marc. et Luc. evangeliis comparato.
Hague, 1816.

STEIN, K. W.—Authentia Evangelii Johannis contra Bretschneideri dubia vindicata.   Brandenburg, 1822.

 A vindication of the genuineness of the writings of John against Bretschneider's objections.

WEBER, M.—Authentia capitis ultimi evangelii Joh. hujusque evangelii totius et primæ Joh. epistolæ argumentor. internor. usu vindicata.   Halle, 1823.

CROME, F. G.—Probalia haud probabilia. Oder Widerlegung der von Dr. Bretschneider gegen d. Aechtheit und Glaubwürdigkeit des Evang. und der Briefe des Joh. erhobenen Zweifel.   Leyden, 1824.

THOLUCK, A. F. T.—Die Glaubwürdigkeit der evangelischen Geschichte, zugleich eine Kritik von Strauss' Leben Jesu; für theologische und nicht-theologische Leser dargestellt. 2nd Ed.   Hamb. and Gotha, 1838.

16

242 APOLOGETICAL LITERATURE ON JOHN'S GOSPEL.

FROMMANN, G. C. L. T.—Der Johanneische Lehrbegriff in seinem Verhältnisse zur gesammten biblisch-christlichen Lehre dargestellt. Leipzig, 1839.

LANGE, J. P.—On the Indissoluble Connection between the Individuality of the Apostle John and the Apocalypse. *Vermischte Schriften*, Vol. II. p. 173 ff.
Leipzig, 1840—41.

THENIUS, O.—Das Evangelium ohne die Evangelien. Ein offnes Sendschreiben an Herrn Bruno Bauer.
Leipzig, 1843.

EBRARD, J. H. A.—Das Evangelium Johannis und die neueste Hypothese über seine Entstehung. Zürich, 1845.

BLEEK, F. v.—Beiträge zur Einleitung und Auslegung der heiligen Schrift: *Beiträge zur Evangelien-Kritik*, p. 107 ff.
Berlin, 1846.

LUTHARDT, C. E.—Das johanneische Evangelium nach seiner Eigenthümlichkeit geschildert und erklärt. 2 Parts.
Nuremberg, 1852.

NIERMEYER, A.—On the Writings of the Apostle John. *Verhand. van het Haagisch Genootschap tot Verdediging der christ. Godsdienst*, Vol. XIII. 1852.

COSTA, ISAAC DA,—De Apost. Joh. en zyne Schr.
Amsterdam, 1854.

MAYER, G. K.—Die Aechtheit des Evangeliums nach Johannes. Schaffhausen, 1854.

EBRARD, J. H. A.—Johannes der Apostel: Art. in Herzog's *Real-Encyclopædie*, Vol. VI. pp. 722—737.
Stutt. and Hamb., 1856.

STEITZ, G. E.—Pascha, christliche und Pascha-Streitigkeiten: Art. in Herzog's *Real-Encyclopædie*, Vol. XI. pp. 149 —169. Stutt. and Hamb., 1858.

VAN OOSTERZEE, J. J.—Het Leven van Jesus. 2nd Ed. Vol. I. pp. 127—156. Utrecht, 1863.

ASTIÉ, J. F.—Explication de l'Evangile selon Saint Jean.
Paris, 1864.
The Preface presents the special reasons for selecting John's Gospel to meet the religious wants of the day ; and the Introduction argues in favour of the authenticity of this Gospel against recent objections.

WEIZSÄCKER, C. H.—Untersuchungen über die evangelische Geschichte, ihre Quellen und den Gang ihrer Entwickelung.
Gotha, 1864.

GODET, F.—Commentaire sur l'Evangile de St. Jean. 2 vols.
Paris, 1865.
An excellent apologetical work.

THENIUS, OTTO.—Das Evangelium der Evangelien. A Letter
to Dr. Strauss. Leipzig, 1865.

TISCHENDORF, C.—Wann wurden unsere Evangelien verfasst?
Leipzig, 1865.
English Translation: When were our Gospels Written?
London 1866, and New York, 1867.

ZÖCKLER, O.—Die Evangelien-Kritik, etc., p. 33.
Darmstadt, 1865.

FISHER, G. P.—Essays on the Supernatural Origin of Christianity. Ch. II.: *The Genuineness of the Fourth Gospel,*
pp. 33—152. New York, 1866.

HASE, C. A.—Vom Evangelium des Johannes. Eine Rede an
die Gemeinde. Leipzig, 1866.

RIGGENBACH, C. J.—Die Zeugnisse für das Evangelium Johannis neu untersucht. Basle, 1866.

STEINMEYER, F. L.—Die Wunderthaten des Herrn in Bezug
auf die neueste Kritik. Vol. I. Berlin, 1866.
The Raising of Lazarus, pp. 197—210.

UHLHORN, G.—Vorträge über die modernen Darstellungen
des Lebens Jesu. Lecture III. pp. 69—103. 3rd Ed.
Hanover, 1866.
English Translation. Boston, 1868.

JONKER, H.—Het Evangelie van Johannes. Bedenkingen
tegen Scholten's Hist. krit. onderzoek. Amsterdam, 1867.

LUTHARDT, C. E.—Apologetische Vorträge über die Grund-
wahrheiten des Christenthums: *Die Evangelien,* etc.,
pp. 210—225. 5th Ed. Leipzig, 1867.

SCHULZE, L. T.—Vom Menschensohn und vom Logos; ein
Beitrag zur biblischen Christologie. Gotha, 1867.

DIEHL, J. C.—15 Nisan oök volgens Johannes de Sterfdag
van Jesus. Thiel, 1868.

GRAU, R. F.—Zur Einführung in das Schriftthum neuen
Testamentes: On the Peculiar Nature of John's Gospel,
and its Importance for the Church of the Present Day,
pp. 183—234. Stuttgart, 1868.

GROOT, HOFSTEDE DE,—Basilides als erster Zeuge für Alter
und Autorität neutestamentlicher Schriften, insbesondere
des Johannesevangeliums. German Ed. Leipzig, 1868.

16*

GUERICKE, H. E. F.—Gesammtgeschichte des neuen Testaments; oder neutestamentliche Isagogik. Der historisch-kritischen Einleitung ins N. T.: *Aechtheit des Evangeliums Johannis*, pp. 170—205. 2nd Ed. 1854; 3rd Ed.
Leipzig, 1868.

Compare also the Introductions to the Commentaries on John's Gospel by Olshausen, Ebrard, Tholuck, Lücke, Meyer, and especially by Lange (Bibelwerk): Das Evangelium nach Johannes. 3rd Ed.   Bielefeld, 1868.

•

———

ROBINSON, E.—The Alleged Discrepancy between John and the other Evangelists respecting our Lord's Last Passover. *Bibliotheca Sacra*, Vol. II. pp. 405—435.
Andover, 1845.

GRIMM, C. L. W.—On the Gospel and First Epistle of John as the Work of One and the Same Person. *Studien und Kritiken*, Part I.   Gotha, 1847.

WEITZEL, K. L.—The Fourth Evangelist's ' Testimony of Himself. *Studien und Kritiken*, Part III. p. 578ff.
Gotha, 1849.

STUART, M.—Exegetical and Theological Examination of John I. 1—18. *Bibliotheca Sacra*, Vol. VII. pp. 13—53; 281—327.   Andover, 1850.

The Logos of St. John. *Journal of Sacred Literature and Biblical Recorder*, Oct.No.   London, 1856.

STOWE, C. E.—The Four Gospels as we now have them in the New Testament, and the Hegelian Assaults upon them. *Bibliotheca Sacra*, Vols. VIII. pp. 503—524; IX. 77—108.   Andover, 1851—52.

ABBOT, E.—On the Reading "Holy Begotten *God*" in John I. 18, with Particular Reference to the Statements of Dr. Tregelles. *Bibliotheca Sacra*, Vol. XVIII. pp. 840 —872.   Andover, 1861.

GROOT, HOFSTEDE DE,—The Antiquity and Authenticity of John's Gospel according to External Witnesses before the Middle of the Second Century. *Waarheid in Liefde*, p. 593 ff.   1868.

The Most Ancient Traditions on our Four Gospels. *Revue Chrétienne*, Dec. 15. Paris, 1863.

BONIFAS, J.—Sur l'humanité de Jesus-Christ selon l'Evang. de St. Jean. *Bulletin Théol.* of the *Revue Chrétienne*, Dec. No. Paris, 1864.

LEWIS, T.—The Regula Fidei; or, the Gospel of John. *American Presb. and Theol. Review*, Vol. II. pp. 46—63. New York, 1864.

Recent Literature on the Gospels. *British and Foreign Evangelical Review*, Jan. No. 1864.

The Genuineness of the Fourth Gospel. *British and Foreign Evangelical Review*, April No. 1864.

Modern Criticism on St. John's Gospel. *London Quarterly Review* (Wesleyan). July No. London, 1865.

GRAF, E.—The Authentic Features and especially the Portraitures of Character of the Fourth Gospel. *Der Beweis des Glaubens*, Vol. I. pp. 435—502. Gütersloh, 1866.

GRAF, E.—Ueber die Aechtheit von Joh. Cap. VII, 53—VIII, 11. *Vierteljahrsschrift für deutsche und englische Theologie*, Vol. III. pp. 152—179. Published by Dr. M. Heidenheim. Zürich, 1866.

GROOT, HOFSTEDE DE,—A Witness of the Longest-Lived Apostle as the First Witness of the Antiquity and Authority of the Books of the New Testament, together with other Witnesses thereon before the year 138. *Waarheid in Liefde*, p. 449 ff. 1866.

MOMBERT, J. I.—The Origin of the Gospels. *Bibliotheca Sacra*, Vols. XXII. pp. 353—384; XXIII. 529—564. Andover, 1866.

PAUL, L.—The Time of the Lord's Supper according to John. *Studien und Kritiken*, Vol. II. p. 362 ff. Gotha, 1866.

ZÖCKLER, O.—On the Importance of Miracles in Nature and History. *Der Beweis des Glaubens*, Vol. II. pp. 65—85. Gütersloh, 1866.

CRAMER, J.—Is the Fourth Evangelist an Historical Drama? *Bydragen op het gebied van godgeleerdh. en wijsbegeerte*, p. 204 ff. Rotterdam, 1867.

GROOS, F.—On the Idea of Judgment (κρίσις) John. *Studien und Kritiken*, Part. II. Gotha, 1868.

ANTIQUITY OF THE GOSPELS.—*North British Review*, Vol. IV.
p. 347.

HISTORICAL CRITICISM ON THE GOSPELS.—*British and Foreign
Evangelical Review*, Vol. XII. p. 515.

JOHN THE EVANGELIST.—*American Biblical Repository*, Vols. III.
299 ff.; VII. 440 ff.

THE GOSPEL OF JOHN.—*Princeton Review*, Vol. III. p. 569.

THE GOSPEL OF JOHN.—*Kitto's Journal of Sacred Literature*,
Vol. II.

INDEX.

250 INDEX.

IGNATIUS, of 2nd century, acquainted with John's Gospel, 52.

Impotent Man, miraculous healing of the, 140—142.

Intellectuality, not always confined to higher classes, 40.

Invention of Christ's divine character more incomprehensible than historical reality, 210.

Irenæus, citing John's Gospel over sixty times, 53.

JOHANNEAN Christ, the church never recognizing conflict between the synoptic and, 61. Difference between him and the synoptic Christ owing to different circumstances and purpose, 67—70; 84, 85. Treated at length, 177—240. Objections on the ground of sudden and complete appearance as a heavenly phenomenon, 184, 185; answered, 186—190. Both his origin and character more than human, 186—190. Sceptical objection that he is only the Logos in a human body, 193, 194; that he is exalted above all human emotion, 194—196. Did not possess double consciousness, 204. His human emotions, 195. His divinity revealed in his humanity, 196, 197. His human development, 198—200. The God-man, 203. The invention of him morally impossible, 212. Internal evidences of the truth of John's account, 212, 213. Comprehensibility of him, 215—217. Difficulties increased by rejecting him, 218, 219. The

alleged difficulty of understanding him, 220, 221. How can our age be brought anew to him?, 233—239.

John the Baptist, record of, more majestic in John's Gospel than in the synoptics, 80; explanation, 81.

John the Evangelist, self-testimony of, 17. His purpose in his Gospel, to keep in the background, 17. His characteristics, 18. Culture and intellectual development, 29. Energetic Boanerges character, 30. Harmony in all his writings, 30—32. Acquaintance with him from tradition, 32. Impression received on reading his Gospel, 32. Personality, 40. His love for Christ, 40. Compatibility of the ideas found in his Gospel with his origin, 40. Residence in Ephesus, 41. His knowledge of Greek, 41. His adoption of the philosophy of his day, 41. Illumination, 42. His design in his Gospel, 42. His Picture of Christ fundamentally the same as that of Peter, Paul, and all the Apostles, 42—44. His perception of Christ's supernatural character, 44. He calls Christ The Word as Paul calls him The Son, 44. His elevated christological representation met with in Paul's writings, 44. His harmony with Peter and Paul, 44, 45. Essay of Niermeyer on the difference in his writings, 46, 47. Coincidences declare the same author, 46. Recent works upon his writings, 47. His expressions not borrowed from the Alexandrine philosophy, 42. His love for the Master alone sufficient to prevent him from misrepresenting him, 82. His acquaintance with the first three Gospels, 102. Assumption of their acquaintance by others, 103—105. Does not make the impression of a writer of romances, but of an eye-witness, 210.

John's Gospel, J. P. Lange cited on, 1. History of the growth of opposition to it, 12, 13. Opposition commenced by Evanson, an Englishman, 12. Authenticity defended by German theologians, 13. Cause of mistrust, 14. Old weapons only used in opposition to it, 14, 15. The opposition partisan, 16. The author a Jew living in Palestine at the time of our Lord, 19; acquainted with and cites from the Old Testament, 19; acquainted with the Alexandrine Translation and original Hebrew text, 19; with Galilee, Judea and our Lord, 19; speaks as an eye-witness, 19; his alleged animosity to the Jews, 19; friendship for Jesus, 21; vividness and minuteness of his description, 22, 23; importance of his chronological indications, 23, 24; must be sought in the Apostolic circle, 24; proofs discovered in the language, 25, 26; he is John, the son of Zebedee, 27, 28. Internal proofs in the 4th Gospel, of John's authorship of it, 28,

from the synoptic accounts and Paul's epistles, 28. Silence of John a proof of his authorship, 30. Harmony with the First Epistle of John; the authenticity of the latter not being denied, 31. Agreement of the Prologue of 4th Gospel with the Apocalypse, whose Johannean authorship is unchallenged, 31, 32. Objections based on historical, geographical and statistical mistakes, refuted, 34; cannot outweigh the proofs, 34; found in doubtful passages, 35—39; their unimportance, 39; important ones adduced, 39, 40; the philosophical introduction of the Gospel, 40; its philosophical color, historical material, and doctrinal character, 40; John's use of the Logos, 42; its illogicalness, 42. Design of John in it, 42. His picture of Christ, the same as that of the other Apostles, 43—45. The supernatural character of Christ, 43. Objections on account of the miraculous deeds and experiences of our Lord, 45. Unauthenticity alleged from dissimilarity between the Gospel and the Apocalypse, 45—47. Importance of the last two verses of John's Gospel, 50. Authenticity not doubted in the 2nd century, except by the Alogi, 51, 52. Cited by Irenæus, 53. First quoted under his name about A. D. 180, 53. More threatened at the present time than ever before, 56. Comparison of John's Gospel with the others, 62.

254 INDEX.